The Co

from his quiver. Fra..., he could and grabbed for the whip looped over the pommel. His fingers clawed at the horse's blanket trying to pull the saddle toward him. It did not budge. In one instant he heard the twang of the bow and in the next watched an arrow quiver in the roan's body.

Boy shuddered, struggled for a moment; then, relaxed.

"Oh, dear God," No-Chance groaned aloud. Stunned at hearing his own words, he straightened. This was the second time in twenty-four hours he had called on God, something he had not done since he was fifteen! Like a flight of swallows, images of his mother, White Cloud, and the baby, flitted through his mind. Maybe his one good deed would redeem him with his father's God.

Today he would die with dignity. He was many things, but not a coward. No-Chance pulled open his jacket and shirt to expose his scarred chest.

"The Comanche finds honor in killing a crippled man!" He cleared his throat. "I spit on such honor."

No-Chance clenched his teeth as he watched the warrior find his heart as a target.

Praise for M. Carolyn Steele

"From the Creek Indians on the Trail of Tears to the Great Plains of the Comanche, M. Carolyn Steele's *SPIRIT OF THE CROW* is a skillful blend of high adventure, authentic history, touching romance, and the love of a half-breed fugitive for a child that brings to life the Indian experience of America's early 1800s."

~Charles W. Sasser,
author of the military classic ONE SHOT-ONE KILL
and sixty other best-selling books and novels
~*~

"M. Carolyn Steele's vivid imagery and period details plunged me into this story of one man's quest for survival amid removal from his homeland to a harsh and unwelcoming land....*Spirit of the Crow* is a deeply moving, lyrical tale of struggle and tenderness, fortitude and redemption that will delight lovers of historical fiction and especially those who enjoy Native American history and folklore. I loved it!"

~Carla Stewart, award-winning author of
STARDUST and A FLYING AFFAIR
~*~

"M. Carolyn Steele has gone all out in her debut novel. She moves you right into the cleansing of the Creek tribe from the southern states and dumps them in the land out west after a "journey" that becomes a death march. Carolyn has found a reality in her characters that emerge from the pages of this novel in a strong form. You must read it."

~Dusty Richards, Two-time Spur Award winner and
author of the Chet Byrnes Western Series

Spirit of the Crow

by

M. Carolyn Steele

Spirit of the Crow

Cover Art by *Rae Monet, Inc. Design*

The Wild Rose Press, Inc.
PO Box 708
Adams Basin, NY 14410-0708
Visit us at www.thewildrosepress.com

Publishing History
First Mainstream Historical Edition, 2017
Print ISBN 978-1-5092-1286-6
Digital ISBN 978-1-5092-1287-3

Published in the United States of America

Dedications

To my mother, Melba Kent Kalkins,
who held this story in her heart.
To my husband, Carl,
who never lost faith in my abilities.
To my daughters, Teri and Traci,
who are my biggest cheerleaders.

Acknowledgments

I never wanted to be a writer. But my mother did. Inspired by her love of Native American lore, she and I would spread a quilt outside on summer nights and craft stories around the adventures of a half breed named No-Chance. Later, when she was ill, she made me promise not to let this character die with her.

The heart is tender, and it took awhile to revisit the wild half-breed I'd grown up with. Over the years, *Spirit of the Crow* developed into something I think she would have liked. Along the way, I count myself fortunate to have received encouragement and guidance from more people than I can possibly remember. Just a few of these wonderful folks:

The Crossroads Critique Group, under the able direction of Steve Amos, patiently sat through a number of rewrites.

Friends Carla Stewart, Derrick Bullard, and Mary Patterson pored over the entire manuscript in its various rewrites. Dusty Richards gave me the first rays of hope that my story was good. Julie Kimmel-Harbaugh, sprinkled her magic (and commas) throughout the pages.

Ted Isham, my teacher of the Muscogee Creek language, checked usage of the Creek sentences to ensure authenticity.

When I strayed into other writing projects, my husband, Carl, and daughters, Teri and Traci, gently pushed me back to this manuscript. I had a promise to keep, and they didn't let me forget it.

Finally, a thank you to my editor, Allison Byers, who patiently led me into the world of publication.

Chapter 1

John MacGregor tried to shrink his body away from the clinging wetness of his clothes and concentrate on the soft music of silver disks adorning his roan's bridle. A dog howled, and the sound was lonely in the gray hour before darkness.

He tugged at the brim of his black felt hat. Mist settled like a layer of cloth over Mother Earth and her children. Earlier it had been rain. Now it was heavy air, threatening to become colder and wetter.

Whispers of human suffering mingled and melted together becoming one solid, miserable sound. Horses snorted as they sloshed through mud. Wagons rumbled and creaked. Cooking utensils clanked together in the faltering rhythm MacGregor had listened to during the weeks of removal.

Eighteen thirty-six had not been a good year. Beelzebub, himself, perched on MacGregor's shoulder, stirring his wrath. He wasn't sorry he killed a drunken sergeant back in Pensacola. Only sorry to be caught up in the latest treachery of the white man, the forced march to Indian Territory.

He wasn't particularly sympathetic toward the Mvskoke, these Creek Indians who shared his present misery, either. They should have been prepared. It was only a matter of time before the relentless push of the whites would force them off the land of their ancestors, out of their homes. They had been warned. Such thievery had been happening for years. No one knew that better than he.

McGregor gritted his teeth at the bitter memory and snugged his heel into the roan's side. Trained to respond to every shift of his body, the slightest sound of his voice, it seemed the large horse could read his mind. He trusted this animal as he trusted no man.

Trudging feet of hundreds of poor souls kneaded the ground, bloated with winter rain, into a thick morass. Mud sucked at the roan's hooves and splattered several children struggling through the mire. They looked up through young eyes grown old.

MacGregor cursed the children's parents for their stubborn faith that the latest treaty would be honored, that no one would remove them from their beloved homeland. Go far away, west of a river called the Mississippi, the Great White Father had said. There the land was fair, the grass green and the water always ran. He glanced at the gnarled trees lurking in the shadowy forest. They had lost their hair and been made ugly by winter's killing breath.

The children huddled together in the center of the road. MacGregor jerked the reins to circle them and bumped another horse. Impatient, he frowned at a young woman astride a chestnut mare.

Startled, she grabbed the saddle pommel to steady herself. Silver bracelets around her wrist clinked when she pushed wet strands of black hair from her face to look at him, then dropped her hand to rest on her swollen belly.

"I am sorry," MacGregor murmured in the language of the Creeks and spurred the roan ahead. He shifted to look over his shoulder at the beautiful woman and noted the beaten silver gorget necklace, a symbol of importance, hanging about her neck. Her condition prevented the closure of her decorated coat.

Everyone suffers, he mused, high born, low born, young and old, as long as they are Indian. A tired smile crossed the woman's face, and he realized he was staring—impolite in any society, but especially among the Creeks.

He nodded to her and turned his attention to several men struggling to free a small rig mired in the mud. The roan plodded off the road and into a shallow gully of water to avoid the wagon. Large chunks of ground crumbled beneath the horse's hooves as it regained the road.

An old man stopped to lean on his cane in a coughing fit. MacGregor slowed his horse to a walk. He had no wish to call attention to himself. With the wide brim of his hat pulled low, he had remained hidden on the edges of this mass of moving humanity for weeks. In a few days, they would be in Indian Territory, and he would keep moving. Texas maybe, or California.

A chill gust bit at his back and screamed in his ear. He turned in the saddle. The cold air was thick with the din of misery. The sweeping wind sounded especially human, pitiful and agonized. He reminded himself that it was only Father Wind crying for his suffering children. Besides, even if the scream was human, it was not his affair. At least not as long as he could remain hidden in their numbers.

A woman stopped in front of him to readjust a cradleboard. Her calico skirt clung to her legs in sodden folds. He halted the roan. Ahead, the uniformed figure of a sergeant spurred his horse toward them. MacGregor glanced over his shoulder to see another soldier skirting the mired wagon. He swore beneath his breath at being caught between the two.

On impulse, he reached to relieve the mother of her crying infant. She looked up, reluctant to release her burden. His long braids fell forward as he put his hand on hers and said in her language, "I will carry the baby."

The haggard woman nodded. He rested the cradle in the bend of his arm. A small brown face with intense black eyes peered from the rabbit fur lining. Its lips quivered with weary sobs.

"Shhh." He jiggled the cradleboard. MacGregor nudged the horse to a walk again, pulled a paper packet from his pocket, and ran a thumb under the edges of the fold to open it. Carefully he pulled loose a strip of black licorice with his teeth, refolded the paper, and tucked it away.

He angled the cradle so it would shield his face from scrutiny and pushed the end of the candy into the infant's mouth. Trudging next to the roan, the child's mother clutched the stirrup for support. With a sigh, he reined his mount and pulled the young woman up behind him. She rested her head against his back. They would be a burden, these two, if trouble developed.

A soldier, young and most likely a private, galloped past to meet the oncoming sergeant. MacGregor peered from under the brim of his hat to watch them in animated discussion, then looked down and wiped drool from the infant's chin with a finger as the roan plodded toward the two men.

"I'm telling you, Sarge, the people can't go one

more step." The private's voice echoed above the miserable sounds of the march. "The horse must have lost its footing when the woman fell. The worst of it, she's in a delicate way."

"Ah, saints above, son." The sergeant screwed his face into a frown. A cigar-butt wavered between clinched teeth. "I told you don't let 'em stop. You hear me?" He took the cigar out of his mouth and spit pieces of tobacco. Pointing the stub at the young private, he continued, "Now, get on up ahead and bring Russell and Jacobs back with you. And that no good Seminole, too. What's his name?"

"You mean the scout, Coache?" The private peered down the unending line of people.

"Yeah, get him and be quick. The captain don't reckon to make camp for another couple hours. It'll be dark soon, and there'll be hell to pay if we lose any more stragglers. Gotta keep 'em moving."

Shifting the cradleboard in his arms again, MacGregor chanced a quick glance at the soldiers as they passed. The private spurred his horse and disappeared into the line of wagons ahead.

The sergeant chomped on his cigar, looked from the infant to MacGregor. He noticed the stalled rig and yelled, "Get that jackass going, 'fore I shoot her in her traces. Can't you see you're blocking this sorry excuse for a road?" His burly voice receded as he moved away. "What's the matter with you idiots?"

Contented, the baby sucked on the limp strip of licorice. Black drool escaped from the corners of its mouth. It was none of his affair, MacGregor told himself again. These are not my people.

The sergeant's shout cut through the air. "Come

on, pull, you good for nothin' hag, or I'll shoot you where you stand."

Keep in the shadows, MacGregor reminded himself. Keep to yourself. The soldiers think you are a Creek, and the Indians, in their tightlipped way, will not tell them different.

Four horsemen came trotting down the line of slow-moving people toward him—three soldiers and the Seminole named Coache. Clever, he mused as the scout passed; the army uses a brother to watch a brother. Only *these* brothers, the Creeks and the Seminoles, hate each other.

The scout, with his bright blue turban, red and yellow striped jacket, and knee-high beaded moccasins, presented a colorful contrast to the dull blue of the soldiers' army uniforms. Unlike the Creek Indians he guarded, the Seminole carried a rifle across his lap.

"What does Sarge think I could do?" The young private's voice rose as he pulled his collar up. "Tell that pregnant woman lying there, all still like, to get up and keep walking? Wish I could quit right now."

MacGregor watched the men pass and continue along the trail. The once-mired wagon finally moved, blocking his view of a growing disturbance. He settled back in the saddle and shifted the cradle to rest on his other arm. The Creeks could expect no sympathy from the scout, and less from the soldiers. The plight of these people was not his, yet the thought of leaving an *almost-mother* alongside the road stirred a vague memory. A familiar flush of anger heated his bones.

Wrestling with indecision, MacGregor halted the roan. There was much hardness on the removal. Why should he care about one more injustice? He had stayed hidden by not caring. No good would come of starting now.

"I must go back," he murmured to the woman and shifted to help her dismount.

She slid to the ground and reached for the infant he handed down. Her whispered thanks, "*Mvto*," was almost lost in the moan of the wind. He circled the woman and nudged the horse toward the commotion.

Flames flickered in the mist as a number of Creeks fired torches and surrounded the soldiers. An orange glow gave an illusion of warmth in the gathering grayness. MacGregor pushed his horse into the fringe of light. Pawing the soft ground, a chestnut mare snorted. Mud streaked her shoulder and front legs.

MacGregor stared down at a young woman lying in a shallow pool of dirty water. Fingers of blood traced a path down her face. An old Indian shivered as he knelt and forced his own blanket beneath the woman's head.

"Look boys, can't you keep 'em moving?" The sergeant stood from his examination of the woman and waved the people back. Few budged.

The Seminole shouted a command in the Creek language, "*Yvkepes! Yvkepes!* You walk! You walk!" His horse pranced back and forth, pushing the reluctant Indians onto the road. When MacGregor did not move, Coache repeated the command.

In the Seminole language, MacGregor said in a low voice, "This woman must be important. Assure these people she will not be left alone, and they will move."

"Bah, they drop like flies in first frost. If I did that with all who fall by the wayside, there would be none left to reach Fort Gibson." Coache moved his horse next to the roan so that he sat face to face, knee to knee with MacGregor. "Who is it that speaks to me as a brother?"

A screech interrupted the confrontation, and they turned to find the old Indian kneeling in the mud. His wavering voice, half moan, half song, rose above the murmur of the gathering crowd. The young woman's face contorted in pain as she clutched her swollen stomach.

"Surely you see that her child comes." MacGregor ignored the scout's question. "Leave a woman to help her and her husband to guard her."

Coache shook his head. "My heart is not stirred by a people who have hunted the Seminole." He leaned close. "Ah-ha!"

MacGregor, knowing summer blue eyes betrayed him, steadied his gaze to meet Coache's stare.

"Why does a white man hide beneath likeness of an Indian?" The scout moved the rifle barrel from the crook of his arm. "And why does he seek to fool me with inflections of my own language?"

Coache pointed the rifle at MacGregor's chest, probing past his coat and shirt to expose a jagged scar. "Unless he is bad half-blood known as," the corner of his mouth went up in a smirk, "No-Chance."

Chapter 2

MacGregor stiffened at the sound of his earned name: No-Chance. In his fifteenth summer, people ceased to call him John MacGregor. At first, he ignored the whispers that One-Who-Gives-No-Chance comes among us. Now, after ten years, the name was as much a part of him as the Celtic weapon that earned it.

Without taking his eyes off Coache, he slipped his foot from the stirrup and leaned back in the saddle, away from the rifle prodding him. He hoped his knee's upward movement would not be noticed and dropped his hand to his leg.

"I thought only to prevent trouble for a brother Seminole." His fingers sought the handle of the Celtic knife hidden in the top of his boot.

"You give the Seminole a bad name." Coache shifted in the saddle and rested his rifle in the crook of his arm again.

"Coache," the sergeant fumed, "what's this mad man doing? He's hollering like a crazy banshee."

The old man kneeled in the mud and chanted as he shook a gourd rattle over the injured woman.

Tired and grim-faced, the marchers ignored the soldiers' orders to keep moving. Wrapped in blankets and ragged clothing, they stood in the mist watching one of their own beseech the night spirits for help. Old men and women leaned on canes and each other.

Mothers hugged children to shield them from the wind, and the men stood, arms folded.

"Coache, get over here." The sergeant's face reddened. "We're paying you to translate. Now tell this mad man to get back in line."

When the scout turned his horse and trotted toward the soldier, No-Chance eased back in the saddle.

"He is *a heles haya*, a medicine man." Coache looked at the gathering crowd. "To heal is matter of honor. The only way he will stop is if you put bullet in him."

The sergeant's eyes narrowed. "Is that right?" His hand went to the gun at his hip. He wallowed the cigar from one side of his mouth to the other, finally remounting his horse in disgust.

"Jacobs, bring that mule licker over here. Lay it across that fool Injun there. We'll see how much honor he has."

No-Chance sat up straight and nudged the roan forward. He pulled his hat down until the band rested on his eyebrows. Moisture, gathering along the edge of the brim, reflected the golden glow of the torches.

"But…but, sir," the young private stammered as he guided his horse into the circle, "the lady…what if she gets," his voice went up, "hit?"

"First off, this ain't no lady. She's an Injun!"

No-Chance clenched his fist and swallowed. He barely dared to breathe in an effort to stifle flames of anger building in his head. He knew the pain, the power of a snake biter. His own whip lay coiled and hidden in his saddlebags.

"Second of all," the sergeant continued, "I gave you an order. I didn't ask for no opinion."

"Sergeant," Coache interrupted, "it matters not what you do with this worthless medicine man. The old ones slow the march. But this clumsy girl is someone important in her tribe."

The scout pointed with the rifle barrel. "See the necklace she wears? Her husband or, perhaps her father, is a chief." He nodded toward the crowd. "And they will fight for one such as her."

The sergeant turned to study the haggard line of people.

A young warrior guided a gray dun through the throng of onlookers. He slid off the horse before it came to a halt and ran to the fallen woman.

"Now look'it here, Coache," the sergeant growled, "I don't care a thimble's wit if she's the Queen of England. You tell that fella to get moving, or it will go hard on the whole miserable lot of 'em."

Coache dismounted and rested his rifle in the crook of his arm. He shifted from one leg to the other, talking in a slow, measured voice to the newcomer who stood over the moaning woman.

The young man waved the scout away. His loud refusal, "*Mvnks*! No!" rang out above the medicine man's song.

Coache spit on the ground and grabbed his saddle pommel to remount.

"Soldier!" The sergeant turned to the private. "I won't tell you again. Lay that mule licker into these people," he ordered, pointing to the whip.

"Yes'sir." Jacobs sighed and allowed the coiled weapon to spiral to the ground; then jerked his stiffened arm forward, up over his head and back. The end of the whip arched through the air landing behind him. Just as he stood in the stirrups to send the snake's lethal tongue lashing out, No-Chance jabbed his heels into the roan's sides and pulled back on the reins.

The roan's loud whinny unsettled Jacobs, and he dropped the whip. The horse reared again, hooves clawing the air. The private ducked, lost his balance, and fell sprawling in the mud.

"What the devil's going on," the sergeant's voice boomed.

The warrior leaped toward Jacobs.

No-Chance jumped from his saddle, landing in front of the Indian. The two men stood face to face, neither taller than the other—one in white man's clothing, one in calico and buckskins. The warrior's dark eyes glowered.

"If you harm this soldier, your *almost-child* will be fatherless." No-Chance put his hands up, palms forward, and spoke in the Creek language. He nodded toward the cigar-chewing sergeant aiming a pistol at them.

The warrior stood, arms folded, cords bulging on either side of his neck until the injured woman cried out in a spasm of pain. With a quick glance at the soldiers, he returned to the woman's side.

No-Chance sighed in relief and gathered his horse's reins.

"Sergeant," Coache said, "it is clear these miserable people will revolt if we leave her behind." Leather creaked as he shifted in the saddle. "That back end of a horse is her husband. Leave him and the medicine man. If they all die in the cold, it will be a good thing."

Coache motioned to No-Chance. "That man is a

fellow Seminole. He came along to learn the route. Wants to be a guide for the white man's army." He lifted an eyebrow at the bold lie. "I have his word he'll see these people catch up by daybreak."

No-Chance dropped the retrieved reins and straightened, biting back a protest.

"Coache," the sergeant interrupted. "If I leave them here, it will set a, what'cha call it, a bad example. Every time someone falls out, they'll expect to be pampered."

"Look at this sorry pack of two-legged dogs. Do you think your whip scares them? Most are beyond caring whether they live or die. A revolt will live in the memory of your superiors. They will say Coache did not do his job."

The sergeant slid his gun under his wide belt, removed his hat, and slapped it against his leg, sending drops of water aloft. He took the cigar out of his mouth and jabbed it toward No-Chance.

"His word, he catches up by daybreak?"

"Yes, his word." Herding people back onto the road, Coache glanced back at No-Chance. "His word is good."

****

"Miserable low-down worm. Filthy rotten yellow-bellied coyote. Stinking no good lover-of-dogs." No-Chance's cursing was answered by the soft hoot of an owl. Sudden dread enveloped him, and he shuddered. The feathered square-head brought the shrouded visitor of death.

"Shut up!" No-Chance yelled at the owl nestled high in a hackberry tree. With a screech the bird fluttered from his perch and disappeared.

"That no good, black-hearted Seminole weasel!"

He kicked scattered branches into a pile. "Expecting me to ride herd on these, these"—he glanced over his shoulder at the campsite—"these miserable beaten-down souls." Torchlight blinked through the tangle of trees and bushes.

Heavy clouds thinned and exposed a sky alive with the star spirits. No-Chance looked at the face of Grandmother Moon. "Why'd that carrion-eater have to go and give my word? He had no right." Arms loaded with broken limbs, he struggled through the underbrush into the clearing.

The medicine man glanced up through reddened eyes. Canyons of grief lined his weathered face as he resumed sorting through dried roots and herbs spread on a blanket.

No-Chance dropped the wood next to the old man and assembled stones into a layer to hold a fire above the wet ground. Sputtering and smoking, damp kindling flickered to life. Thankful the wind had gone to sleep, No-Chance sat back on his heels, adding broken limbs to the growing flames.

The warrior had moved his wife under a lean-to. Speaking softly, he sat stroking her hair. The young woman, belly huge and swollen, rested spraddle-legged on a mat of withered grasses and twigs.

No-Chance closed his eyes against a memory that forced its way from hidden depths of his mind. Years ago, his mother had the same thick black hair. He saw it splayed out on white cotton bedding as she gripped his hand with each surge of pain that heralded the journey of a child into the *now-world*.

The young woman's cry shook him from his memories. A woman's pain, his father said, was a reminder of the sin of Adam and Eve. Holding his hands over the fire, No-Chance turned to the medicine man fingering a meager collection of medicinal herbs.

"You have something that will help her?"

The old man nodded and attempted to quell a rattling cough. He blew his nose between two fingers before wiping them across his leg. With a trembling hand, he reached for two dried plant roots and held them up.

"A tea of Blue Cohosh will hasten journey of *near-child*." His face dissolved into a thousand wrinkles with the next deep cough rolling up from his chest. The path from the old land was littered with victims of the coughing sickness.

No-Chance winced, stood, and walked to his horse. Stroking the roan's long neck, he whispered, "We'll be in the land of green grasses soon." He untied his blanket and fished in the saddlebag for a small pot, canteen, and tin of soda crackers.

The withered Cohosh roots sank to the bottom of the pot as tiny bubbles ran up its sides. Between spasms of coughing, the old man continued a low chant to the four directions and Mother Earth. The simmering water turned brown. No-Chance tried not to hear the moans of the young woman. He slid crackers from the tin and held them out.

"Soon I will feel no hunger," the medicine man said, shaking his head. A grimace exposed gaps of missing teeth. His voice wavered as he pushed the pot from the hot stones. "Before Grandfather Sun comes, Maker and Taker of Breath will take me to be with ancestors. My head will not rest in new land."

No-Chance pulled a blanket over his ears to muffle

the sounds of misery and mumbled, "Before Grandfather Sun comes, I will be gone, too. But not to the darkening land."

Chapter 3

The campfire crackled in the nighttime stillness. No-Chance shifted his position on the ground and yawned. He stood, searching the night sky for the position of the Seven Sisters. Dawn was still hours away.

Slumped forward in sleep, the young husband cradled his wife's hand in his own. The medicine man had abandoned his chant and sat hunched in a blanket. No-Chance added wood to the fire, grabbed the empty pot, and made his way to the roan. The horse snickered softly as he stored the pot and blanket in his saddlebags.

A wail of anguish froze him and lifted the hair on the back of his neck. He squeezed the saddle pommel and buried his face in the roan's mane. Another tortured moan rose. There was no mistaking the meaning of this cry. It sent him spiraling back in time and shattered his heart.

"Damn that miserable scout."

The roan's musky smell filled his nostrils as he leaned into the horse. He would not look at the woman. He would just leave. It was not his affair.

Again, an agonized cry tore at No-Chance, draining him of the strength to mount. A distant past, haunted and painful, held him frozen to the spot. Taking a deep breath, he turned to face his memories.

The warrior bent over his wife cradling her head

and shoulders in his arms. She gripped his sleeve. The medicine man remained hidden in his blanket.

"Wake up!" No-Chance shouted and shook the old man causing him to fall sideways. His legs and arms unfolded in a slow slide from under the blanket. The beaded pouch tumbled from his hand. Eyes closed, mouth agape in a silent cough, the wrinkles of his face relaxed in a gentle sag.

No-Chance sank to his knees and covered the *gone-away* one with the blanket. He glanced at the shelter. The young woman gritted her teeth, emitting a long groan. Her husband hugged her close and looked up in an unspoken plea for help.

"Coache could have left a midwife," No-Chance offered. The woman grimaced and another wail filled the air.

"Her pains come close together now. It is a hopeful sign." No-Chance looked into the weary eyes of the young man. "Have you ever birthed a baby?"

The warrior shook his head. "That is work of women."

Numerous small shells sewn to the laboring woman's coat clinked softly as she gasped for breath.

"My mother was Ester Little Wing, a Seminole woman of the Alligator Clan." No-Chance sat back. "In her name will you accept the small help I offer?"

The young man nodded. "I am Chickamauga of the Upper Creeks. My wife is White Cloud, daughter of Chief Black Storm." He frowned. "Her fall...she wanders in and out of dream world."

"A woman should do this," No-Chance grumbled. He grabbed the hem of one pant leg and nodded for Chickamauga to do likewise. Together they tugged until the leggings loosened enough to drag over her stomach. Colorful designs decorated the length of each leg. An image of No-Chance's mother flashed through his mind again as he ran a fingernail over the intricate beadwork.

Water inched its way from under White Cloud's skirt and between her bare legs. No-Chance dropped the leggings down in an effort to soak up the liquid. White Cloud groaned and arched her body with the next ripple of pain.

Pushing back his own panic, he directed Chickamauga to kneel above his wife and cradle her head and shoulders on his legs, and then positioned himself opposite. Time and again, White Cloud clung to her husband's arms and, with her feet, pushed against No-Chance's knees until the pain subsided. Exhausted, she collapsed into a fragile rest until, minutes later, the next spasm roused her. The Seven Sisters inched across the heavens.

White Cloud drew in a mouthful of air, and a moan forced its way between her teeth, swelling into a scream that ended in sobs as one pain melted into another. She struggled to breathe. Finally, the critical moment arrived.

A wave of inadequacy washed over No-Chance. He groped back to his childhood.

"Our Father which art in heaven…"

The top of the baby's head appeared.

"Hallowed be thy name." Sweat dripped from No-Chance's forehead and stung his eyes. "Thy kingdom come. Thy will be done." He faltered. "Thy will be done."

White Cloud's voice lifted in a shriek.

The prayer died on No-Chance's lips. His braids

fell forward as he stretched his arms between her open legs. A small head pushed defiantly out into his cupped hands. Another contraction, another scream, and the baby slipped from its warm confines into the chill air.

"Ah, Chickamauga, you have a fine son." He lifted the tiny form, turning it to face its parents. The light of the campfire softly illuminated its glistening skin.

No-Chance laid the child between White Cloud's legs and tore at the knot of his kerchief. Exhilaration turned to alarm as he wiped blood and mucus from the baby's face. He placed his fingertips on its chest. It didn't breathe, didn't cry.

No-Chance cradled the limp infant, balancing its head in one hand, body in the other and blew warm breath into its face. He turned the baby over gingerly rubbing its back and tiny buttocks until a sharp angry wail broke the tense silence.

"Listen, this new one has the howl of our loudmouthed brother, the wolf." No-Chance said as he tied the umbilical cord with a piece of rawhide fringe. He pulled his knife and held it to the cord, then hesitated. Chickamauga cradled White Cloud's head on his knees. The two men stared at each other. It was a sacred thing to separate the bond of mother and child.

No-Chance bit his lip and made a swift cut. He tied the kerchief around the baby's middle and reached for White Cloud's leggings bunched between her legs. Alarmed, he jerked his hand back. Blood crawled across the surface of the soft white buckskin turning it a bright crimson.

"This great loss of blood is a natural thing," he said, unsure of the fact.

White Cloud, long black hair plastered in wet

strands against her pale face, didn't stir when the infant was placed on her chest. Her gaze shifted from the infant to No-Chance. There was a knowing in her dark eyes—an anguished look of grief. A tear escaped from the edge of her eye, slowly descended down the side of her face and dropped off the silver ring in her ear.

"What a fine son you have." No-Chance placed her hand on the baby's back. "He will make a great chief for your clan someday."

She continued to look at him.

He put a finger to her face to interrupt the path of a second tear. "The heart of your father will be glad again when he sees this grandson. Does not your husband burst with pride at this great thing you have done?"

White Cloud's bracelets clinked softly as her hand slipped off her infant son and slid in one graceful movement to the ground. No-Chance glanced down at the upturned palm and held his breath. Had he not chased away the owl? Wasn't the medicine man's death enough sacrifice for the night?

He forced himself to look into White Cloud's face. Her unseeing eyes stared back. Shock filtered through his body, and a great sadness crushed him, holding him rooted to the ground. The untended fire sputtered, leaving the small group in the night's cold shadows. Last memories of his mother surged through his mind and exploded in an agonized scream.

"NO!"

Chapter 4

"Mother's gone turtle hunting,
She'll be back soon.
Sleep baby sleep,
She'll be back soon."

No-Chance paused in his lullaby to kick another branch into the campfire. The newborn lay snuggled inside his shirt and jacket, warm against his chest. He could feel the faint flutter of its breathing on his skin, hear its soft whimper.

Chickamauga sat next to his wife with a blanket over his head and shoulders. His sorrow was silent, as if he, too, had died.

In a low voice, No-Chance began again the lullaby that filled the evenings of his childhood. It was a song of love, a song of warmth, the song of a mother. He walked circles around the blazing fire and watched bright sparks rise and die in the cold air.

Retrieving the medicine man's blanket, he shook it over the flames to remove the chill that resided in its folds. Grandmother Moon and the stars had almost completed their journey in the night sky. In the distance, a wolf howled, announcing his return from the hunt.

No-Chance paused, looked down at the tiny head pressed against his chest, and listened to the shallow breathing of the infant. He ran his finger across the top of the baby's head and ruffled its soft black hair.

"One day you will be a great warrior! You will see many winters and be a wise leader of your people. I think you will not join your mother in the land of dark spirits."

Squatting to catch the light of the campfire, he gentled the baby from his shirt to study its small perfect features. No-Chance bent his head, placed his cheek against the dewy softness of the infant's face, and breathed deeply of the newborn smell—a fragile joy in the night's harshness. He brushed the infant's warm forehead with his lips.

Surprised by the act, he straightened and awkwardly shifted the bundle in his arms. He glanced across the orange haze of flames into the grief-filled black eyes of Chickamauga, who watched from under the blanket's hood.

Irritated at such weakness, No-Chance wrapped the baby in the warmed blanket and laid it on a bed of twigs to lift it from the ground's chill. Do not become attached to this little one, he told himself. Babies are for mothers to suckle and fathers to brag about. He was neither! He was a half-breed and didn't belong in this child's world, just as he didn't belong in the white man's world.

"I never gave my word to help these people." No-Chance swung into the saddle. The roan's ears swiveled with the sound of his voice. "How can a man give the word of someone else? This is Coache's problem."

He nudged the horse past the campfire and looked down at the tiny bundle. The blanket moved as the baby stirred. "It would serve that old belly-crawlin' snake right if he gets called to account. That loudmouth sergeant would chew on him like he chews that cigar." His breath made clouds in the air, and he pulled his jacket closed against the coldness creeping into his bones.

The roan clambered onto the roadbed. No-Chance looked over his shoulder at the blanket-shrouded figure of Chickamauga. In his despair, the warrior continued to sit as motionless as the bodies of White Cloud and the medicine man. Death cast a gloom that even the light of the blazing fire could not warm. Night creatures had returned to their dens, leaving the forest silent in that space between night and day.

"No, sir, I didn't ask to be a midwife, much less to ride herd on these people and deliver 'em back to the blue-coats." Mud sloshed with each plodding step of the horse. "I can't let it get around that No-Chance delivers babies now, can I, Boy?" The horse snorted at the sound of his name.

No-Chance reined the horse and slumped against the saddle's cantle. If Chickamauga, in his grief, failed to keep the spirit of the fire alive, the baby would freeze, and the one good thing he had done in his life would be in vain. With a sigh, he wheeled the horse and returned to the clearing.

Chickamauga, on his hands and knees, dug in the mud with a large stick. He paused and looked up. "Spirit of medicine man told me you would return," he said, voice drained of emotion. He nodded toward a shallow hole gouged into the sodden earth. "I will not let Brother Wolf disturb White Cloud's bones."

No-Chance slid to the ground. He blinked back the image of hundreds of hasty graves in ditches along the trail. The march didn't stop for anything; not sickness, not death, and certainly not for burials.

He added wood to the campfire, retrieved the small pot from his saddlebag and knelt next to Chickamauga to scoop the loosened dirt into a pile. They worked shoulder to shoulder huffing volumes of white air with the exertion of carving a narrow grave from the cold ground.

Mud coated No-Chance's hands and clothing. His back and shoulders ached when he straightened to glance at the eastern sky. "Grandfather Sun brings a new day. We must go or bring the wrath of the blue-coats on us."

"Let them come." Chickamauga threw the stick down. "My heart would be glad to join my *gone-away* wife in the darkening land."

Gummy soil sucked at his boots as No-Chance stepped out of the hole. "Your son has no mother. Would you make him fatherless, too?"

He brushed at his pant legs and shrugged. "Of course, if you want to tempt the evil ones, that is up to you. The baby is a fine-looking boy. Perhaps I will take him. He will be company in my old age."

Chickamauga stared at him.

No-Chance turned and walked over to White Cloud's body. He squatted and gently closed her eyelids. He could not leave them open. If her spirit had not left for the dark world, she would see the dirt fall over her.

Chickamauga knelt and ran his hand down his wife's thick black hair, stopping at the hammered silver necklace on her chest. He guided the necklace over White Cloud's head and placed it around his own neck. With a huff, he lifted her.

Together the two men lowered her into the foreign ground, away from her ancestors, without any rituals. With soft thuds, pails of soil covered the once beautiful face, muting the soft click of tiny shells sewn to the buckskin coat, hiding forever the beaded leggings soaked with blood. The sleeping infant was all that remained of White Cloud.

No-Chance took the pot and scooped live coals from the campfire to scatter across the burial mound. The fire spirit that lived within the chunks of red-hot wood crackled and popped. Its glowing heart would soon collapse into a heap of ash to be blown from place to place by Father Wind.

"Dust thou art and unto dust thou shalt return," No-Chance whispered. He could hear the rest of his father's burial sermon in the crisp clacking of tree branches.

"God shall wipe away all tears from their eyes; and there shall be no more death, neither sorrow, nor crying, nor pain: for the former things are passed away." His father assured mourners that words from the Good Book never failed to comfort. No-Chance looked at the young husband and doubted the power of the white man's words for his red brother.

He patted the coals into the ground with the toe of his boot. Perhaps the effort would prevent the wolves from scenting White Cloud.

Chickamauga dragged the medicine man into the underbrush and heaped broken limbs and debris over the dead body. It seemed a useless thing to do. The crows would alert the forest to his final resting place, and wolves would come to sate their hunger. The easy orgy would mute their keen sense of smell, and the bones of White Cloud would be safe for now. It was the old man's final service to the daughter of a chief.

The sky blushed at the near arrival of the sun when No-Chance finally hauled himself into the saddle. He had lived a lifetime since the previous day, and the experience left him exhausted.

"Why did you come back?" Chickamauga asked as he handed up the infant.

"I don't know." No-Chance took the newborn and tucked it inside his jacket. Did he return for the child or for himself?

The two men followed the wide path of the removal. Here and there bits of cloth fluttered from bushes trampled in the dark. A corn husk doll dropped by a tired child hinted at the native population that passed in the night.

The world was sober in the early dawn as they trotted through stands of cheerless trees and frosted meadows. No-Chance hugged the bundle beneath his jacket with one arm. The infant slept, as if he belonged there. A faint aroma of wood smoke laced the frosty air signaling the nearness of camp. The child whimpered, turning his head, searching.

"He's hungry." No-Chance fished in his pocket for a licorice strip as he slowed the roan to a walk. "What will you name your new son?"

"My gone-away wife did not tell me name she kept close to heart. Her father, Chief Black Storm, will decide."

"If you give the baby a name, surely he would not change it." No-Chance wiggled the end of the licorice between the infant's lips and watched it push at the candy with his tongue.

"A name is an important thing." Chickamauga

nudged his horse close to watch the feeding attempt. "Chief Black Storm lives for this grandson. His land and possessions are gone. Mother of my wife died after march began." He glanced back at the chestnut mare. "Now I tell him White Cloud, his only child, joins mother in dark land."

"So, I hold a future chief in my arms." No-Chance wiped at the black drool on the baby's chin with his finger. "He must have a special name."

"Perhaps he will be last of Creek people." Chickamauga looked up at the pale sky. "I do not see how we survive. The white man, the *wvcenvlke*, strip us, make us a nothing nation. How do I teach son to be proud when white man holds foot on my neck?"

"It is true the white man thinks like our brother, the fox," No-Chance said. "They are clever and cunning. To gain their respect you must know what they know. You must be able to speak like them and read their words. They do not always write on paper what they say with their mouths."

"Chiefs say to learn tongue of the *wvcenvlke* would make our hearts greedy like theirs. It is forbidden."

Disgusted, No-Chance snorted. He had heard the argument before and knew the penalty for speaking English among the Upper Creeks was the loss of an ear.

"If we were to see a Cherokee man there on the road, what would you say?"

Chickamauga shrugged. "*Osiyo*."

"There, you said 'hello' in the man's own language. Why is it wrong to know the tongue of the white man, but not the Cherokee?"

"It is color of man's skin that makes difference." Chickamauga shook his head. "Language of *wvcenvlke*

28

and their writing is forbidden."

"Your chiefs are fools. It will be like being in the forest with no weapons. You will be able to eat only what you can kill with your hands. You will be defenseless, and the bear and mountain lion will not fear you. How can there be a future for your people if the elders take away the weapon of language?"

When Chickamauga did not answer, No-Chance looked down at the now sleeping infant and wiggled the soggy licorice strip from its mouth. Whether these people prospered or vanished was no concern of his.

They topped the ridge of a hill to find the huge camp spread out in a valley. Wagons and tents lined a meandering stream. Strands of smoke rose in the early morning air. Herds of horses nibbled at the yellowed grasses, and blue-coated soldiers walked their mounts around the jagged perimeter of the sprawling camp.

Chickamauga urged his horse into the descent. No-Chance hesitated. If he hung back, he could circle the camp and be in Indian Territory ahead of the wagon train—away from the soldiers. Coache had given him an idea. Should he be questioned, he would proclaim himself a Seminole scout.

The baby squirmed inside his jacket. No-Chance reached to halt Chickamauga when a shrill whoop echoed from the valley.

Chapter 5

The piercing cry hung in the stillness, and then another warrior's savage whoop—the reminder of distant wars—joined the first, rolling one over another. Dismayed, No-Chance watched the blue-coats turn their attention his way. The camp came to life with people crawling out of wagons and tents. Indians near the edge of the encampment scurried to tethered horses.

Soldiers shouted and spurred their mounts to cut off the Indians' rush from camp. No-Chance abandoned the urge to flee, pulled his hat low, and prodded the roan next to Chickamauga as the welcoming Indians engulfed them. Ponies snorted in frosty breaths and jostled each other after the short race across the meadow.

Sitting tall and grim, a blanket-wrapped Indian guided his horse through the boisterous group. Three vivid blue tattoo lines ran down his forehead—one stopped at the bridge of his nose and the other two above each eyebrow.

No-Chance heard again the stories of his father as he studied the imposing Creek. "Aye, ye were just a wee bard when the red devils came swirling out of the forest like a plague of locust, screaming like banshees all the while. The Red Stick Wars they called it. 'Twas Black Storm himself, with his blue-striped face, that burnt our house down around our ears. God, in His mercy, held us in the palm of His hand, else we'd be mightily scorched."

The aging warrior, who earned a fierce reputation fighting alongside Red Eagle, sat sober-faced in the early morning light and stiffened at the faint glint of silver on Chickamauga's chest. The braves fell silent as all eyes shifted to the riderless chestnut mare. The chief clenched his teeth and, with a barely audible groan, lowered his head.

"Father," Chickamauga's voice was soft, "you have a grandson."

No-Chance unbuttoned his jacket and carefully removed the small bundle snuggled next to his chest. The sleeping infant sucked at its lower lip.

Black Storm moved his horse forward and reached for the child as a number of soldiers approached the group. No-Chance comforted himself with the thought their eyes were on the chief and not him. Black Storm allowed the edges of the blanket to fall away, exposing the naked child to the cold.

The sergeant barked, "What do you think this is, boys, a bloomin' tea party? Get these people back to camp."

A tiny wail answered the harsh command. The chief lifted the flailing baby over his head. Soldiers and warriors alike laughed at the insistent crying.

"Come on, get 'em down there, like I told you boys," the sergeant commanded.

One by one, the riders turned their horses and trotted back to the encampment. Chickamauga and Black Storm followed. Neither looked back.

No-Chance tugged on the brim of his hat, pulled his jacket closed, and urged the roan downhill. What had he expected? A thank you?

The colorful scout pulled alongside the roan. "I did not think that One-Who-Gives-No-Chance would return."

"You gave my word, didn't you?"

"Wah, so the half-breed is a man of honor." Coache's laughter was thin and mocking. "It is a rare thing with one who has blood of the white man running through his veins."

"My father fed many a Seminole and Creek at his table and hid a heap of them from the militia." He did not tell Coache the price of a bowl of boiled meat and corn cakes was a sermon on the love of God.

The sergeant escorted Chickamauga and Black Storm until they disappeared into the camp, then wheeled his horse and trotted back.

Coache's smirk dropped. "The medicine man?"

"Dead. Coughing sickness, most likely."

"And the woman?"

"Bled to death."

Coache pointed with his rifle. "The feed wagon is there in the center of the camp. Fill your stomach with something hot. My eyes will not notice if you disappear." The scout moved his horse to intercept the sergeant.

The soldier's gruff voice questioned, "I suppose the old man and the woman are dead?"

The scout's response was lost as No-Chance urged the roan between wagons and into the camp. He paused to watch two rib-skinny dogs fight over a bone. A woman, fringed shawl tight around her shoulders, stirred a boiling pot over a campfire. The sour smell of corn sofke wafted in the air.

Wet wood hissed in hundreds of campfires coming to life. A thin layer of smoke hung low over the encampment. The aroma of coffee and bacon announced the chuck wagon. Soldiers squatted on their heels or leaned against the wagon eating from tin plates. A line of ragged Indians waited docilely for the soldiers to finish.

No-Chance slumped in the saddle. His bones screamed for rest. His eyes ached, but worst of all, the knot in his stomach burned. He yawned and watched a soldier drain his cup and hold it out for more. The cook's helper lifted a huge coffeepot from the fire and poured steaming brew. The two men laughed.

Was it wise to risk being questioned or recognized? He avoided the feed wagons, always eating alone, never bedding down near the same family more than once. He sighed and rubbed the back of his neck.

All but one soldier left. The cook turned to serve the line of Indians. No-Chance slid off the roan and walked toward the chuck wagon. He pulled his hat low and stood in line, idly fingering the leather reins.

"Breath Maker clears the skies and sends sun today," said an old man in front of him. He rested his hand on the head of a young girl. She fidgeted with a bright red blanket wrapped around her shoulders.

Head still down, No-Chance moved another step forward. The rumbling in his stomach grew louder, more insistent.

The little girl peeked around at him with wide eyes and giggled. The old man bent down. "It is not polite to laugh at another's hunger." He looked into No-Chance's face to begin an apology and then straightened.

The half-breed sighed. He had inherited his mother's thick black hair, but his light blue eyes gave clue to Scottish ancestry. He shrugged his shoulders. "Maybe it is better to laugh when you can't do anything else."

The old man turned his back. The little girl grinned until a hand firmly turned her head forward.

No-Chance shifted his weight, aware that others in the line had suddenly become conscious of an impostor. He could hear their muttering.

"Soldiers think they fool us with a spy."

"He is probably outlaw from his people."

His stomach rumbled again, and he twisted the reins in his hands. He still had a few stale soda crackers in his saddlebag. Perhaps he should go.

The old man turned and spoke sternly. "Be quiet! You stir an interest in us. Soldiers take offense at smallest things. Who would give blue-coats satisfaction of taking anyone? Not I!"

Cold silence enveloped those in line. No-Chance dared not look toward the soldier. Head still lowered, he moved forward a few paces. The little girl reached up, accepted a bowl of hot hominy mush with a happy smile, and marched off, dragging her red blanket in the dirt.

The aroma filled his nostrils, tantalizing him as he stepped up to the chuck wagon. From under his hat brim, No-Chance saw the offer of steaming mush with a strip of fat meat. He took hold of the plate, but the mess cook did not release his own tight grip. The plate hung suspended in a tug of war. Alarmed, No-Chance raised his eyes slowly and met those of the beefy, red-faced cook.

"Ha! I thought so! Your face is showing, Breed. Only one reason a man with a gussied up horse would be waitin' in the handout line. You're on the run, lookin' to get lost in this mess of Injuns," the cook sneered. He glanced over his shoulder at the soldier and lowered his voice. "Now, for a few silver coins I could forget about this!"

No-Chance stared at him. He felt the warmth of the food through the tin plate.

"Or now…I'll accept that horse instead. I ain't partic'lar." A rolled smoke dangled from the cook's lower lip, and as he talked, ashes filtered onto the plate of food.

"I heard how good you boil mush." No-Chance forced a smile. "Thought to mosey over and see for myself."

The cook roared with laughter causing his apron to dance over a quivering belly. The soldier and the helper looked up from their conversation. Finally, wiping his eyes, the plump man snorted and leaned forward.

"Like I said, I ain't partic'lar."

"Sorry, won't give up the roan," No-Chance said under his breath. "And don't have money," he lied.

"Then guess I gotta do my duty." The cook's tiny pig eyes narrowed. He spit the smoke butt into the kettle of bubbling mush. "Such as callin' over that there soldier!"

No-Chance struggled to control his rising anger. He eyed the steaming food. With a forced smile, he whispered, "I could tell you of a big deal. Ever hear of a killer named No-Chance?"

Chapter 6

"No-Chance?" The cook frowned. "What about him?"

"You're looking at him!" No-Chance straightened his shoulders and pushed the brim of his hat back to meet the man's stare. Barely breathing, he allowed his right arm to hang loose, his fingers tense, ready to find the hidden knife.

"You ain't him," the cook retorted. "That fellow killed a dozen men."

"Never killed a man that didn't deserve it." No-Chance flexed his fingers and fixed the man with a scowl. "They all had their chance. Besides, it's more like five dead. The woman don't count."

The cook's voice lost its belligerence. "Aw, you can't hornswoggle me. They say that breed's plumb loco, and you don't look…"

"Try me," No-Chance said without altering his stare. Coldness crept back into his bones—the kind that left a man steady, ready to fight.

A bead of sweat popped out on the cook's forehead. "You…you say you'll make a deal?"

"I might." No-Chance paused to let his words simmer. "You let go this plate"—he tugged on the tin—"and you got a chance at eyeballing another sunset."

"Haw, haw." Pretending to laugh, the cook's beady eyes narrowed. "How you gonna kill me?" The grin vanished. "You ain't packin'."

"Been a lot of men thought that."

The cook's mouth quivered.

No-Chance set his jaw. The man was a coward. They all had that look—weak eyes with a nervous twitch. It disgusted him. He leaned forward. "Ever hear a man try to scream with his throat cut? He just whistles, especially when the air is cold."

"Here, take the damn thing." The cook shoved the plate forward. "Ain't no skin off my nose," he mumbled and wiped his mouth with the back of his hand.

No-Chance didn't move. He gestured with his head toward the heavy frying pan. Snorting, the cook speared several strips of pork and flipped them onto the plate.

"Now, I'll be right over there for a spell." No-Chance broke eye contact. "Don't do nothing stupid." He clucked for Boy to follow and kept the horse between himself and the nearby soldier. A few feet away, he squatted against his heels and scooped cigarette ashes from the steaming food.

The roan nuzzled his back. No-Chance fished out a strip of pork, sucked the hot juices off, and spit it back into his palm. He held his hand open as the horse lifted the meat with his lips.

"That overstuffed bastard will squeal on us with nary a backward thought, Boy." He watched the cook who kept looking from him to the soldier. No-Chance shoveled in spoonfuls of warm mush, easing the knot of hunger. The roan noisily wallowed the pork along his back molars.

Without taking his eyes off the chuck wagon, No-Chance scraped the spoon across the bottom of the plate. Whether it was the hot food or the sense of danger, he felt alive again, freed of the previous night's emotions.

"Just as soon as that blue-coat leaves, we'll mosey down the road like we're scouting. Then we'll find some dry hole, and I'll get that saddle off, maybe sleep clean through to spring."

The roan spit the pulverized mass of pork out. No-Chance looked down at the gray lump.

"You're right, Boy; it weren't that good." The taste of salt hung in the back of his throat, and he glanced at the coffeepot hanging above the fire.

The loitering soldier drained his cup and turned to leave. Cook put his arm out as if to stop him.

"Don't do it, fool," No-Chance said under his breath, dropping his plate on the ground. He retrieved the hidden knife and stood, feet apart.

Cook glanced over, flashed a weak smile, and shrugged. He slammed the soup ladle into the cooking pot while the soldier, hands pushed deep into his pockets strolled past, whistling.

No-Chance breathed a sigh of relief and pierced the last piece of meat with the point of his knife. A slight tremor ran along the soles of his feet, and he looked beyond the jumble of wagons. Three mounted men emerged from the tree line, clattered across the wooden planks spanning the creek, and slowed to pick their way around campsites.

No-Chance stuffed the pork in his mouth and secreted the knife in his palm. Pulling his hat low, he watched the riders trot past, leather creaking and metal jingling. Two of them wore black woolen coats and the youngest, a blue plaid mackinaw covering him, as well as his horse.

Although he saw no weapons, he knew they wore guns. It was in the manner they rode—with a slight lean to the left to allow for a pistol tucked in their belts or strapped to their legs. The riders didn't slouch but sat stiff and cocky—with an air of authority and the means to back it up. He grimaced. No doubt about it. Lawmen!

"Hey, you," one man yelled at the whistling soldier who turned to watch their approach, "get your superior. We need to line up any stray riders travelin' with this bunch of Injuns. Got word to watch for a couple of fugitives."

No-Chance spit the pork out and looked over at the cook.

"Hey," the cook yelled and reached into the back of the chuck wagon. Sunlight bounced off the metal barrel of a rifle as he waved at the receding lawmen, then pointed toward No-Chance.

As if it had a mind of its own, the cold blade of the Celtic-handled knife slipped into position between No-Chance's fingers. He knew its weight and balance. In one swift moment, the weapon hummed silently toward its target.

Stunned, the cook fumbled with his rifle and staggered. Eyes wide, he clutched at the knife handle protruding from his throat. His mouth dropped open in a mute scream before he fell against the wooden serving table. Plates, spoons, and the kettle slid down the collapsed table and clattered to the ground.

The huddled Indians turned from their food. None moved. Chest pounding, No-Chance stole a glance at the riders as he reached under the roan to tighten the cinch.

The three lawmen looked back at the disturbance.

Trudging from the stream, the helper yelled, "Damn, Otis, you been drinking already this morning? Don't expect me to be cleanin' up that mess."

With a shake of their heads, the lawmen chuckled and moved off through the maze of wagons and tents.

Daring to breathe again, No-Chance picked up the plate, then holding the roan's bridle led him to the chuck wagon. He felt naked as a newborn babe without his knife and didn't fancy leaving it behind.

Head down, the young helper struggled with two sloshing buckets of water. No-Chance wiggled the toe of his boot under the cook's shoulder and strained to push him over. He knelt and jerked his knife free.

Eyes bugged large as plates, Cook struggled to breathe. Warm blood spewed from the severed windpipe and steamed in the chill air.

"Are you daft, man? I warned you." No-Chance pried the man's grasping hand from his sleeve. "Did you think I'd let you turn me in?"

Cook's tongue trembled, voice a hiss. Blood bubbled from the wound and into the folds of his ample neck until the hissing stopped.

"It is good," No-Chance whispered in the dead man's ear. "I will not hear your voice from the grave." He wiped the knife blade along the man's coat sleeve before slipping it back into its hidden sheath and tucked a towel under the cook's chin.

The helper set both buckets down with a thud and bent over, hands on his knees, panting. "Now look here, you tub-o'-lard, you can just lay there all day. I ain't falling for that 'I'm hurt crap' again."

No-Chance nestled his hat low on his forehead,

stood, and walked over to the freckle-faced young man. "That fat man don't look good." He handed the helper his empty plate with a casualness he didn't feel. "Must've been something he ate."

"Ohhh shii-it!" the helper whined. "No telling where the sick wagon is."

No-Chance stepped onto the muddy road. Don't hurry, he told himself. Just walk to the stream; once across and into the trees, let Boy set his own pace. The horse likes to run. He scratched the roan's muzzle and stopped, hand in mid-air.

On the other side of the stream, two soldiers paused in their patrol to talk. No-Chance turned the horse and walked back to the chuck wagon. Somewhere straight ahead were the three lawmen. Retracing the previous night's path would leave him out in the open. Only one hope of escape—cut around the chuck wagon and get lost among the Indians.

"Hey, mister, I don't think Otis is breathing."

The cook gazed up at the sky, mouth agape.

No-Chance kicked scattered plates from his path. "Nah, kid," he struggled to sound calm, "the food ain't that bad." Despite the cold, his palms were sweating.

He avoided the broken table and worked his way through the group of Indians still huddled over their food. Several paused in the act of running their fingers around the rim of tin plates and glanced up. Tight-lipped, the old man held the little girl in his lap and stared directly at No-Chance. Cook's death was no secret from the grandfather.

"Hey, somebody, come 'ere!" The helper held up a bloody towel.

The child looked up and smiled. No-Chance

winked at her and hastened through the group.

"Help! Otis is kilt!" The boy's panicked voice pierced the rumblings of camp.

A patrolling soldier shouted from the perimeters, "What's wrong over there?"

No-Chance swung into the saddle.

"*Ehake!* Wait!" a voice hissed from the shadows.

Chapter 7

No-Chance jerked at the command to wait.

Coache stepped from behind a canvas wind shelter and caught hold of the roan's bridle. "So, it is true! You carry the spirit of the troublemaker, our blue-feathered brother, the jay, with you," he sneered.

No-Chance leaned forward and dropped his arm against his leg, fingers ready to find the knife.

The scout raised his hand, palm forward. "It is a good thing, this time what you have done." He let go of the bridle. "Upstream where the water falls, there is a crossing. Beyond, grandfather oak shelters a hidden path on the other side." He stepped back. "Go! I will come when it is safe."

No-Chance stared at the flapping canvas and nudged the horse to a walk. It would be foolish to follow the advice of the scout again. Does one reach to pat a dog that has bitten once?

The excited voice of the helper grew louder interrupting his thoughts. "I didn't see nothing. Some fellow just said Otis was sick. Ask them Injuns what happened."

No-Chance twisted in the saddle. A redheaded officer stomped into the circle of resting Indians. His voice was loud, angry. Other soldiers stayed mounted, rifles across their laps.

The old man and the others would say nothing. Of

that, No-Chance was certain. Their stoic silence would infuriate the blue-coat, and they would be punished with all the righteous indignation that the officer could muster. An image of the little girl's smile flashed in his mind. He ran a hand under the flap on his saddle bag and removed a coiled leather whip.

No-Chance turned his horse to face the soldiers and took a deep breath. "Ah yaheeeeee!" He felt invigorated as the spirit of his Seminole ancestors filled the ear-splitting yell. If he died today, it would not be an unexpected thing. He had walked on the edge of death many times.

"Hey, you there," the officer bellowed. "Stop!"

No-Chance jerked the roan around and spurred him to action. The horse lunged ahead.

"Shoot him, damn it. Shoot!"

Loud cracks of rifle fire split the air and reverberated through the encampment. No-Chance flattened himself against the neck of his horse as it bounded over the tongue of a wagon. Several bullets tore through the canvas covering. People scattered as he searched for a path through the confusion. A jumble of Indians and settlers, tents and wagons, horses and cattle, campfires and steaming kettles blurred into a giant barrier. He wove his horse through the moving mass of humanity.

"There he is! After him!" Soldiers' angry shouts cut through sounds of crying children and screaming women. "After him!"

No-Chance bobbed from side to side, glancing over his shoulder in time to see an old woman throw a large basket in front of a horse. The animal stumbled throwing its rider.

"Clear a path!" he shouted in Creek. *As long as they do not see my white father's eyes, my braids make me one of the tribe. The Maker of Breath gives me an advantage.*

Mothers grabbed children, and items out of the way. As soon as he sped past, men swatted a cow or pulled a cart into the newly-made opening to slow the pursuing soldiers. The big roan cleared campfires and cut around obstacles with a sure-footedness born of many such chases.

No-Chance caught sight of a soldier racing along the stream to cut off his escape. With an earsplitting yell, he pulled himself erect in the saddle, allowed the whip in his hand to uncoil, and headed straight for his attacker. The yell built into a crescendo of rage, unnerving the panicked young recruit, who faltered in his charge and struggled to pull his rifle from its scabbard.

Standing in the stirrups, No-Chance arced the whip back over his head and sent it forward with a mighty snap. The tightly-braided leather slashed across the soldier's hand. Without pausing, No-Chance drew abreast and slammed his forearm into the astonished soldier, sending him backward off his horse.

No-Chance slowed the roan and turned in the saddle. Several soldiers and lawmen had regained their mounts and were treading their way through the camp's disorder.

Deprived of weapons, hundreds of Indians peered from under wagons at a fight they dared not join. Interference in the chase would not go unpunished. No-Chance ran his fist skyward. A grateful thank-you rang out.

"*Mvto! Mvskokvlke!* Thank you! Mvskoke people!"

Defiant whoops answered back as No-Chance leaned forward and urged the horse to full stride. Swollen by winter rains, the stream churned and swirled around rocks. The rush of water would have dug invisible holes. He dared not cross to the shelter of the wooded area beyond the stream.

A bullet ripped past almost before he heard the sharp crack of rifle fire. Just ahead, the stream poured over a rock slab, creating a shallow waterfall. Coache's advice flooded back with the next scream of bullets.

Then it came, the sick thud of lead tearing through flesh. The roan whinnied and stumbled. Snorting, he regained his footing and forged ahead.

No-Chance swerved the horse to cross the stream on the flat ledge of rock. He chanced a glance at the four riders bearing down on him. Conspicuous in his colorfully striped jacket, Coache raced behind the soldiers.

The roan splashed across the stream, onto the bank, and through an opening in the trees. Layered with a deep carpet of leaves, the narrow trail led No-Chance into the gloom of a sleeping forest. Thickly-massed trees laced their branches together creating a canopy.

Boy's labored breathing and muffled hoof beats broke the silence. Leaves scattered in the wake of his unsteady gait.

No-Chance searched the woods for a hiding place. Ahead, a giant oak reached tangled branches in all directions as if to beckon the anxious rider to safety. He eased the limping roan into a walk and approached the tree. Scanning the ground, he ducked under limbs sheltering the road. A few steps past the massive trunk,

No-Chance stopped and looked backwards.

There it was! Beyond the tree, a slight break in the underbrush suggested a path that angled off the road. Dare he trust the scout again? The roan's hindquarters sagged. It would be heartless to push the animal. He dismounted and led the horse through the slim opening into the dense woods. Brambles and bushes tore at his pant legs as he struggled to get deep into the foliage.

The ground trembled in advance of the pursuing soldiers. No-Chance grabbed the bridle and pulled the roan's head low.

"Easy, Boy. I'll find us a dry hole and get that bullet out of your hip. Poultice it with a little camphor."

Trees shuddered, sifting a sprinkle of yellow leaves as horsemen thundered past the large oak. No-Chance caught only blurs of riders through the forest's thick camouflage. He waited until the sound of hoof-beats and creaking leather, the smack of whips across horses' rumps and clink of metal died away before daring to breathe.

The roan's eyes were wide with pain, and No-Chance ran his hand down its long forehead. "I'll fix you up right as rain, you'll see," he soothed. Sidestepping deer droppings and deflecting the sting of slender branches, he led Boy along the narrow path. The trail ended at the brink of a steep slope of land. So this was it—a ravine, the perfect hiding place.

Wildlife had left deep ruts down the incline. Mindful of soft ground, he urged the horse over the edge. Boy's hindquarters slumped, and the roan slipped. Reins tore through No-Chance's hands as the heavy animal struggled against the rapid descent. With a frightened squeal, the horse slid to the bottom of the slope.

No-Chance's feet went out from under him, and he tumbled through the mud and wet leaves. He grabbed at dangling roots and vines in a futile attempt to avoid a collision. No-Chance skidded into the roan as it collapsed.

Sharp pain ripped through his legs, forcing an agonized scream that echoed down the ravine. Pinned beneath the horse, No-Chance steadied his breathing and coaxed, "Up, Boy. Get up!"

The roan thrashed in a useless attempt to rise.

No-Chance grit his teeth as he managed to free one leg. Bile rose in his throat at the torment movement produced, and he collapsed backward into a mound of leaves, the right leg still trapped under the horse's broad rump.

"Whoa, whoa, whoa...be still," No-Chance gasped, trying to soothe the animal's suffering. "Never did I think we'd end up like this!" He closed his eyes and clenched his fist against a wave of pain.

Bare branches clacked in the wind and mingled with the rustle of leaves. The horse whinnied, and No-Chance opened his eyes. Did he hear a sound? He listened with every nerve and scanned the sides of the ravine. The roan, breathing labored, raised his head.

"Yes," No-Chance whispered, "I hear it, too!" After weeks on the removal, he had grown deaf to the constant shuffle of feet, coughs, and moans. Had his ears forgotten the sound of forest spirits as they moved from tree to tree? No, there had been a noise this time, a twig cracking underfoot.

No-Chance stared up the embankment. The throb in his leg caused his whole body to pulsate and vision to blur. He shook his head and focused his eyes again.

A leaf drifted like a sinking butterfly into his lap. Squinting, he studied skeleton tree branches fanned against the gray sky. There, directly above, the shadow form of an Indian with a long bow.

"Coache?"

Leaves rustled as No-Chance shifted for a better view. A creeping fear dulled all pain with his discovery.

Looking down, a red-painted warrior scowled back.

No-Chance's gaze froze on the line of scalps sewn across the yoke of the Indian's tunic. Comanche! No-Chance swallowed. Horse thieves. Comanche were damn horse thieves.

"Not my horse," he hollered. "You're not getting my horse."

On instinct, he reached for the knife hidden in his right boot. He tried to wiggle his hand under the horse. Teeth clamped tight, he put his left foot against the roan's rump and pushed in a futile attempt to free his trapped leg.

The Comanche drew an arrow from his quiver. Frantic, No-Chance stretched as far as he could and grabbed for the whip looped over the pommel. His fingers clawed at the horse's blanket trying to pull the saddle toward him. It did not budge. In one instant he heard the twang of the bow and in the next watched an arrow quiver in the roan's body.

Boy shuddered, struggled for a moment; then, relaxed.

"Oh, dear God," No-Chance groaned aloud. Stunned at hearing his own words, he straightened. This was the second time in twenty-four hours he had called on God, something he had not done since he was fifteen! Like a flight of swallows, images of his mother, White Cloud, and the baby, flitted through his mind. Maybe his one good deed would redeem him with his father's God.

Today he would die with dignity. He was many things, but not a coward. No-Chance pulled open his jacket and shirt to expose his scarred chest.

"The Comanche finds honor in killing a crippled man!" He cleared his throat. "I spit on such honor."

No-Chance clenched his teeth as he watched the warrior find his heart as a target.

Chapter 8

"Go ahead, you bastard. Kill me!" Rage was alive in the shouts echoing along the ravine. "You low-down stinking skunk."

No-Chance exhausted his white man's curses and began to hurl insults in Mvskoke, the Indian way. "Your ancestors will turn their eyes away from such," he spit the word out, "bravery!" Breezes chilled his bare chest as he held his jacket open.

The Comanche twirled the arrow in his fingers and studied the flint arrowhead. A faint grin played on his lips as he notched the arrow in the bowstring.

"What are you waiting for?" No-Chance screamed. He picked up a stone and threw it toward the Indian. "You have the pizzle of a dog! Coward! Did the Maker of Breath forget to give you balls, too?" He stretched for a handful of rocks and began throwing one after another. They peppered the edge of the incline at the Comanche's feet and bounced back onto the dead horse.

"A sissified woman, that's what you are. I'll bet you dig up graves to get your scalps!"

The red-painted lines on the Comanche's face wrinkled into a smile. He lifted the bow into position and made a great show of pulling on the twisted sinew string until it was taunt. Still smiling, he sighted downward.

Furious, No-Chance continued to shriek and throw stones. He would go to the nightland cursing his enemy, not begging for mercy. It did not matter that this Comanche did not understand his words.

A loud ka-boom thundered through the trees. Birds scattered into the sky. No-Chance put his arms up to shield himself as the Comanche tumbled down and landed sprawled across the roan. Fresh pain ripped through No-Chance's leg, and he choked back a wave of nausea.

The warrior's long greased braids, wrapped in beaver skins, dangled in No-Chance's lap. Arrows slid from the Indian's quiver, clicking against one another like sticks in a child's game.

A voice mocked from the top of the ravine. "I think that now you need a new name, One-Who-Roars-Like-a-Bear. This Comanche did not hear my moccasins behind him because of your loud mouth."

No-Chance fell back on his elbows and squinted up at the colorful image above him. The red and yellow stripes of the scout's coat came into focus.

No-Chance forced a smile. "I thought you followed the soldiers."

"They ride long way past big oak. I come back." Coache crept down the hill on the sides of his feet. "It is good thing. I think your friend wanted another scalp."

"If I'd had my whip…that son-of-a-coyote was lucky getting the drop on me like that."

Coache raised an eyebrow at the boast. The scout grabbed the Comanche by the leg and pulled him off the horse. No-Chance swallowed back the taste of salt pork that rose in his throat with the renewed jarring of the roan's body.

"What is that dog-eater doing here?" he groaned.

"Horses and cattle lure them. There is much honor when they steal from under noses of blue-coats." Coache smiled, bent, and lifted one of No-Chance's braids. "Your scalp would be unexpected prize."

The scout whistled for his pony; then secured one end of a rope to his saddle pommel and the other to the hind shanks of the roan. No-Chance clinched his teeth as the heavy weight inched off his injured leg.

"It is not so bad," Coache said as he slit open No-Chance's pants, exposing the swollen leg. "Bone does not come through skin. You walk good again. But not today." He folded his arms and frowned. "You much trouble, Seminole. What do I do with you? I come back later."

Coache tossed a blue and white striped blanket and wooden canteen to him. "There will be others." He nodded toward the Comanche. "This one was a scout. Horse thieves do not travel alone. I must warn the wagon train." He picked up the warrior's broken bow. "Soldiers will not question why I fired my rifle with this."

No-Chance shivered and hugged the blanket up to his chest as he watched the scout leave. Within minutes, only the sound of Father Wind whistled through the trees.

"Coache thinks to fool me with his promise to return," No-Chance said to the wind. He studied his swollen leg, then reached for the arrows. "Maybe he will lead the soldiers back here. He would look like a big man when he shows them a Comanche scout and an outlaw." He retrieved his knife and sawed flintheads from the shafts. "Or maybe he will leave me here to freeze to death." He tore strips from the blanket and used them to tie the arrow shafts into place around his leg.

Drained of everything but the throbbing pain, he eased back onto the ground and closed his eyes. He would rest, allow his mind to clear. With sleep, a plan would come.

The raucous calling of crows intruded into No-Chance's troubled dreams. "Shut up," he mumbled. "Nothing but trouble. Always into Mother's corn." In the distance a lone crow called. The note was familiar somehow. The crow called again, closer this time.

"Father? Yes, I know it's you. You can't fool me!"

No-Chance sat up and held his hand out to the tall bearded figure striding through a swirl of falling leaves.

"Aye, Laddie, ye never did master the crow, did ye? But a fine student of many another call, ye were. In those days, ye did me proud, John! A blessing sent to me in my old age from the Almighty."

No-Chance dropped his hand and stared into the familiar face of the man kneeling beside him. The deep upturned wrinkles around his father's blue eyes gave hint to the smile hidden behind his beard. The Reverend MacGregor always gave the crow's caw to announce his arrival home from his preaching circuit.

"Why did you leave us, Father? You knew it was close to Mother's time." No-Chance's voice hardened, momentary happiness replaced by bitter memories. "We needed you. All night, I prayed and listened for you to come."

"Laddie, it was time to begin me rounds. Satan had his seat amongst the people for too long. Dun'na ye see, too many drunken unconverted heathens would bring down the Almighty's wrath to the wicked and the innocent alike. The Lord put it in me soul to build up the believers and to offend the wicked. And that I did all to the glory of God's holy name. Ye must trust that it was in God's great plan to have me where He called."

"No! If Mother and I were blessings from God, why would He have you leave us when we needed you most? The white doctor told me everyone knew Indians were like dogs and could birth their pups alone. And the Upper Creek women…they wouldn't come Father, because of you. No one would help—the doctor, because Mother was an Indian and the Creeks, because you were white."

"The sin of hate is theirs, John, and not mine. And for that sin, a beautiful woman died, just as our good Lord died."

Sobbing, No-Chance shook his head. "But Mother died in pain and alone. I didn't know how to help her."

"Laddie, she wasn't alone. While ye held one hand, God held the other and, in death, gave her everlasting life with Him in Heaven where there is no pain, no hate."

"And you, Father, why then did God take you and leave me alone? I had no one. I belong in no one's world!"

"John MacGregor, ye were never alone." His father's voice mellowed. "If ye had put aside your hate and listened, God was with ye. Has it not been His angels that have kept ye safe in this wicked world? In my life, I preached to a goodly number and do humbly trust that many were converted to believe in His holy word. The Lord was satisfied and gave me rest. That is all there is to it. And ye Laddie, it is up to ye to make your own place in the world. The Almighty gives us each a path to walk, and He is eternally with us to help carry our burdens!"

"The Almighty has turned his back on me." No-Chance rubbed the pulsing ache in his leg. "My soul is black. I am lost to His eyes."

His father drew back, voice booming with a loss of patience. "Lost, is it, ye say? Nay, no child o' God is lost 'til he breathes his last lungful o' air. There be good in ye John. Why do ye hide it so?"

"Good?" No-Chance struggled with exasperation. Were there no windows in Heaven? Did his father not see his sins? He shook his head. "I have forgotten how to be good."

"Kindness starts with one wee act. Do one kindness that gains ye nothing. Give something and expect nothing in return." Warmth returned to his father's eyes. "Aye, 'tis not a soft task, I be askin'. It gets easier with practice and the good Lord's help."

Exhausted, No-Chance sank back into the cushion of leaves. He watched his father rise, turn, and disappear into the receding fog.

"No, wait," he called, "don't leave me."

Even Father Wind held his breath in the crushing silence. The terrible loneliness that had been No-Chance's companion for years crept back into his soul. He folded his arms tight across his chest and sobbed at its return.

Chapter 9

The aroma of Mother Earth mingled with that of wet leaves and decaying bark. No-Chance breathed deep, comforted by the familiar scent. He shifted his leg in an attempt to relieve the dull throb rousing him from sleep.

Sudden memory of the Comanche jolted No-Chance awake. He squinted into a noon sun and a group of black crows calling to one another in the trees. The crescendo of caws reached frenzied alarm as a hawk landed on the dead roan. The predator dug its talons into the horse's flesh. No-Chance grabbed the canteen and slung it at the hawk.

"No, get away you bastard!" The outburst created an explosion of flight from the surrounding trees. He rubbed his leg, shifting about for a comfortable position. It had been years since he thought of his father. Why had he dreamed of him now? Or was it a dream? Indians would say it was a vision. Dream or vision, words from the dead were sacred.

No-Chance ran his tongue along cracked lips and searched out the canteen. Clenching his jaw, he scooted over to the roan, reached for the container, and quenched his thirst in large gulps. Exhausted, he settled back. A broken leg, a dead horse, a strange country— could anything else go wrong?

The wind stirred leaves piled in crevices of the

bank. No-Chance watched them dance in large circles and settle to the ground. It seemed they moaned at being disturbed. He sat up and stared at the Comanche.

Frowning, he studied the slight movement of the Indian's back. Blood soaked through the buckskin shirt and glistened in sun filtering through tree branches. The Comanche groaned again, and this time, his hand moved.

"Dammit, Coache! You didn't even check to make sure he was dead," No-Chance muttered as he felt for his knife. "So, you would kill a man while he was as helpless as a rabbit in a trap, huh? Well, an eye for an eye, the Good Book says."

A lone crow settled on an overhead branch. His hoarse caw seemed to say, "Wrong, wrong." The crow spread a fan of black feathers and folded them back into its body.

"Father, I was a stranger. No danger to him and he tried to kill me."

The echo of his words sounded hollow. Another crow flew overhead on silent wings. The branches rustled and clacked as one crow after another floated in to take its place among the trees. In mute harmony they fastened their glare on him. A whisper sent chills down his spine.

"John, love even your enemy."

"I cannot do so!" No-Chance shouted. "I cannot do so." For a long while, he sat lost in memories. Nothing stirred, not the wind, not the leaves, not the birds.

A moan from the injured Comanche released No-Chance from his thoughts. With a sigh, he slipped the canteen strap around his neck and, ignoring the throb in his leg, scooted over to the wounded Indian. The

Comanche opened pain-dulled eyes, fastening his gaze on the canteen.

"You want water?" No-Chance taunted and balanced the Celtic knife in his hand. "Won't ask for it, will you?" He sat back and met his own soul in the Comanche's stare. There would be no pride in this death.

Reaching for a pebble, he held the small stone up, then pushed it into the soil. With the point of the knife, he flipped it out of the dirt.

A flicker of understanding crossed the Indian's face. No-Chance leaned over the injured man's back and tore the blood-soaked shirt away.

"You must be fool-headed, addle-minded crazy." He studied the swollen and bruised skin around the wound. No telling how deep the bullet went. His hand trembled as he probed for the bullet with the tip of the knife. Fresh blood gushed with the effort. The Comanche groaned and slipped into unconsciousness. No-Chance held his breath and eased the ball of lead out of the wound.

The injury continued bleeding. No-Chance cut a strip of material from the torn leg of his pants, dropped the makeshift bandage over the wound, and leaned on it.

"What were you thinking? Just because you birthed a baby, don't make you a doctor." He continued to press the wound until it clotted, cut the strap from the canteen, and tied the compress into place. The Comanche's eyes flickered open.

"Don't go getting any thoughts about us being friends," No-Chance grumbled as he rolled the Indian onto his back and handed him the canteen. Secure in knowledge of the other man's weakness, he relaxed back to the ground's hard comfort and pulled his jacket closed, touching a small fringed bag hanging around his neck. He removed it and played his thumb across rows of red and white beads. Funny his father should live in his thoughts again. Why now?

Eight tiny gems sparkled in his palm as he shook them from the pouch. They were not mere stones, but personalities. He knew every reflection of light each cast. His inheritance. Untainted by blood or lust. The only things left of an honest life. In an ancient time, the jewels had lent their beauty to the hilt of a mighty Highland sword. His father left Scotland armed with this small fortune for the new country—a land where the name MacGregor was not cause to be hunted down.

No-Chance closed his eyes remembering the story behind each glittering gem. They were to build a kingdom for a beautiful Seminole wife. The stones sparkled in the afternoon light. No kingdom was built. The jewels remained hidden away in a buckskin pouch.

He lifted his favorite, a light blue sapphire, and caught its brilliance in the sun. Intrigued, the Comanche watched as the jewel cast its spell.

No-Chance put down the favorite, picked up a small ruby, looked at it, then placed it in the Indian's palm.

"My father brought this across the great waters. It reminded him of the precious blood shed by the Son of God for the sins of us wretched mortals."

The Comanche frowned.

"Like blood, you see…" He grabbed the bloody sleeve of the Indian's shirt. Pointing to the sun, he urged, "Look through it."

The Comanche held the ruby high and turned it between grimy fingers. Long twisted silver earrings swung as he nodded. The jewel gleamed in the dark upturned palm as the Comanche held it out.

No-Chance struggled with the sermon that exploded in his mind. Do one kindness that gains you nothing. Give something and expect nothing in return. "Lord, I feel as if the devil and one of Your angels wage war inside my head." He looked up at the sky. "Why would I possibly give a gift to the heathen that would take my life? Why?"

Finally, he reached over and closed the Comanche's fingers over the ruby. He slid the rest of the gems back into the small leather pouch and clasped his hands together in the sign for peace.

"One-Who-Gives-No-Chance makes a gift to his enemy."

As soon as the words were out of his mouth, he regretted the gift. He fought to protect this inheritance. The spirit that forced such words from his mouth must be truly strong. He looked up at the crows hunkered among the trees.

"Father, if hatred has cursed my soul, then do not expect too much of me. The good Lord may have said to turn the other cheek, but that damn sure seems as if it would be a good way to get yourself killed." He tucked the fringed and beaded bag inside his shirt and lay back on his arms.

The Comanche stared down at his closed fist, then over to No-Chance. The two studied each other until the repeated call of an unfamiliar bird broke their unspoken communication. The Comanche eased up and listened.

No-Chance tensed. Another trilling note, much

closer, sent a chill down his spine. Panic dulled the pain in his leg as he dragged himself across the ravine to a deep crevice in the sloping bank. He glanced back at the Comanche, who had turned his attention to the top of the ravine.

No-Chance dug in the soft dirt with his knife, dislodging clumps of bushes. The smell of fresh earth filled his nostrils as he pushed deep into the hillside, pulled the thick brush over himself, and peered through the brambles.

A series of whistles and shrieks reverberated through the air. The wounded Comanche gave an answering warble. Within seconds five stout Indians, bedecked in feathers and scalps, appeared. Their faces, smeared with red and yellow paint, differed so much from the civilized Creeks that No-Chance shivered. Even with his knife, could he handle five men? He flexed his fingers, suddenly aware they were empty. The Celtic weapon lay somewhere at his feet.

Two Comanche lifted their comrade while others examined the dead horse and prepared to strip the animal of the silver harness.

No-Chance's leg throbbed, and he shifted. The snap of a twig echoed through the air like the sound of a falling tree.

Not daring to breathe, he peered through the tangle of brush. Armed with a hatchet, a yellow-faced Comanche followed the body tracks through the dirt and reached to pull away the bushes. Too late, No-Chance spied the glint of a steel blade among layers of decaying leaves.

In an instant, one Comanche became four. No-Chance pressed his back against the bank in a useless attempt to stand and face his attackers.

The yellow-faced warrior reached down, dragged him to his feet, and held the hatchet to his throat. He could feel the bite of the cold blade against his windpipe. A man can't scream with his throat cut.

"*Nein, nein*! No, no!" the wounded Comanche shouted.

Warriors turned at the command. Sagging against a comrade, the Comanche opened his palm to show the ruby, sentences spilling out in the strange guttural language of the scalp-takers. Then, he patted the canteen strap securing his bandage.

A rough shove sent No-Chance crumpling to the ground. He ran his hand through the leaves to retrieve his knife as the Comanche backed away. They abandoned their plunder of the dead horse, caught the wounded man under his arms, and struggled up the incline.

No-Chance watched them disappear into the trees and heard the sound of retreating hooves. He sat frozen with relief as the wind puffed through the ravine, chilling sweat on his face. Weary, he became aware of the radiating throb in his leg.

Trees rustled with the return of birds. No-Chance scooted over to the dead roan and grabbed his coiled whip. In a fight, he would rather have the snake-biter in his hand than another man at his shoulder. It was careless of him to be trapped without a weapon.

A cloud obscured the sun, and No-Chance nestled into a mound of leaves, scooping armfuls over his body. Gusts of air stirred dead foliage again, adding and subtracting from the pile.

The hum of Father Wind through tall grasses lulled

him, and he closed his eyes. A dove cooed in the distance. Squirrels chattered. In the chorus of woodland sounds, a horse snorted.

Chapter 10

No-Chance bolted up through the quilt of leaves. An unwilling groan escaped as he struggled to one knee, ready to let loose the snake-biter. He stared in relief at two riders trotting down the ravine—Coache and Chickamauga.

"I almost got my hair lifted! The Comanche...you didn't kill him!" No-Chance huffed.

"Why didn't *you*?" Coache asked. "You killed cook—a good thing."

No-Chance eased off his knee. "Why was that a good thing?"

"He brought shame to my sister's daughter and fled, taking two black brothers." The scout leaned across his saddle pommel. "Rewards for runaway slaves bring us much trouble." Coache's eyes narrowed. "Even though he was a thief among his own people, my complaints fell on deaf ears. Indians cannot give testimony against a white man."

He straightened. "You avenge your tribesman's honor, Seminole." Without waiting for a reply, the colorful scout urged his horse up the bank.

No-Chance shifted his leg. His motive had been self-preservation when he killed the cook. If Coache wanted to think he had done a favor, fine.

Chickamauga dismounted and held out a bundle. "When man hides in forest, he must look like forest.

Soldiers chase someone in white man's clothing. Now soldiers must see only man in calico and buckskins."

No-Chance nodded, eased out of his pants, and smoothed the loose fitting leggings over his throbbing leg. He had done nothing honorable. He had simply killed a man that would have killed him.

Chickamauga held out a pair of moccasins. The shape of another man's foot still lived in the leather. No-Chance reached for them and sat back. A sunburst of white beads decorated the top—most likely sewn by White Cloud. It would not be polite to mention the gone-away one. He loosened the rawhide ties and eased a moccasin onto his swollen foot.

A row of tiny cowrie shells down each sleeve of a buckskin tunic whispered as No-Chance tugged it over his head. He closed his eyes and remembered the sounds his mother made when she walked—the clink of silver bracelets on her arm, the talk of shell necklaces, and the tease of bells sewn to the hem of a colorful ribbon skirt.

"You missed seeing the Comanche," he said at last. "Bloodthirsty savages. Enough to give a man nightmares."

"We were beyond when we heard their calls."

"You were?" No-Chance raised his eyebrows. "Why did you wait so long to show yourself?"

"You were in small danger. The wounded Comanche would not let his brothers harm you. Coache thinks he told them you speak to spirits, and you gave him a stone that makes blood strong. Comanche think you crazy man or shaman. To kill either would bring bad medicine." Chickamauga crossed his arms. "Coache and I would have avenged your death."

"Crazy, huh?" No-Chance struggled to stand on one leg. "What do you think?"

"Your name travels before you." Chickamauga hoisted No-Chance into the saddle and handed him the reins. "All know you live by the knife. I know you spoke for my wife in time of need. I know you gave help to scalp-taker, one who would take your life."

Chickamauga fashioned a blanket into a sling, attached it to the saddle horn, and helped ease No-Chance's leg into position. "I do not know what manner of man does this. You need prove nothing to me. You have honored place at my fire."

Coache appeared at the top of the slope and motioned for them to follow. A sense of loss filled No-Chance as the mare circled the body of the golden roan. The big horse had proved to be brave and steadfast, and that, after all, was more than he could say of most men. He halted the mare and glanced down into the ravine. He was leaving behind a companion and, he resolved, the spirit twins that resided in his soul—anger and hatred.

The three men followed the trail of the Removal, searching for signs of the Comanche as they galloped through the somber woods—a flash of red or yellow, a sudden flight of birds from a tree, knowing Comanche would not be seen unless they wanted to be. The torturous jolting to No-Chance's leg kept him alert, ready for a second encounter with the party of scalp-takers.

At dusk, wood smoke announced the nearness of camp. Coache waved, leaving the other two behind. No-Chance and Chickamauga took shelter in a stand of warty hackberry and ancient oak trees. They dismounted and sat back to back, listening for the crack of a twig that spoke of something larger than a night creature. Neither dared close their eyes. It was said a Comanche could crawl within six feet of a sleeping man who had tethered his horse to his wrist, cut the rope, and be gone without ever disturbing him.

Chapter 11

No-Chance jerked awake, a heavy hand on his shoulder. With his old sense of danger, he lunged away from the touch, twisted, and came up, knife in hand. His leg gave way in a searing stab of pain. He fought for balance and fell.

The surprised face of a huge Negro split into a broken-toothed smile as he spoke in slow English, "I only wake you, Knife Man!"

No-Chance stared at the grinning black man, his sleepiness dissolving, memory returning. They had slipped past the guards and found Black Storm's group in the night. Exhausted, he fell asleep propped against a wagon wheel, knife hidden beneath the folds of his blanket.

"Sorry," No-Chance murmured, "but you ought not come up on a man like that!"

"Yes, suh. I be Stvluste, head man fo' de Chief." The Negro bent and poked the campfire into vigorous flames under a boiling pot. A gray-haired old Negro sat on a tree stump, cleaning a rabbit carcass.

No-Chance stretched his injured leg and pulled the blanket around his shoulders. Fragrant wood smoke joined the thick haze of hundreds of other early morning fires.

Stvluste straightened. A scar on his cheek extended down to the corner of his mouth giving the appearance of a lopsided smile. "We eat once moah, Knife Man. Nice little rabbit done been caught by ole Nick's snare."

"No-Chance. I'm called No-Chance."

"My chief, he ain't never eat in de white line, and he ain't goin' to with ole Nick around." He flicked his gaze toward the wiry little man who dropped pieces of rabbit into the boiling pot, and added, "Me, Ah had some beans fo' de pot, too, been soakin' 'em all night. Ah gets close to de soldier food sometimes, helps with de heavy liftin' just like Ah was one of their regular boys. De boys, they looks at me and don't say nothin'." Stvluste bent, hand on one knee, and stirred the pot.

"So you take a few beans for your help, huh?" No-Chance reached for his saddlebags and extracted a pipe and tobacco pouch.

"No suh, dem beans jumps in my pocket, dey does. 'Sides, ain't stealin' if'n it from de soldier's grub."

No-Chance glanced at the campfire a few feet away.

"Say, you be wantin' a start-up, Knife Man?" Stvluste wiggled a burning stick from the flames.

"My name is No-Chance, and yes, I'd be thankful for a light." He reached for the offered stick. "Nothing better than the smell of food cooking and a fine pipe." He leaned against the wagon wheel and clamped the pipe in his mouth. Brilliant orange-red flames jumped along the edge of the stick, and he sprinkled a handful of dirt over it to tame the fire. The perfume of burning wood and tobacco mingled as No-Chance sucked at the pipe stem. One more breath would ignite the tobacco. He put the tip of the flame back over the bowl.

An impatient *humph* interrupted the effort to light the pipe, and he looked into Black Storm's stern countenance, tattoos a vivid blue in the morning light. The stout old man stood arrayed in a bright calico shirt stretched across his barrel chest. A tawny catamount skin pouch with the tail attached hung from his sash, giving the appearance of a strange animal clinging to his waist.

No-Chance dropped the glowing twig and grasped the wagon wheel to stand. Leaning against the wagon, he attempted to look Black Storm square in the face. His father insisted that to avert one's eyes suggested a man of little worth. But his mother taught that to stare into another's face was a sign of disrespect. He clenched his teeth in an effort to ignore the throb in his leg.

The chief pulled the catamount tail through his hand in a slow, deliberate manner. The two men stared at each other until No-Chance lowered his gaze. At last, the chief seated himself and pulled a bear robe around his shoulders. A slight breeze stirred two eagle feathers dangling by rawhide strips from a thin plait of long hair.

No-Chance lowered himself to the ground. Under the chief's intense glare, it felt as if his skin were being stripped away, exposing past sins. He would not be humbled by the unflinching old man and stiffened his back. This family was owed his gratitude, but if he had minded his own business, he'd not be in this sorry condition.

A fragile wail from inside the wagon startled both men, and the silent battle was broken. In relief, No-Chance shifted his position and looked down at the unlit pipe in his hand. He sighed and, extending his arm, offered it to the chief.

"It would be an honor to share tobacco with Black Storm, wise and beloved chief of the Wind Clan."

Black Storm nodded and accepted the offer. Nick brought a fresh light from the campfire, and soon the chief's head was encircled in a cloud of smoke. Chickamauga climbed out of the wagon with the crying infant and strode to a neighboring campfire.

The chief cleared his throat. "Many moons ago I fought as a Red Stick Warrior to save sweet hills of my ancestors from *wvcenvlke*. I cried as my brethren died all around me at Horseshoe Bend and wondered why Maker and Taker of Breath left me behind. Singing Woman bound my wounds and said it was because I was to lead my people into far-away land. I did not believe my wife. I did not wish to leave land I loved. My heart forgot her vision."

Black Storm paused, as if lost in memories. No-Chance glanced at the Celtic pipe in the old man's hands.

"Singing Woman did not forget. In month of Green Corn, she packed wagon so we might be ready when soldiers came. My wife, and now, my only child, have died on long walk." Black Storm's shoulders sagged, and the shell necklaces clinked softly as he adjusted the robe.

With a heavy sigh, the deep voice continued, "My son-in-law has told me all things about you. You brought forth my grandson. For this I have great happiness. But I have a great fear, also. It bad omen for one of my family to be helped into world by white man."

No-Chance opened his mouth to protest. The chief held up his hand and continued, "I do not allow white blood in my village. You have done a kindness. I am not ungrateful. I welcome you to my wagon and, later, my village until safe for you to go. Chickamauga say lawmen seek you. He believes Seminoli blood of mother runs deep, and you will keep our ways."

Nick placed a bowl of stew in front of the chief. The steam unfolded upward in an enticing column.

"My people will protect you and will share all but one thing. For you to remain among the Upper Creeks, you must agree to what I ask."

Black Storm cleared his throat. "You may claim no woman among our tribe."

No-Chance grimaced in an attempt to control his rising anger. Black Storm did not want his white blood to weaken the bloodline of his tribe. No matter what he did, he would belong in no one's world. His Indian blood would always be at war with his white. Pursing his lips tight, No-Chance nodded his head. These people were not his concern. He wanted no woman from them.

Black Storm frowned, distorting the straight lines of the blue tattoos. "In the mists of time, my father watched *wvcenvlke* come from great distance to claim lands of our ancestors for their kings. We fought. It was useless. They were like locusts devouring all in their path. Their words were like leaves before a wind and soon gone. You make promise to keep our laws and not dilute my people with your seed. But it is made with half the heart of a *wvcenvlke*. This troubles me and makes me suspicious." A wisp of smoke curled from the bowl as Black Storm held the pipe out.

No-Chance knew the old man would not accept the sincerity of his words until they shared tobacco. He clasped the familiar mouthpiece between his teeth and sucked at the stem. Warm, pungent smoke filled his mouth, and he savored the sweet bite. Sharing tobacco gave a man time to think. He opened his lips to release the smoke and wave it back into his face.

No-Chance cupped the warm pipe in his palm. His sense of anger ebbed as he studied the glow in the bowl. Perhaps they needed a Solomon, for how could a man divide himself in half.

Above them, a familiar caw sounded. With a flutter of wings, a crow settled onto the top branch of an oak tree behind the chief.

"Father, what trail do I take now?" No-Chance whispered as he stared at the shiny black bird preening its feathers.

Puzzled, Black Storm turned and looked up at the crow. The silent sentry fastened its glare on the men below.

The flash of anger gone, No-Chance spoke in a soft voice. "The Creek have many brothers that the *wvcenvlke* call Indian: the Seminole, the Chickasaw, the Cherokee, the Seneca, the Sac, the Choctaw, the Pottawatomie, the Iroquois. Too many to count. Even the Creek nation is two halves: the Upper and the Lower. Just as not all red men are the same, not all white men are alike. My father was neither English, nor French, nor Spanish. He was from the Scottish clan MacGregor, who suffered because of their bloodline, like your people, at the hands of the English."

No-Chance leaned forward. "I cannot separate my Scottish blood from my Seminole blood. Both are honorable lines. It is from all of me that you must accept my promise to keep the laws and look for no woman among your people."

In the following silence, a single feather floated in the air, catching the light appearing first purple, and then black, as it tumbled down. It landed on the ground between the two men. Both looked up to search the empty tree for the bird that had presided over their meeting. Neither disturbed the feather, knowing the crow might one day return for it.

Black Storm nodded. "It is done. I have your promise." He lifted a spoonful of food to his mouth.

No-Chance turned the pipe in his hands. The pleasure of the smoke was gone and the stew, cold. There was no place in the world for a half breed.

Chickamauga strode back to the campsite and handed the baby to Nick, who immediately hefted the child to his shoulder, and crooned a wordless lullaby.

"Stvluste, you and Nick look for hickory nuts as we go. No woman has enough milk to suckle the baby." He accepted a bowl from the large Negro and sat down. "The food is good?" he asked motioning to the stew.

No-Chance nodded. "Best I've had in a while. How's the baby going to eat a hickory nut?"

Chickamauga chuckled. "Women force milk from nut when can no longer suckle little ones." He lowered his voice, "You are welcome in Black Storm's camp?"

"I've promised to follow the laws of the tribe." No-Chance set his empty bowl down. "And I've promised to take no woman as long as I stay."

Chickamauga stopped eating. "You promised what?"

Chapter 12

No-Chance sat untangling his thick braids before the fire, his injured leg atop a folded blanket. A mane of black hair billowed in the breeze as he massaged his itchy scalp. The hot soapy bath at Sadie's Laundry and Bath House in Pensacola was a distant memory. He would settle now for a sandy-bottom stream where he could scrub away grime with a handful of grit and clean water.

The clamor of pots and utensils melted into a steady din that grew louder with soldiers' commands. He looked down at the baby nestled in his lap and hoped the blue-coats kept their distance.

Old Nick squatted, holding out a bowl of dark liquid. "Soup from de pot. Done picked out pieces of rabbit. See if'n de little'n take it. Dey be some strength to it."

No-Chance nodded and touched the bowl's edge to the infant's lips. Warm soup filled its mouth and spilled over. The baby strangled, gasping for breath.

Nick grabbed the infant. "Land's sake, feed 'em, not drown 'em." He patted the squalling baby on the back.

Stvluste paused in his chore of filling the wood box. "Knife Man, don't you know nothin'? All God's creatures start out suckin' at dey mama's tits 'afore dey can swallow."

"I know that." No-Chance glared at him. "Do I look like I have a mama's tit hiding 'neath this shirt?"

"No, suh!" Stvluste's mouth lifted in a lopsided grin. "You suppose to make one."

"Make one? How do I do that?"

Stvluste shrugged his shoulders and gathered up harnesses. "You jus' sittin' dere. Ponder on it a spell. I gotta help bring in dem mules."

Whoever heard of making a tit? No-Chance reached for his saddle bag, emptied its contents and rifled through the items: the tightly-coiled black snake whip, chip of salt-block, tin of camphor, pieces of string, his Celtic pipe and tobacco pouch.

The infant continued to cry as Nick shuffled around the campfire prompting No-Chance to hurry his search: battered tin plate and small pail, crumbling Pensacola newspaper, almost-empty whiskey bottle and parfleche bag containing three withered slices of dried apple.

"What you doin' down dere?" Nick demanded.

"What do you think? I'm making a tit!" No-Chance grabbed the whiskey bottle, uncorked it, and breathed in the sharp aroma. One good swig left.

Arms flailing, eyes shut tight, the baby gasped for breath between cries. Its voice rose above Nick's crooning. Others stopped to stare.

"Next, we'll have an all-fired visit from the soldiers complaining about that infernal racket," No-Chance muttered. He grabbed the bowl of broth and poured it into the bottle swirling two liquids together. Whiskey, the best sleep-inducer known to mankind. After detaching the flap on the parfleche, he punched a small hole in the center with the tip of his knife and tied the make-shift nipple over the opening of the whiskey bottle.

"Now, Nick, I do believe I've got us a mighty fine tit here." No-Chance turned the bottle upside down and watched the liquid turn the pale leather dark brown. A drop slowly seeped through the hole. He motioned for the sobbing child. "The little one won't even know the difference between this bottle and the real thing." He snuggled the baby in the crook of his arm and touched the leather nipple to its lips. The screams softened to sobs as the infant sought the broth-soaked leather.

"You do make a dandy mama." Nick chuckled, turning to lift the kettle from the fire.

Stvluste led four mules into camp and looked down at him. "Land's sake, Knife Man, I most believe you have de touch. Don't baby look sweet nestled dere like a 'possum in its mammy's pouch?"

"I'm no nursemaid and the name's Noooo-Chance."

Chickamauga squatted to touch a finger to the baby's wet cheek.

"Who speaks English here?" The question from an unfamiliar voice was a definite command.

Chickamauga stood and faced two men. Not fellow tribesmen, not soldiers—lawmen.

No-Chance allowed his unbound hair to fall over his face. He fought rising panic. There was a reason the Maker of Breath didn't intend for men to suckle their young. An armful of baby was a disadvantage. He studied the spidery fingers gripping his thumb and felt his stomach sink. He would offer no resistance if called out.

Stvluste relayed the question to Chickamauga in

Creek, nodding afterward to the tall Indian's instructions.

"Yes, suh, I speaks good English." He straightened his shoulders. "Masta says to listen and answer best I can."

The lawman hooked his thumbs in the gun belt that held his heavy coat closed. "I'm Marshal Bob Armstrong. We suspect outlaws are hiding among you Creeks. We're talking to everyone, and if you've seen anyone suspicious or know anything, well, it's best you speak up." He drew his words out as if bored with the speech.

"No, suh!" replied the giant black man, rolling his eyes. "Why we be wantin' to hide 'spicious outlaws here? We just be poor ol' Creek folk."

The lawman nodded and glanced around. Chickamauga, arms folded, shifted to block his view of No-Chance.

"You know there was a baby born a day or so ago. Quite a fuss about it, too. Seems the mother died. Then, there was that trouble at the feed wagon." The marshal made a point of skirting Chickamauga and studied the pair at the smoldering fire.

"That your baby?" he asked.

No-Chance didn't look up. He was caught like a rabbit in old Nick's snare. Only the sucking sounds of the infant broke the silence.

"That fella hard of hearing or something?" The younger man, wearing a blue-plaid mackinaw, asked.

"Yes, suh, he shore is. Can't hardly hear a thing," Stvluste volunteered. "Deaf as a post, he is."

Both men skirted the campfire. No-Chance studied their worn boots for a second, then gave a quick glance up through his mop of hair and down again as if intent on comforting the bundle in his arms.

"That…your…baby?" the marshal asked, raising his voice.

"Yes, suh, it's his." The falsehood rolled off Stvluste's tongue without hesitation.

"Where…is…its…mama?"

Stvluste hustled close. "She done gone…ahhh…lookin' fo' milk."

The marshal looked at the whiskey bottle. "Can't she nurse the papoose?"

Stvluste straightened his huge frame to its full height. "No, suh. She mighty poorly. All the womenfolk is."

The younger man reached down and touched the baby's head. "Sure is little, ain't it, Bob?" He ruffled the ample shock of soft black hair. "Say," he shouted, "what's the baby's name?"

Stvluste stuttered, "It's…it's…ahhh." He turned toward Chickamauga and then No-Chance, repeating the question in Creek.

No-Chance kept his eyes on the infant. Special, the name for a future chief should be special—like the feeling of standing on the sandy shore of the great salt waters, like opening your arms to embrace Father Wind and smell the promise of far-away lands on his breath. Yes, the name should be that special.

No-Chance spoke slowly, "*Tampa pipuce hocefkvt os.*"

The lawmen glanced around for a translation.

Stvluste stuttered, "De, de baby's name," he paused, "Tampa, suh."

"Tampa, huh? I reckon that's a mighty nice name.

Has a good sound…"

"Come on," the marshal interrupted. "Once these folks get movin' it will be harder to talk to everyone." He pointed his finger at Stvluste. "You see anything, let me know. Might be some grub in it for you." The men turned to go, doffing hats toward Black Storm, who had just entered the campsite.

Stvluste cleared his throat and nodded to Nick to get busy. The chief glared, eyes narrowed and lips tight. Name-giving was an important ceremony, usually the privilege of a favorite uncle or tribal elder.

Chickamauga knelt. "A name from land of Seminoles! Could you not think of good Creek name?" Broth seeped from the corner of the infant's mouth as it ceased sucking and fell into an easy sleep in No-Chance's arms. The young father stood. "You have named him. He will be known as Tampa."

"Never!" exploded Black Storm.

No-Chance looked down at the tiny form cuddled in his arms and back to the glowering chief. "Let him keep the name, and my hands will help build a shelter to protect him from winter winds when the new land is reached. He will be warm and grow strong."

Black Storm's nostrils flared. He stood straight, shoulders back, an unmovable mountain ready to erupt.

"It is true that you are a great chief," No-Chance continued in an attempt to quell the old man's anger. "You have much to teach him about the laws of the tribe, about the honor and bravery of his ancestors." He nodded to Chickamauga. "And you will teach him to be a fearless hunter and to love the land."

No-Chance sat the whiskey bottle down. "The old mothers will nudge their daughters and say, 'Cast your eyes in the direction of Tampa, for his seed is the best in all the nation'."

With his jaw set in a rigid grimace, Black Storm stood slapping the catamount tail against his leg—the soft thwacks, a steady beat amidst the camp's noise.

No-Chance sighed. He had not softened the old man's heart. "Let him keep the name, and I will arrange for someone to teach him English when he is older. He will need such knowledge to hold his own against the many white men who will come among the people. Times are changing. To protect the tribe, the child will need to know more than the ancient Creek path. He must understand the ways of the whites and their words. He must be able to read their talking leaves."

"Never!" shouted Black Storm. "Words from mouth of *wvcenvlke* are like honey from a hive. As they fall, they become like rushing of a great water that wears away stone. There is no music in such language. It hurts my ears."

He lifted his chin and continued, "The Maker of Breath gave the talking leaves to the white man. The Indians, he made children of the earth and brother to the animals." The old man shook the tail of the catamount. "No, learning such things will change our people. Do not *wvcenvlke* send their fool's water to rot minds of our young men and replace honor with evil thoughts?"

Black Storm pointed his finger at the whiskey bottle. "Even now you pollute the child."

No-Chance willed his voice to remain calm. "The bottle is only a means to feed the baby a little soup. Does he not sleep with a full stomach now?" The old chief could not know about the swallow of liquor mixed with the broth. "There is truth in what you say. You have much to teach him that is good. But the path ahead is unknown. He must learn both languages if he is to keep the people safe."

"Nothing from *wvcenvlke*!" Black Storm turned and stomped toward the tethered horses.

"Then you rob your grandson of the chance to be a great leader!" No-Chance raised his voice as the old man mounted. "Without this knowledge, he will be betrayed like his grandfather and left with a bitter heart."

A wagon rumbled past. Black Storm, sitting stiff-backed, guided his horse into the procession of travelers.

"Wasting my damn breath, that's what I'm doing." No-Chance relinquished the sleeping baby to Nick. "These aren't my people. Why should I care?" he mumbled and grasped a wheel spoke to pull himself up. "Where does he think this wagon and that kettle come from, if not the white world? He closes his ears to reason and closes his eyes to what is real."

"Father of gone-away wife has much hatred." Chickamauga slipped an arm around No-Chance and helped him into the wagon. "Many wrongs have been done to our people."

"If there is one thing I understand, it is hatred. It burns hottest in the heart and consumes all that is good in a person."

Chickamauga looked at him for a minute, then lifted the tailgate and bolted it shut. Woven baskets, empty of their supplies, stacked one inside the other took shape in the darkened interior. Wooden bowls and spoons, bone scrapers and pottery jars crowded against an iron pot. Worn clothing and once-colorful blankets now frayed and torn, lay folded atop a barrel. Beaded pouches hung from knobs driven in the tall wooden sides.

"Go'on!" Stvluste's voice rumbled above the slap of leather across the mule's rumps. "Go on 'fore we be left behind."

The wagon lurched forward, and No-Chance braced himself for the bumpy ride as he studied the people trudging behind the wagon. Wrinkled and gaunt, all were huddled against the cold in an assortment of blankets, animal skins, and white man's clothing. They hugged bundles close for the warmth their burden offered. Most held threadbare moccasins together with mud-crusted rag bindings. Only dogs large enough to strap packs on their backs remained on the march.

Stubborn, that's what they were. These Creeks were stubborn as a mule with its ass planted in an ant hill. No matter how hard you pulled, it would sit there being eaten alive, braying all the while.

Wooden slats groaned, and clay jars jostled against each other, tapping out an uneven rhythm. Chickamauga trotted his gray dun up to the wagon. A young boy sat in front of him and another behind. He lifted the children through the canvas opening. They huddled together, staring wide-eyed at No-Chance. He moved his splinted leg off the bear skin where the baby slept and bent over to pat the fur. Both boys scrambled to snuggle into the warm spot.

No-Chance's injuries ached with each bump. He tilted his head to one side and divided a handful of thick hair between his fingers to braid it. How long would it take to be fit again? Hair slid through his fingers as he wove sections together. He clamped the end of the braid in his teeth, cut a strip of leather from the fringe on his tunic, and tied it around the braid.

Tilting his head to the opposite side, he ran his fingers through the remaining loose strands and began the process again. Yes, he would trade one of his father's jewels for a horse and supplies. Light out for Texas. Or maybe California.

Chickamauga lifted two more children over the end of the wagon. A little girl crawled in and sat with her knees pulled up under her chin, arms wrapped around her legs. No-Chance sighed and handed each child one of the blankets that pillowed his back.

"You are comfortable?" Chickamauga pushed wisps of hair under his turban.

"Yes," No-Chance lied as he rubbed his aching leg. "It is out of the wind. I am grateful."

"Good."

"As soon as I can, I will not trouble your family." No-Chance shifted his weight. "My heart is glad for the sanctuary you offer."

Chickamauga jutted his chin toward the sleeping infant. "It small thanks for what you have done."

"It was nothing."

"It is right one who breathed life into child should name him. Tampa is good name."

"Even if Black Storm doesn't like it?"

Chickamauga nodded and settled back in the saddle. "I think on your words. It troubles my heart I must answer white man through mouth of my slave. That makes my spirit small. I do not want son to be a nothing man."

He motioned toward those trudging behind the wagon. "We go into strange land. Our wealth was homes, land, cattle. We are like helpless children dependent upon soldiers. We do not understand their words."

He leaned forward. "Stand beside me as brother and guide son. He will not distinguish between us! Together, we prepare his path. Someday he stand strong and wise. Think upon words, friend. Give answer when we reach fort."

Chapter 13

Black Storm's wagon groaned and creaked its progress along the rutted military road to Fort Gibson, Indian Territory. No-Chance sat lost in thoughts, disturbed only when another child was lifted into the wagon.

Stand beside me as my brother and guide my son. He will not distinguish between us! The words pulsed in No-Chance's mind. The young father must be desperate for the future of his son to defy the chief and make such a promise. But why ask a wanted man, a half-blood, to guide the child? What was it that Chickamauga saw in him? True, his reputation had been exaggerated. He never killed without provocation and had not lived these last ten years without extending small kindnesses.

No-Chance studied the children huddled in shadows and between stacks of baskets. Clothing tattered, feet wrapped in rags, robbed of their smiles by hunger, they stared back through weary eyes. Pacified by the broth-diluted whiskey, Tampa slept nestled in the matted fur of Black Storm's bearskin.

"Thank you Brother Bear for your warmth," No-Chance whispered, though it was hardly necessary. Whoever made the kill would have asked the four-legged's forgiveness. The Indian was brother to the animal. In this, Black Storm was right.

He buried his face in his hands. If he gave his word

to Chickamauga to stay and teach the child, he would be obligated for years. He possessed few virtues, but a sense of honor was one of them.

Outside the wagon, the unmistakable aroma of burning wood permeated the air. A chorus of voices grew with excited shouts from those in front. The traveling wall of sound echoed and rolled past as he crawled between the napping youngsters to peer around Stvluste.

In the distance, lay rambling log and stone buildings—Fort Gibson, the long awaited destination, nearly one thousand dreary miles from the comforts of Alabama and Georgia. To the west, the Neosho River flowed blue-black in the gloom of winter light. Stands of cherry laurel and cedar, the only color in the December landscape, stood out amid the ice-crusted branches of sweet gum, oak, and hackberry.

Plumes of smoke curled toward the gray sky. The road cut a dark path through pristine snow. Soldiers poured from the fort and directed wagons onto the tree-stump studded plain surrounding the stockade.

Stvluste flapped the reins. "Go'on. Dis nightmare 'bout be over." He looked over his shoulder. "Yes, suh! Masta find us a nice little piece o' land. Soon Stvluste not be sleepin' on cold ground any more. My bones been talkin' to me all dis long way."

The wagon lurched off the road and rolled to a stop next to a lightning-struck oak. Stripped of limbs, only the charred and split trunk remained. No-Chance eyed it through the rear opening of the canvas as he lifted children down to whoever claimed them. Only those with bad thoughts need fear the power in trees kissed by lightning. Still, to be safe, he would keep an arm's distance from the scarred trunk.

By the time Grandfather Sun disappeared in the west, the slaves had picketed the mules and horses, erected Black Storm's tent, and set a kettle of water boiling. The snow-covered prairie sparkled in the orange glow from hundreds of campfires. The air was festive as people went about fetching water from the river or gathering wood from the surrounding hills. The terrible march was over.

No-Chance sat on the wagon's open end, scraping a length of wood free of snags. His injury left him vulnerable—helpless as the baby. He glanced at Tampa curled next to him on the bear rug and eased off the wagon to test the crutch.

"I've been lookin' for your bunch." The young lawman spoke from astride his horse and fumbled with something under his blue-plaid mackinaw.

Startled, No-Chance stumbled and fell against the dead tree. He glanced over at the campfire, where Nick stood beside the kettle with a wooden ladle in his hand. Stvluste dropped his armful of wood. Black Storm and Chickamauga scrambled to their feet.

"Here." The rider smiled. From under his mackinaw, he pulled a jar with brown paper tied over the opening. "Take it." He pointed to the infant. "For the baby."

Using the crutch, No-Chance struggled to stand, then reached for the container. He sniffed the top of the glass bottle—rich wholesome milk.

Louder, the rider repeated, "It's…for…the…baby."

No-Chance remained in the shadows and nodded.

"Good luck to you folks," the lawman shouted. He tipped his hat and nudged his horse, disappearing in the jumble of people, wagons, and tents.

No-Chance held the jar up. "He brought milk for Tampa."

Black Storm stomped over, took the jar, and tore the paper lid off. "Where was this man when children cried for bread from *wvcenvlke* standing beside road with hands in warm pockets? We are walking skeletons. They saw us with unfeeling eyes. Now this man hopes to make excuses to his God."

The old man scowled, brows furrowed over black eyes intense with anger. "We take nothing from *wvcenvlke*!" He dropped the jar and stalked off into the darkness.

Pain surged through No-Chance's leg as he dove to the ground and grabbed the container up. A puddle of milk glistened in the warm glow cast by the campfire and slowly disappeared into the thin crust of snow.

"Damn crazy old man." No-Chance leaned against the dead oak. Several swallows of milk remained in the bottom of the glass. The chief's hatred was beyond reason. He would never allow Tampa to learn English if he couldn't even accept milk from a white man. What chance did the child have?

Chickamauga knelt.

"Let me be." No-Chance shook off the offered hand. "Your father-in-law's heart is filled with hate. It makes him crazy like the wolf whose mouth bubbles white."

Chickamauga nodded. "Bad spirits entered his head during the long walk. I grow tired of it." Despite the shadows, it was easy to see the young father's anguish, his frustration—mouth set in a rigid line, quiet rage blazing in his eyes.

Spirit of the Crow

"If I stay among the tribe after my leg heals, Black Storm's anger will grow worse. For me, it will be a small matter. Will your heart grow bad, too, if you are banished for accepting me as a brother?"

"The old ones say that to follow the light-path is not easy." Chickamauga sat back on his heels fingering the silver disk on his chest. "My heart misses gone-away one. What would she do? She loved her father, but she loved child inside her, too. It makes little sense to sacrifice our young to old ways."

"Here, brother." No-Chance rubbed dirt from the side of the glass with his thumb. "Before Black Storm returns."

A smile spread across Chickamauga's face as he took the milk. He reached into the wagon for the baby and empty whisky bottle and returned to the warmth of the fire.

No-Chance ran his hand down the blackened trunk of the lightning-struck tree, dislodging a piece of bark. He turned the charred piece in his palm. His skin didn't blister or burn or split open like fired wood. It wasn't even warm. Pleased, he closed his fist and leaned back. The spirit that lived in such trees knew his motives were good.

****

"Um…um…um. Never did see de like. Pitiful, pitiful."

No-Chance shifted onto his side and pulled the blanket over his head to muffle Stvluste's complaints. Doubts had crept into his dreams and left him sleepless. How old had he been when his parents died? Fourteen? Fifteen? For ten years, he lived trusting no one, white or red. Had he taken leave of his senses? What did he

91

know of being a family? What about Texas? Or California?

"What you mean, no rabbits here 'bouts? We gots to have meat. And it ain't gonna be none of dat wormy beef soldiers be handin' out this mornin'."

No-Chance rolled over and peered from under the wagon. Stvluste's hulking form bent over the kettle, scraping corn kernels from a cob with savage fury, while Nick wound cord around a stick.

"If de country here 'bouts is hunted out," Stvluste huffed, "it be hunted out."

No-Chance sighed and crawled from under the protection of the wagon. He had more peace and quiet sleeping in the rooms above Red's Whiskey Parlor in Pensacola.

Pointing a cob at Nick, Stvluste ordered, "Fetch a piece o' that good fo' nothin' beef they handin' out at de fort. And don't let masta see you 'ceptin' somethin' from white soldiers, neither. He have both our hides."

With the aid of the crutch, No-Chance lowered himself next to the fire. "Don't you think Black Storm will know the difference between rabbit and beef?"

Stvluste rolled his large eyes and continued to run a curved bone scraper down a cob. Withered corn kernels flew in all directions. "Once I doctor it with a smidgin' of vinegar an' dab o' wood lye, chief won't know what he eatin'."

The fire's warmth dulled the ache in No-Chance's leg. He brushed a kernel of corn from his hair and flipped it in the pot. For the first time in a week, the sun shone with enough intensity to give the illusion of a pleasant day. He leaned forward, massaging his leg, and watched Chickamauga trudge back from the Neosho.

Morning sun, at the tall Indian's back, haloed his figure and sparkled in his damp hair.

"Wash Sleep Bringer from your eyes." He set a sloshing bucket down. "We go among the people."

Sharp prickles chased from his fingertips to his elbows as No-Chance plunged his hands into the bucket, splashing water in his face. Another thing about Red's Parlor: for an extra copper, a fellow could get a basin of hot water.

"Have you spoken to Black Storm?" He rubbed his hands together over the fire.

Shivering, Chickamauga wrung water from the ends of his hair. "No, all the chiefs and elders gathered as soon as Grandfather Sun appeared."

"You know you will not be welcome among the people if I am at your side."

"That is why you go with me." Chickamauga pulled No-Chance up. "Friends will decide for themselves if you have heart of eagle or one of coyote."

Together, they wound their way around wagons and tents. Men huddled at campfires, and women bent over their chores. At each campsite, talk was the same. The water of the Neosho River tasted different from the waters of their homeland. There, the flavor of the land lived in the Coosa, the Chattahoochee, the Ocmulgee, rivers that fed the streams where they built their homes. Here, air burned the lungs, and low hills disappointed the eyes. Nowhere did they see the sheltering longleaf pines or beloved giant oaks draped in gray moss. Yet, Grandfather Sun shone on Mother Earth as he did back home. And there was hope.

They paused at a low brush shelter beside a flickering campfire. Inside, a woman's voice wavered in a mournful wail. "My friend," Chickamauga called, "I have come to tell of sorrow in my heart for your woman."

A stout Indian peered out, eyes narrowing in the bright light. Four deep scars ran down the right side of his face and neck. He crawled through the entrance and motioned for Chickamauga and No-Chance to join him at the fire. They sat listening to the soft voice of sorrow spilling from the shelter. Those in neighboring campsites walked on silent feet. The scar-faced Indian pulled his blanket tight and stared into the sputtering flames.

Chickamauga cleared his throat. "Every family has been touched by sadness on long walk. This morning, my ears hear of your loss."

The answering voice was harsh, like the whisper of a bear. "Two suns ago, someone went to be with the ancestors. My wife is missing someone. Our son suckled only once at her breast. Now, Chade aches with fullness. Her heart is empty. My words do not soothe her." Slumping, the stout Indian looked down at his large hands. "My arms do not comfort her."

"There is someone who is missing his gone-away mother." Chickamauga bent toward his friend. "Now he cries with an empty stomach."

The man looked up. "Your wife?"

Chickamauga nodded.

"I am sorry. Grief covers my ears. Maker and Taker of Breath is angry with our people that he visits us so."

"I bring my brother, One-Who-Gives-No-Chance, to meet my friend, Crazy Bear."

The stout Indian looked across the fire, a flash of

curiosity in his dark eyes. No-Chance returned the glance and pleased that he did not read disapproval in the man's face, nodded.

Flames consumed a tangle of twigs and danced along a branch of scrub oak. If he listened hard enough to the fire's crackle, he would not hear the sorrow in the woman's voice. Cries of hunger, of grief, of anger filled each day for weeks. He wished to be away from it all.

Finally, Crazy Bear stood. "I will speak to my woman."

There was no question that, despite her sorrow, Chade would nurse Tampa. Each child born into the tribe was loved and had many mothers and fathers. Crazy Bear's guttural voice carried through the thin layer of brush.

A young woman emerged from under a cloth strung across the entrance and stood blinking in the sunlight. Tears sparkled in red-rimmed eyes. Thick black hair flowed down her back like a shroud. With awkward tenderness, Bear put a blanket around her thin shoulders.

"Chade. Great sadness visits my heart to know of your loss." Chickamauga stood and looked down at his feet. "My son is wanting comfort of woman's arms."

Wordless, Chade took a halting breath and nodded.

No-Chance struggled to pull himself up with the crutch. "Go on." He nodded to Chickamauga. "Turtle calls me brother these days, and Tampa is hungry."

He watched the three leave and sighed at his infirmity as he hobbled toward the road. The past evening's crisp layer of snow was now churned into mud. Cold penetrated the soles of his moccasins. He stopped to smile at the little girl from the chuck wagon.

"*Hensci*," he greeted.

Giggling, the child reached out to touch the crutch and then scampered toward the road, red blanket fluttering across her back.

A growing rumble, rising above camp noises, caught his attention. Four straining horses pulled a lumbering wagon toward the fort. The driver's stricken "Whoa," was audible above the clicking of wagon tracings and pounding hooves.

A flash of red caught No-Chance's eye. Wet mud sucked at his moccasins, and his crutch sank into slush as he limped toward the little girl, who stood frozen in the middle of the road. He planted the crutch to propel his body forward in a mighty lunge and reached into space falling, grabbing, rolling.

Curled into a ball, his arms encircled the frightened child. The ground shook as the wagon roared past. An explosion of pain in his injured leg left him gasping for breath.

Dozens of hands helped him sit. An old man, puddles of flesh sagging beneath sunken eyes, pushed through the crowd and squatted. No-Chance released the girl into the arms of her grandfather. Terror on the old man's face melted as he cradled the crying child.

"Old Father, you need to keep a rope on her."

The grandfather smiled and nodded.

"He did a brave thing," someone murmured. Another straightened his leg to examine the loosened splints. No-Chance sucked in his breath at the renewed torment.

"See? This one carries an injury, too." An old woman lifted one of his braids and hit it against her hand to dislodge a clump of mud.

Chickamauga, who had worked his way through the throng of people, held out his hand. "You always find trouble when I leave you alone."

"It was good this one here," another declared, retrieving the crutch.

A muddy wheel track graced one corner of the child's red blanket. Clinging to Chickamauga, No-Chance picked it up and handed it to the little girl.

"What's your name?"

Tears moistened her cheeks. "Cesse," she whispered and turned into her grandfather's chest.

Everyone laughed. The sound was good.

No-Chance studied the circle of smiling people. One by one, they patted his shoulder and returned to their chores.

Does no one notice the color of my eyes, he wondered.

Chapter 14

"What you doin', Knife Man? Playin' in mud?" A lopsided grin spread across Stvluste's face.

"Haven't you heard? I was doing a brave thing." No-Chance eased down next to the campfire and pulled the soiled tunic over his head.

"Um, um, listen to him, Nick. Braggin' hisself up."

"Nearly got run over." No-Chance tossed the buckskin to Stvluste. Shivering, he pulled a blanket tight around his shoulders and watched the Negro scrape mud from the garment and then, stretch it to dry before the fire.

Chickamauga nodded toward a rider approaching the fort. "That is messenger from Chief Roley McIntosh. He'll be here soon."

"How do you know that?" No-Chance paused in the process of scrubbing his moccasins.

"You have been away from your people too long," Chickamauga said. "Nothing is hidden from eyes of Indian."

"I thought McIntosh was dead." No-Chance readjusted the rabbit fur in the bottom of his moccasins.

"No, William, his brother, died. Killed for breaking tribe's law and signing treaty to give away land. Now, Roley is chief of the Lower Nation." Chickamauga swirled a brown osprey feather in his hand. "I was a boy. We thought them foolish to leave land. Maybe we foolish ones."

"Maybe," No-Chance said. Even his father's farm hadn't escaped the white man's raids. He took a deep breath. "Nick, fetch my saddle bag from the wagon. I need to go into the fort and buy a horse."

"No, brother, you cannot risk it." Chickamauga stuck the feather into the folds of his turban and stood, arms folded across his chest, one shoulder lowered. White Cloud's hammered-silver necklace glimmered at his throat.

"The Lower Nation has been here for ten years. Soldiers are used to breeds. Heck, there's probably no full-bloods left among them." He rummaged in the saddlebag and pulled out a knotted kerchief. "Who knows what's beyond the fort. Might be no other place to get supplies."

He unfolded the cloth and studied a collection of coins. A half-dozen coppers, three Spanish reales, a picayune, eight gold eagles, with the design nearly obliterated, and five silver dimes. Not much. He retied the money and slipped the kerchief in his waistband.

"Unless the chief is hiding tools someplace besides the back of that wagon, we'll need to bargain for our own or plan on ripping trees up by their roots." He shimmied the cleaned buckskin over his head.

"We were not allowed time to gather tools or weapons." Chickamauga looked over at the fort. "Soldiers said we would get plows and axes here."

"Did they?" No-Chance arched an eyebrow. "Let's go find them."

"I go." Chickamauga helped him up. "I go alone."

"Come on, old mother," No-Chance teased. "You need me to translate." He hobbled toward the fort where a gathering of Indians waited for corn being handed out to the new arrivals. He kept his head down when they passed the sentry at the gate. Many Indians wandered in and out of buildings unable to understand the soldiers who tried to keep order.

No-Chance stopped in front of the runaway wagon that had roared through the camp earlier. "That your wagon?" he asked a man toweling off one of the horses.

"Yeah," the man nodded, shaking the towel out. "Sure is."

"We saw you come in. Got those horses lathered pretty good."

"Afraid they got away from me." The man stopped working and motioned to No-Chance's leg. "Say, you need to see the doc? It's gonna be awhile. My wife's having trouble birthing. Thought we might not make it."

"I can come back." No-Chance softened his tone. "Good luck."

He and Chickamauga continued down the boardwalk, accompanied by the heavy thump of the crutch. They stopped at the general store's open door. Inside, the proprietor tried to understand Indians wanting to bargain for supplies. Flustered, he scurried around tables, taking blankets out of the hands of first one, and then another, replacing canned goods on the shelves, fussing at children who pressed their noses against the glass bins.

"They aren't going to steal." No-Chance leaned on his crutch. "They're cold and starving."

"*Humph*," the storekeeper snorted, tugging on his bow tie. "Well, they don't have money, and I ain't in the charity business. The government's supposed to take care of them."

Glaring at the plump little man, No-Chance turned and grabbed the arm of a young woman holding a silver bracelet. *"Naken ceme kvsapkv?* What do you want?"

She glanced toward a loaded table. *"Vtcetv hokkolen.* Two blankets."

"She needs blankets. I think this bracelet is worth a couple, don't you." He tossed the bracelet on the counter. It glittered as it spun in circles.

"Well, uh… It's pretty, I suppose."

"Sure it is." He turned to the woman, held up two fingers, and nodded toward the blankets, *"Lvpecicvs!* Hurry!"

She selected several and backed out of the door muttering, *"Mvto.* Thank you."

No-Chance felt a tug at the hem of his jacket and swung around. "Ho, Cesse. *Estonko?* How are you?" The grandfather stood next to the smiling child and held out a small carved eagle.

"Nakete? Fune eco? What is it? Deer bone?" he asked.

The old man shook his head. *"Rvro rakko, vcule-mahe.* A large fish, much old."

"It's whalebone." No-Chance studied the piece of scrimshaw and held it out. "Probably been in his family for a long time. Some officer's wife would love to have this sitting on her table."

"Humph." The proprietor studied the carving, tracing his fingers along its curves.

No-Chance turned to the gray-haired old man again. *"Poca, naken?* Grandfather, what do you want?"

The grandfather pointed first at the blankets, then a woolen cap, jerky, and a small hatchet.

"Fair trade?" No-Chance asked.

The storekeeper nodded, still rubbing the yellowed piece.

Silver bracelets, earrings, hair combs and beads, carvings, and a small reed basket cluttered the counter. The proprietor ran his hands through his hair, as Indians pointed at what they needed and No-Chance translated their needs. When all had traded, he limped out of the store with Chickamauga hurrying after him.

"You didn't trade."

"I'll come back." No-Chance touched the lump at his waist. There was no sentimental value attached to the clump of coins.

They retraced their steps to the doctor's office. Horses, still hitched to the wagon, chomped at their bits. The door slammed open, and the driver rushed out.

"Hey, everyone, I've got baby girls, two of 'em. I've got me two beautiful girls." He grabbed No-Chance's hand and shook it, then grabbed Chickamauga's hand and pumped his arm, as well.

"Congratulations." No-Chance smiled. "He and I have a new son, too."

"I'm Reverend Wade." The driver released Chickamauga's hand. "Settin' up a church down on the Canadian. Hope we'll be friends." He turned to shake the hand of another man passing by.

Wooden boxes lined the inside wall of the fort and with careful maneuvering, No-Chance hoisted himself onto one. Chickamauga leaned against the wall and watched the exuberant father as he laughed and talked with all who came near, Indian or white.

"He is like your medicine man," No-Chance said. "Takes care of the white people's religion and helps them when they are in sorrow or trouble. He's pretty happy now. His wife just had two babies—both girls!"

"Two!" Chickamauga's eyebrows went up. "He's in trouble now."

No-Chance chuckled, nodding in agreement before turning his attention to a commotion on the other side of the parade grounds.

Officers and a group of chiefs filed from a log building. The Indians mounted horses and rode in solemn procession out of the fort. Some wore cloaks trimmed in fur and faded ribbons, others, simple cloth coats belted with woven sashes. Shell, bead, and silver adornments flashed. Several older men were tattooed: one with a black line down his forehead and nose, another with red and black lines running across his cheeks. Black Storm, blue tattoos dominant, filed past and gave no notice of his son-in-law and No-Chance standing at the gate.

The two were caught up in the wave of Indians following the chiefs from the fort. Those at their cooking fires hurried to join the parade until the road was packed. Many spilled into campsites, moving forward, in and around wagons and tents, like an army of ants.

In the distance another procession of Indians came into view. Loud whoops announced the arrival of Head Chief Roley McIntosh and the resident tribe of Lower Creeks. No-Chance was jostled and bumped as those in the rear attempted to see ahead.

"The people grow impatient." Chickamauga positioned himself to buffer the crowd's push. "Many have friends or relatives that married into the whites and joined McIntosh's tribe."

No-Chance glanced at the sea of bronze faces. The wind stirred the feathers and ribbons adorning their clothing and hair. Smells of fur and buckskins and the scented pomatum women used to shine their long hair mingled in the closeness.

Chief McIntosh ushered the immigrants away from the fort and the watching soldiers. He led them deeper into wild Indian Territory, land that was to be theirs as long as their descendants tread upon its green grasses. Near the mouth of the Neosho River, where it emptied into the Arkansas, they stopped to celebrate.

By evening, a great encampment of the two nations of Creeks settled in large groups under hundreds of brush arbors. Fires blazed from numerous campfires. Roasting deer meat and bubbling pots of corn sofke welcomed the newcomers.

After devouring the portions brought to him, No-Chance leaned back and watched torch bearers wander in and out of campsites in search of friends and relatives. Through drowsy eyes, the flickering lights looked like fireflies darting about on a summer night. Laughter mingled with the drone of muted conversations.

"Ho, his stomach is full, and he sleeps like a baby!"

No-Chance struggled to sit. "I wasn't asleep!" He opened his eyes to find Chickamauga grinning down at him. Chade held Tampa. She had put her grief away with the acceptance of the child that needed her. Crazy Bear held a firebrand high, creating a warm circle of light.

"Well, maybe, I was." He laughed as the others settled into a circle. "How is Tampa?" He reached over and pulled the blanket from the baby's face. Tampa's lips puckered at the touch, and he turned, rooting for milk. "Hungry, I see."

Chade's straight black hair fell forward as she bent and cooed at the infant. She loosened the ties to her print blouse, and soon, soft sucking sounds replaced the whimpering.

"All the chiefs are in council again." Chickamauga stretched his legs. "They decide what must be done. Where to settle. We must be careful when we choose. Here, the streams do not respect their banks and rush out to carry everything away, in the time of fresh leaves."

"They say the buffalo are gone." Crazy Bear, voice deep and raspy, leaned forward. "I wanted to hunt the great beasts. What good is this country we have been driven to?" A necklace of bear claws clicked as he shifted his weight. "The chiefs are angry. Soldiers do not have axes and saws for our people. It was promised, but it is not so."

No-Chance glanced at Chickamauga, who met his eyes. Neither said a word.

Drums sounded as the night darkened. An old woman in a calico dress stood before the campfire. The fringe on her long blue shawl swayed as she turned and shuffled around the blazing logs. A dozen turtle shells, filled with dried peas and strapped to her calves, shushed in a soft rhythm. One by one, others fell in behind her enlarging the circle, accompanied by the steady drum beat and whisper of turtle shells.

"Chade." No-Chance reached for the sleeping baby. "You and Bear join the dancing."

Chade handed over the child and walked with

Crazy Bear toward the line of dancers. He was stocky, his leather leggings soiled to a dark shine with wear, and his wild hair tamed with a rolled scarf tied around his forehead.

Chickamauga nodded toward the two. "Bear is an honorable man and has done many brave things to prove himself."

"Let me guess! He killed a bear by the scars on his face."

"Four," Chickamauga corrected and scooted over to look at Tampa. "One sliced open his throat, and now his voice is like the four-legged's growl."

Crazy Bear stepped in behind his wife and began the familiar sliding toe, heel step, of most Indian dances. Silky strands of Chade's thick black hair lifted in the evening breeze and fluttered across her face. Her smooth movements were a pleasing sight among the crowd of dancers.

Chickamauga reached over and poked the fire into a blaze. Flames jumped into the air. "Many little ones suckle at dry breasts. Chade is yet full of nourishment. And she is from Wind Clan. That should soften Black Storm's heart."

"If we had a good shelter for Tampa, maybe your father-in-law would not protest our leaving the fort."

Chickamauga did not answer. No-Chance sighed. Black Storm would never willingly see them leave, no matter who cared for Tampa.

Chade left the line of dancers and sagged next to the fire. "My strength has vanished like morning mist before the sun." She hugged her legs, resting her head on her knees, and picked at frayed ribbons sewn to the bottom of her skirt.

One by one, the newcomers, energy spent, drifted away from the circle. Soon, only Crazy Bear, in his buckskins, remained dancing with McIntosh's Lower Creeks, in their white man's coats and pantaloons. The beads at their necks and feathers in their hats were all that remained of their Indianness. Finally, Crazy Bear returned to the campfire.

No-Chance pulled out his pipe, tamped down shreds of tobacco, and handed the pipe to Chickamauga, who puffed the tobacco to life. The young father passed his hand through the smoke, waving it into his face. Satisfied, he handed the pipe to No-Chance who did the same and in turn, gave it to Crazy Bear. The men sat cross-legged, sharing the smoke in quiet friendship.

Pulling the knot of coins from his waistband, No-Chance hefted them in his hand. "Bear, if you and Chade come with us, I will buy an ax and saw so we will not be dependent upon the soldiers for shelter. Together, we can get through this winter." He looked at Chickamauga who nodded.

"You mean leave our people?" Crazy Bear looked at his wife asleep with Tampa nestled in her arms. "We have nothing but blankets."

"I mean leave the shadow of the fort and the eyes of the white soldiers."

The scar-faced young man stared into the fire for long minutes; then grunted his approval and curled next to his wife. Snuggled in their blankets, the steady beat of drums lulled the tired group to sleep until the early morning chill stirred No-Chance awake. He shifted about, hoping to quell the ache in his leg, as well as the growing doubt of his decision. Could a half-breed outlaw ever find a home?

Finally, he roused and reached for another log to add to the glowing embers. He squinted to peer through the pre-dawn grayness at a distant campsite where a large group gathered. Angry voices rose and ebbed in the stillness.

"Wake up," he whispered. "Something is wrong."

"Huh?" Chickamauga yawned.

"Listen! Over there. They're fighting."

Chapter 15

Fingers of fog crawled up from the Neosho River and slithered around trees and sleeping bodies. It shrank from campfires that blazed away the moisture giving it life. In the distance, through stands of trees bare of their summer covering and thick tangles of brush, angry voices pierced the tranquility. Dark forms rose from the mist and moved toward the commotion.

"That is where chiefs held council last night," Chickamauga said, peering into the dark.

"Our people fight among themselves." Crazy Bear shook off his blanket and trotted toward the noise, leaving swirls of fog in his wake.

Chickamauga hurried after the stout Indian while No-Chance groped for his crutch. Yawning, Chade sat up and shook her dark mane of hair. With her movement, Tampa whimpered, then wailed in earnest.

"Little one," No-Chance said abandoning his attempt to stand, "your cry will chase the sun away."

Chade smiled. "He has appetite of a bear cub." She opened her blouse and lifted the fussing infant. Tampa turned his face to the full breasts, moist with the leakage of milk.

"Where did my husband go?"

"There is a fight, I think, with the chiefs." No-Chance settled next to the fire and fed dry sticks into the embers.

Women from neighboring campsites came to warm themselves. They sat and worked tangles out of their hair and smoothed wrinkles from their skirts. Ignoring the women's chatter, he studied their anxious faces, their deep lines enhanced by the fire's flicker. Chade was maybe twenty winters, perhaps younger. The hardships of the removal, hunger, exposure and sadness, aged everyone, especially females.

"Ho, old woman, you missed a fight." Chickamauga walked into the circle of light, interrupting No-Chance's thoughts and the hum of conversation. Crazy Bear, lip bloodied, stalked behind him.

Old woman? No-Chance sighed and looked for his crutch. "Who was fighting? What was it about?" Chade deposited the baby into his arms before he could stand and rushed to her husband.

"You are not going to be able to eat with such an injury," she scolded, dabbing at Crazy Bear's lip. "Are there not enough four-leggeds to wrestle? Must you fight your own people?"

"The old bitterness is not forgotten." Chickamauga slumped down, rubbing his shoulder. "The nations cannot live together."

"Bitterness? What are you talking about?"

"The Lower Creek leaders signed away our homeland! They opened door for flood of people we could not stop. It is a true thing, new land is rich with tall grasses and fine timber, but Mother Earth is not pleased to have her children here. Summer goes from burning droughts that wither grasses, to rains that eat away land. In time of bare trees, clouds fall from sky and covers land in snow and ice."

He looked around at the wide-eyed women. "They say summer brings fever that takes young and old and weak. To be forced from comfortable green hills of our fathers to country that does not love us brings back old anger. Bad words were spoken."

Crazy Bear brushed Chade's hand away. His words rumbled out. "It is not enough that *wvcenvlke* push us from place of our ancestors. Here, Osage bind us on the north, Pawnee in the west, Comanche to the south. To hunt great beasts, we must go among fierce tribes."

"So," No-Chance interrupted, "we will hunt as a group for buffalo. We are all brave men."

Chickamauga shook his head. "Lower Chiefs say we are not free to leave our new lands to hunt. Great Father in Washington will protect us and provide for our needs."

The group sat in silence. No-Chance pushed another branch into the crackling fire. The Great Father provided but a single blanket and food fit only for dogs, nothing more. And when people walked through their moccasins, they tore ends of their blankets to wrap bleeding feet. Desperate mothers knew only one word of English. The word, bread, was repeated over and over to spectators who watched them pass.

"This can be fixed." Chade pulled Crazy Bear's torn sleeve up to his shoulder. "I must find a needle."

"Leave it!" The stocky Indian jerked his arm away. "Soon we will be naked. We will starve. Our bones will whiten in sun!"

Without speaking, the visiting women rose and returned to their own campsites, blankets draped about slumping shoulders.

"We will not ask permission to hunt." No-Chance

shifted the infant in his lap and looked up to find the others staring at him. He shrugged, surprised they had not thought of the solution.

"Do the soldiers have eyes everywhere? Will birds whisper our comings and goings to the blue-coats? Soldiers are only men with bigger weapons." He reached over and clasped his friend's powerful shoulder. "Tell me Brother Bear, how many felt the strength of this arm?"

"I did not count." A grin sprouted a fresh trickle of blood from Crazy Bear's lip, and he held a fist up. "My blows sent them toward the Osage and Pawnee and Comanche."

"I had to duck or be struck by flying bodies," Chickamauga said, imitating the fact.

"It took five light horsemen to hold me." Crazy Bear puffed his chest out and reached to help No-Chance stand.

"Chiefs have decided." Chickamauga kicked dirt over the fire. "Creek people will remain separated. The Lower Nation has settled along the Arkansas River. We will build our homes on a different river called the Canadian."

They joined the line of Indians retracing their path to Fort Gibson. In the absence of hope, the wind seemed colder, the day duller. Without tools and provisions, the new immigrants would spend the winter huddled under the watchful eyes of the soldiers.

All, thought No-Chance, *but one small group*.

****

"You will need me." Chickamauga looked through the entrance of Fort Gibson at the soldiers inside.

No-Chance shook his head. "My money won't buy

much. Bear can help me. Gather your possessions and meet us here. Chade says good-bye to her friends now."

He watched the young father walk away and felt a shiver of guilt. Chickamauga would face Black Storm alone. Head down, No-Chance limped through the gates, Crazy Bear at his side.

"Good morning to you," a familiar voice called as they passed the doctor's office. Reverend Wade hopped down from his wagon, a grease bucket in his hand. "It looks like another cold day. I pray the good Lord holds the snow until I can get my family home."

No-Chance smiled and, favoring his leg, leaned against the wagon. "Did you say you had a place near the Canadian?"

"That I did." Reverend Wade put a handful of grease on the axle wheel. "Leaving soon as I get loaded and horses hitched."

"We're heading for the Canadian, too. See'n as how we don't know this country, do you mind if we follow along?"

The minister set the bucket of grease down. No-Chance could see indecision in his eyes as he looked at Crazy Bear's scarred face and bruised lip.

"Well…how many are there?"

"Just a few. Me 'n' my brother and our baby. Crazy Bear, here, and his wife. We won't slow you down. I just have to get supplies."

"Reckon to be leaving in a couple hours." Reverend Wade pulled a rag from his pocket and wiped grease from his hands. "Can you be ready? Don't want to spend more'n one night out. Want to make it home before another storm sets in."

"We'll be ready, waiting at the gate." No-Chance

spun and hurried toward the general store, his crutch thumping against the wooden planks.

The minister's voice followed him, "Did you say 'our' baby?"

No-Chance nodded and waved, then paused in front of the general store.

The proprietor, a stack of shirts in his arms, looked out at them. "I don't need any more bracelets if that's what you've got to—" The plump man's eyes shifted from No-Chance to the formidable Indian at his side. "Say now, I don't want no trouble."

"Neither do we!" No-Chance walked in and plunked his bundle of coins on the counter. "I've got money!" He moved about the store picking up an ax, tobacco, jerky, coffee, beans, flour, cornmeal, and salt. Crazy Bear stood, arms folded, and stared at the proprietor.

No-Chance plucked licorice strips from a glass jar and looked about. "Got any saws?"

"A couple." Sorting the coins, the storekeeper shook his head. "But you don't have enough money."

"Count again. I'll take one off your hands." He peered into a glass case and pointed to a display of silver sewing needles. "And one of those, too."

"But, but…" the storekeeper protested.

"This is my friend." No-Chance gave a two-handed saw to Crazy Bear. "He's killed four of the most vicious four-footed creatures God ever breathed life into. You don't want me to have to tell him you won't sell us supplies, do you?"

Crazy Bear lifted his chin, not taking his eyes off the proprietor.

"Oh, no…no." Flustered, the storekeeper dropped

supplies into several gunnysacks.

"Good." No-Chance smiled and nodded for Crazy Bear to pick up the supplies. "Nice to do business with an honest man."

"Anytime." The storekeeper muttered, fumbling with his bow tie.

No-Chance limped out the door and glanced about for the blacksmith's barn, spotting the structure across the parade grounds. Soldiers and blanket-clad Indians hustled about in the cold air, each avoiding the other.

With the crutch under his arm, he maneuvered off the boardwalk and hobbled between the buildings, motioning Crazy Bear to follow. Secure in the shadows, he lifted the small pouch from his neck, poured the jewels into his palm, and chose a purple-hued ruby. His father, Alexander MacGregor, spoke of the heather covering the rugged hills of his beloved Scotland when holding this stone. "'Tis a grand country," he would sigh, "one that breeds men with the strength to wield the great two-handed sword called the *claidheamh mor*." It was from the hilt of just such a weapon that the handful of jewels had been plucked decades earlier.

No-Chance dropped the gem back into the pouch. No, he wouldn't part with the heather jewel. He chose a small red ruby, a twin to the one he'd given the Comanche. The old Pretender himself, Prince James Stuart, had given the precious sword to his great-grandfather for services rendered.

Turning the ruby between his fingers he looked at Crazy Bear. "Let's see if this can build us a future!"

The stench of hot metal greeted them as they neared the large wooden structure. No-Chance held his hand up to halt Crazy Bear. A soldier stood in the doorway deep in conversation with the blacksmith.

"Thanks for the repair," the soldier said, dangling a bridle from one hand. "Tell your wife about that remedy for dyspepsia." He barely looked over as he walked off.

The blacksmith nodded, motioning No-Chance and Crazy Bear inside. "Ed's the name. What can I do for ya?" He stirred coals in the forge with iron tongs.

"I'm needing a wagon and horses."

"Wagon? Sorry. Them's hard to come by. Got that cart over there. Horses are out back." The muscular blacksmith, his long hair married into a wooly beard, laid his hammer down and walked toward the rear of the barn.

Four horses moved about the corral and No-Chance studied them for a few minutes. "How about those two, Ed?" He pointed to a roan and sorrel. "Broke in?"

"Sure. Powerful good buy, too."

No-Chance turned to the blacksmith. "I have something that will make you an envied man about the fort. It will make your wife the happiest woman hereabouts. In fact, she'll forget all about the dyspepsia."

"Yeah? How'd you—" Ed narrowed his eyes. "Make her happy? How?"

"I got something you'd have to go clear to St. Louis for. A gen-u-wine ruby!" No-Chance looked around before opening his hand. The ruby gleamed in his palm. "Men kill for a gem like this, and women swoon plumb over."

"Mighty little, ain't it?" Ed took the ruby and held it up between two burly fingers.

"Little!" No-Chance lowered his voice, "I reckon

your wife won't let you out the door in the morning for covering you with kisses, she'll be so wild about this pretty thing." He plucked the ruby from the man's grimy hand.

"Well, I don't know 'bout gems and things."

"I do. Guarantee you'll be getting quite a bargain. Rubies are the favorite jewels of kings and queens. In fact, maybe I shouldn't be trading this. Might be too rich for you."

"See here…" The blacksmith wiped his nose with the back of his hand. "You offered it. Wouldn't be right to take it back."

"Reckon you got a point." No-Chance frowned. "Does that cart have a harness?"

"Well, yeah…could fix something up."

No-Chance clucked to the roan and wiggled his fingers between the horse's lips to squint at its teeth. Permanent incisors. The horse was at least five years old.

"You know, having wealth like a jewel is a big responsibility. Usually only for bankers. These mounts been shoed?"

"Shoed 'em yesterday." Ed combed fingers through his curly beard and puffed his chest out. "An' say, I ain't zackly nobody. Army sent clear to Texas for me!"

"Oh, I see you're a man of importance here 'bouts, Ed. But you know, womenfolk get mushy about twinkly things. Wouldn't want you getting into more'n you can handle."

The blacksmith licked his lips. "Got a canvas you can use. It's gonna be snowin' again soon."

"Look how she sparkles." No-Chance held the stone up to the sun and twisted it between his fingers.

"Need a saddle?" Ed asked.

"Nope, got one with silver studs."

"Well." The odor of onions colored the air as Ed leaned close. "How about two horses *and* the cart."

The three trooped back into the shadows of the building. No-Chance walked around the stubby wagon. Holding the ruby between his forefinger and thumb, he tested the large wooden wheels with his other hand. Seemed sturdy enough.

"Well, got me over a barrel. Help me hitch the sorrel up. It's a mighty good deal you'll be getting."

"Boy, is Minnie gonna be surprised!" The blacksmith quickly fashioned several metal hoops into canvas frames.

No-Chance rolled the ruby in his palm. He'd carried the twelve precious stones next to his heart for ten years. His father called them the twelve disciples, reflecting the light and beauty of our Lord and His goodness. There were times he'd been destitute but never considered parting with one. Now, two of the disciples were gone.

"Whad'da ya think?" Grinning, the blacksmith pointed toward the makeshift wagon.

No-Chance nodded. "A fine job, Ed." He kissed the ruby and put it in the large man's dirty palm. "Good trade you got here. This came all the way from Scotland."

He motioned for Crazy Bear to load the supplies into the cart. "This roan got a name?"

A chuckle began deep in the blacksmith's belly and rolled out with glee. "Thunder. You'll like him."

"Say, might want to close up early tonight." No-Chance winked at the blacksmith. "Save yourself for all that loving you're bound to get."

No-Chance hobbled across the plaza leading the roan toward the gate. Crazy Bear led the sorrel, wheels on the cart creaking and groaning with each rotation. Chade, several bundles at her feet, stood outside the fort gates. A blue blanket, over her head and shoulders, encircled Tampa, too. She jiggled in an attempt to quiet the wailing baby.

The reverend's covered wagon lumbered toward them.

"Where's Chickamauga?" No-Chance yelled to Chade.

His stomach sank when she shrugged. He scanned the sea of Indians milling between tents and shelters. Black Storm's rage would be formidable. Would Chickamauga have the strength to stand against it? Tampa continued to cry. With a sigh of relief, No-Chance sighted the familiar red turban. Chickamauga led his horse and loaded travois through the multitude of people. The black saddle and bridle with silver disks rested on top of the load.

"Chade, what's the matter with Tampa?" No-Chance asked.

"He's hungry and uncomfortable. It is way of babies."

"I could hear Tampa's howl clear to Black Storm's camp," Chickamauga called. "What is wrong with him?"

"Don't you know anything!" No-Chance shook his head. "He's hungry just like babies get! Come!" He pulled the cart's canvas flap open. The saw, ax, and two bulging gunnysacks lay on the floor.

Frowning, Chickamauga reached in and ran his

finger down the wide blade of the saw. "Soldiers told chiefs there were no tools."

"Brother, anything is possible with the white man's money. Now, help me saddle up." He nodded toward a wagon rumbling through the fort's gates. "We need to hurry."

Reverend Wade halted his team of horses next to them.

No-Chance pointed up at the minister. "We're going with him to the Canadian."

Chapter 16

Outside the fort, smoke from hundreds of scattered campfires curled upward and feathered into a gray December sky. Blanket-clad Indians moved about, while children skirted tents and lean-tos or jumped wood piles. The rumbling wagon and cart drew the curiosity of a few who abandoned their campfires to see who dared leave the tribe's security.

Stoic Indians, bundled in threadbare clothing, waited to cross the road. No-Chance shifted in his saddle and tried not to look into their faces. Full bellies from the feast would soon be a memory, and they would be reduced to the Indian agent's meager allowance of dried corn and salt pork.

The dull ache in his leg was constant, impossible to ignore. No-Chance bent to readjust the sling when a small hand reached up and touched his arm.

"Whoa!" No-Chance reined the horse.

Looking up at him, Cesse's wide grin exposed the gap in her teeth.

"Where is grandfather?" he asked.

The child pointed to the frosty-haired man kneeling before a shelter of stretched blankets and cedar boughs. The ax, bartered for a carved eagle, was imbedded in a gnarled branch.

No-Chance rummaged in his saddlebag and removed a paper bundle. Cesse clutched the stirrup leather to watch him pull off a licorice strip. Eyes glistening, she reached for the offered candy.

"Stay away from the road, Cesse," he called as she scampered toward the old man.

The reverend's wagon led the way, followed by Crazy Bear, who tried to maneuver the two-wheeled cart between deep ruts in the road. Chickamauga and No-Chance settled their mounts into an easy walk behind them.

The dark sky seemed to close in on the group, coloring their world a dreary hue. Thankful that Father Wind held his breath, No-Chance tugged at the ruffled collar of his cloth shirt. With the outer protection of a buckskin tunic, he was luckier than most.

A number of old men, some shivering beneath belted flannel shirts that reached to their knees, loitered about in conversation. A proud figure, arms crossed, stepped from the group and stood in the center of the road. No-Chance glanced back at the fort. Would Black Storm create a disturbance, bringing the soldiers running?

"Father," Chickamauga said, "I go now to discover voice of this land."

Black Storm's blue tattoos flashed as he looked at his daughter's chestnut mare and the attached travois.

In a softer voice, Chickamauga continued, "You will see your grandson again. He grows strong. He feeds from milk of his mother's clan. Chade and Crazy Bear travel with us."

The chief slapped the catamount tail over and over in his hand and shifted his glare to No-Chance.

Fingering the crutch that laid across his lap, No-Chance cleared his throat. "I have not forgotten my vow. I will keep your law. Tampa grows close to my heart."

Black Storm, mouth pulled tight, did not respond.

The horses snorted, shifting their weight, until the hoarse caw of a lone crow startled the three and broke their silent battle. The bird skimmed above the wagon and cart continuing down the road. No-Chance followed its flight until it disappeared into the distance. Responding to his master's slight movement, Thunder took a tentative step forward.

With a huff, Black Storm turned and stalked away.

No-Chance urged his horse into the center of the road. Months of forced travel through bogs and swamps, forests and mountains, wearied animals and humans alike. Together they suffered hunger and exposure. Like the Biblical plagues, swarms of insects tormented the body, while grief tormented the soul.

And then in *Ehole*, the month of frost, they prayed to the Maker of Breath to stay the hand of winter. Their prayers to save them from freezing rain and snow were not heard.

No-Chance twisted to watch the fort and settlement of Creeks recede in the distance. Soon threads of smoke were all that remained to mark their existence. He had hidden among strangers, but together, they shared the brotherhood of misery.

"Why do you look behind?" Chickamauga trotted his horse alongside. "Old life is gone. Today, we open eyes as a new baby and, for first time, see sky and trees. Baby does not remember life as spirit. This day is fresh with new beginning."

No-Chance settled forward, content in the thought of a new life.

They forded the Arkansas River into the land designated for the Upper Creeks. Grinding tracks of deer and raccoon beneath their wheels, the wagon and cart traversed the gentle hills on a crude road made by hunters and traders. From a distance they saw a brindle wolf follow a scent and disappear into a thicket.

The roan and No-Chance came to an understanding. He allowed the horse to grab mouthfuls of weathered pea vines peeking through a thin crust of snow. In turn the horse responded to nudges without the use of reins.

"He seems fine horse, easy to learn," Chickamauga observed.

No-Chance ran his palm down the length of the roan's neck. "Thunder may make a fair partner. Sits different than Boy." The horse picked his way with a sure-footedness of one born to running. Low reverberating sounds accompanied his muffled hoof beats on the soft ground.

"Whew! Have we crossed path of a striped tail?" Chickamauga asked.

They scanned the area. A scrubble of undisturbed snow held its pristine whiteness. No-Chance shrugged. "Either that or something crawled off to die." He shortened the sling to change the position of his leg.

The horses resumed their trot. Thunder's stride set an uneven rhythm to the clink of silver disks adorning the bridle. A deep rumble resumed, distinct, sputtering, in sync with the horse's gait.

"You hear something?" No-Chance glanced at the heavy skies.

Chickamauga nodded as they halted. The sound stopped, too.

"Must be a sulfur spring." No-Chance wrinkled his nose and nudged the roan forward. Deep burrups again resonated to the sounds of Thunder's plodding steps, the creak of leather, and jingle of silver.

"Brother!"

No-Chance looked over his shoulder at Chickamauga, suppressing a large grin.

"I know why horse named Thunder."

****

Flames jumped along the length of a downed tree casting light to the dark glen. Shadows frolicked against the wagon's white canvas. A roasting turkey, impaled on a forked branch, popped and spit grease, forcing the men away from the fire.

"I should've known when I saw that blacksmith. I never saw a curly-headed man you could trust. Ringlets are for females and their twisty words, all sweet like." No-Chance took a breath and glanced at the two women fussing with three infants. Chade nodded and smiled as Jerusha, the reverend's young wife, talked, the universal language of motherhood transcending the women's need to understand each other.

"That blacksmith traded me a flatumous horse," No-Chance fumed, much as he had since making camp. "And that slick-talking rascal darn well knew it, too. What's the world coming to when you can't trust a blacksmith?"

His irritation at being hornswoggled was forgotten only when a turkey flew into the branches of a sweet gum tree earlier. The turkey fluffed his feathers and sat, tiny black eyes staring at the intruders, almost asking to become supper. With a quick flip, No-Chance sent his blacksnake whip flying out to grasp the gawking bird by the neck.

"Thunder is fine horse." Chickamauga crossed his arms and watched the turkey roast above the campfire. "Does he not respond to every command?"

"I didn't say he wasn't a smart horse. I said he was flatumous. Windiest animal I ever came across."

Crazy Bear ran his hand down the horse's rump and lifted its long black tail. "He does not speak now."

No-Chance threw his hands in the air and turned back to the campfire.

"Come on boys, this bird looks done. Let us pray." Reverend Wade templed his hands and closed his eyes. "Almighty God, provider for your poor children here on earth, we thank you for your bountiful goodness." His voice rose. "Bless this food that it might nourish our feeble bodies and give us energy to go forth into the wilderness."

Crazy Bear licked his lips and looked over at No-Chance, who put his finger to his pursed mouth.

"We thank you for staying the weather that we might return to our home in safety." The reverend's prayer wavered with passion. "There is much to be done in bringing your lost children into the fold."

The skin on the turkey blackened as flames licked along the surface.

Crazy Bear glared first at No-Chance and back to the minister, who continued, "Open the hearts of your children that they might hear the word of your love and be embraced in the cloak of Christianity. For it is only by receiving the waters of life that they will be able to sup with you in the great banquet halls of heaven."

Eyes still closed, Reverend Wade paused to take a breath.

"Amen!" yelled No-Chance. He jerked the smoking turkey from the fire. Like wolves to a fresh kill, Chickamauga and Crazy Bear pounced on the burnt meat, beating out flames with a rag.

"Amen," the startled minister repeated.

No-Chance settled himself onto a mat of cedar branches. He handed out steaming hunks of meat, saving a leg for himself, then sifted a pinch of salt over its surface and licked at the juices oozing from the skin.

When little more than scattered bones were left, No-Chance searched in his saddlebag for his pipe. "Do you have Indian blood, Reverend Wade?"

"No. Why?" The minister wiped his lips with a hand gloved in grease.

"I wondered how come you're setting up a mission here. The Upper Creeks don't like white folks."

"The American Board of Foreign Missions gets permission from the government to set up schools and educate the children. And churches for civilizing the heathens to Christianity." He hesitated and glanced over at Chickamauga sitting cross-legged. The fire cast a sinister shadow on Crazy Bear's scarred face. Hunger satisfied, both men sat quietly listening to a conversation they did not understand

"Uh," the minister cleared his throat. "Uh, that is, the good book exhorts us to 'Go ye into all the world, and—'"

"And preach the gospel to every creature.' From St. Mark, I think." No-Chance glanced at the minister. "You suppose Jesus meant to preach to even the animals when he said 'every creature'?" He pulled a brand from the fire, touched the flame to the tobacco, and sucked it to life.

Reverend Wade frowned. "How do… I mean, you've been to mission school?"

No-Chance puffed at his pipe. He parted his lips to release the smoke, regretting he had finished the verse. The aroma of tobacco filled his nostrils, heated his mouth. Was it wise to share his past with anyone?

"The Indian already has a religion. They believe in one god, The Maker and Taker of Breath." He handed his pipe to Chickamauga. "And in their world, they're civilized. All the tribes I know have laws. Much like the Ten Commandments, I'd say. They don't abide killing or stealing or taking another man's wife."

He watched Chickamauga enjoy the pipe and hand it to Crazy Bear. "It won't be easy to establish a mission here. Might be easier among the Lower Creeks. Many of them speak English. I don't reckon you speak Creek?"

The reverend ran his hand through his auburn hair. "No. It won't be easy. With God's help, I'll prevail. I'll speak for the Indians when they need it. May God strike me down. I'll not lie to them. These poor folks need someone to show them the way to everlasting life. But how do you know—"

Crazy Bear handed the pipe to the minister, who shook his head.

"Take it. It's a sign of friendship!" No-Chance admonished.

Reverend Wade took the pipe, coughing through several long pulls on the pipe stem.

No-Chance stifled a laugh. "How much farther?"

"Tomorrow noon, I reckon." The minister wiped his eyes and handed the pipe back. "We traveled the whole day, and I never caught your name."

"It's No, uh, it's John, John MacGregor." He smiled. Perhaps there was safety in his birth name.

The minister cocked his head. "Who taught you the Bible?"

"My father, Alexander MacGregor." No-Chance stared into the fire, pushing a stick into the flames, sending tiny bright embers into the darkness. "He was a circuit preacher. Wished to bring Indians into the shepherd's fold, too."

"Your mother was Creek?"

"Seminole."

The minister frowned. "Well, what are you doing in Creek territory?"

"Helping my brother raise our shared son." No-Chance grinned, reached over, and put his hand on Chickamauga's shoulder. "*Honvnwv hvtket Reverend Wade hocefkvt os*. The white man's name is Reverend Wade."

The Indian nodded toward the minister. "*Mvskoke opvnaykvn kerretskv?*"

"He asked if you spoke Creek," No-Chance translated.

Reverend Wade shook his head and extended his arm. "Pleased to meet you."

Chickamauga clasped the offered hand and smiled.

"Uh, so he is Seminole, too?"

"No, he is a son of the Creek nation."

The minister frowned and sputtered, "I don't understand… I mean, what is a shared son? How can you be brothers? Seems I've a lot to learn about Indian customs."

No-Chance hunkered into his blanket and studied the earnest young man. Perhaps, at last, here was someone who could be trusted.

"When White Cloud's time came on the long walk I spoke for her with the soldiers. Together, Chickamauga and I brought a new soul into the now world. My friend's heart is heavy with the burden of his wife's death. But he wishes for Tampa to know the white man's way."

Shifting, he rubbed his leg. "I don't deserve the honor, but together we will raise Tampa to know two worlds. The baby's grandfather is Chief Black Storm who wants the child to know only the old ways."

"Ahh, the Good Samaritan." The minister pulled at his coat and buttoned it. "You not only help a stranger in need, but also until he is able to stand on his own."

"I'm no good Samaritan. They helped me." He looked across the fire at Crazy Bear, who sat stoically in his torn buckskins, oblivious to the cold. "Meet Crazy Bear, Reverend." He held up four fingers. "Guess how many bears he's killed, without a gun, I might add."

"Pleased to meet you!" Reverend Wade leaned forward and stretched his arm toward the solemn Indian. Crazy Bear nodded and clasped the extended hand in a powerful grip.

"They lost their baby before we reached the fort. Chade was still fresh with milk." No-Chance looked down at his splinted leg. "Seems we're tied to each other to survive."

Reverend Wade smiled. "Well, like the Jews who wandered in the desert forty years before finding the Promised Land, the Indians have found their promised land. It is protected for them. There's no white settlers here."

"Reverend, the Indian has no protection from the white man."

"Then, John, your companions are fortunate to have you for a friend."

"I wonder," No-Chance murmured as he hunched deeper in his blanket. The gentle crackle of the campfire mingled with low sighs of a restless wind. Bare tree branches clacked and rubbed. In the distance a wolf howled. Another echoed his call. Somewhere in the thick brush, a small critter rattled the brittle grasses.

He leaned against a tree and listened to the songs of the new land.

Chapter 17

Soft whimpers, much like a new bear cub's mewing, stirred No-Chance from his sleep. The whimper became a whine and then, an angry wail. It was joined by another and finally, a third tiny voice.

The crying of three babies could not be ignored. No-Chance threw his blanket off, sat up, and stretched. Jerusha poured coffee beans into a heavy skillet and placed it on a bed of glowing coals. She wrapped a towel around the handle and jiggled the skillet. The tumbling beans released a strong roasted aroma. Flames caught the loose end of the fabric.

"Ohhh." She dropped the towel and pulled her hand to her chest. No-Chance struggled to his feet and pushed the skillet off the coals with the end of his crutch.

"Are you hurt?" He reached for Jerusha's hand to examine it.

She shook her head with a tight-lipped grimace. "It…it just scared me, I think. Thank you."

"Cooking over a campfire is man's work. Maybe you better see to the little ones." He nodded toward Chade who sat cross-legged juggling all three discontented infants in her lap and arms—two tiny fair-haired girls and one brown-skinned, black-haired boy.

"What do you want me to do with those beans?" he asked as Jerusha hurried to unburden Chade.

"Put them into that pot," she said over her shoulder.

No-Chance peered into a pot of simmering water with six eggs bobbing along the bottom. He smiled as he tilted the skillet and watched the coffee beans slide in among the eggs. How long had it been since he'd had such a treat?

"The Lord blesses us with a fine morning," the reverend called. "Maybe the weather will hold for another day." He led his horses to the front of the wagon and hitched them for the final ride home.

Chickamauga emerged from the wooded thicket, tugging on the halter leads of the roan and gray dun. "This one," he said, and nodded to the roan, "likes to stray."

No-Chance grabbed Thunder's chinstrap and scratched the horse's forehead. "That is a sign of a brave horse. An animal that hangs in close to the campsite is afraid. One that roams knows his strength and will not shy from a fight."

Chickamauga smoothed a blanket over the dun's back. "Maybe he not smart enough to be afraid." A smile crossed his face as he picked up his saddle.

"*Humph*!" No-Chance snorted and turned back to the campfire. Dark craze marks zigzagged around the eggs bobbing about in murky brown water.

"Breakfast!" he called to the others and spooned the hard-boiled eggs, now dyed the color of leather, into a bowl. He wrapped the half-burnt towel around his hand, lifted the pot, and poured the brew into four tin cups.

A swallow of the hot coffee traced a path down No-Chance's throat and spread through his chest. He bit into a bean to release its acrid flavor and handed the steaming cup to Chickamauga. Crazy Bear squatted next to the fire, juggling a hot egg between both hands before he, finally, closed his fist and shattered the shell.

"How long you been out here, Reverend." No-Chance held an egg between two fingers and picked at pieces of shell with his fingertips.

Carl put his coffee cup down and wiped his mouth with the back of one hand. "Since June, and what a summer! Hot as Hades. Had a load of milled lumber brought all the way up the Arkansas by steamer from Little Rock. Without the help of a group of God-fearing gentlemen from the fort, we'd never have been ready for winter." He nodded toward his wife, who tapped a spoon around the center of an egg. "If I'd known she was with child, I'd left her in Philadelphia with her parents."

"Now, Carl," she admonished, "we knew it wouldn't be easy doing the Lord's work out here. We must thank Him for the trials He puts before us."

No-Chance bit into the hardboiled egg and closed his eyes. Pure heaven.

The reverend's voice droned. "We wanted to be completely established by the time the Indians arrived. I must say, there is a great need for us, too." He dropped his cup into a wooden box. "I posted a letter to the elders before we left the fort yesterday, requesting warm clothing as my flock's most immediate priority. I'm sure he'll put the word out to the churches, and they'll conduct a drive."

Jerusha stood and brushed bits of shell from her skirt. "And it will be summer before anything reaches the territory."

With a sigh, No-Chance kicked dirt over the coals and pulled himself into the saddle. He wasn't at all sure the chiefs would accept charity from the white man's holy speaker.

The rumbling of the small caravan and Thunder's intestinal outbursts broke the early morning quiet.

"What does your horse say?" Crazy Bear shouted as No-Chance trotted past.

Chickamauga held his nose. "You and Thunder ride behind wagons. If Comanche or Osage follow our path, they will be discouraged."

No-Chance lifted his chin and spurred Thunder to a gallop. A loud rolling *burrup* followed the horse's burst of speed. If he couldn't do anything else, at least he could outrun the smell.

Quail fluttered from tall grasses in meadows bordered with thickets of sloes and persimmon trees stripped, except for upper branches, of their fruit by deer. The overcast sky made the groves of tall elm, cottonwood, hickory, and oak dreary and cheerless.

The frame of a small church appeared on a distant rise. No-Chance shook his head at the symbol of civilization in such a primitive wilderness. A neat house of milled lumber, with a coat of white wash, sat behind the skeleton of the church. Lace curtains hung at the window beside the door.

No-Chance rode up to the reverend's wagon as it pulled to a stop in the front yard.

"Will you stay awhile?" Carl jumped down. He cuddled an infant in the crook of his arm.

"No. We better be on our way. Won't be dark for another couple hours." No-Chance studied the young man whose beard barely shadowed his face. The minister's faith must be boundless to believe he could persuade an unwilling flock to worship in the white man's church.

Carl reached for the other daughter handed down by his wife.

Jerusha called to No-Chance as she climbed from the wagon. "Don't leave yet. I have something for you folks." A woolen scarf slipped from her head, loosening the pins in her blonde hair, freeing strands to flutter about her face.

"On the other side of the woods, maybe ten or fifteen miles, there's a nice size clearing." Carl pointed past the church frame. "Thirty or forty miles beyond, the hills open up to prairie. This trail will take you all the way to Edwards' Trading Post. How far you going?"

"Not rightly sure." No-Chance shrugged. They'd go far enough to escape detection by the occasional hunter from the fort.

"Well, keep an eye on the weather. It changes mighty fast around here."

The front door slammed, and Jerusha hurried off the porch. She handed a jar to No-Chance. "A little somethin' special to welcome you to the territory."

"Thank you kindly, ma'am." He took the offered jar. Blackberries shifted as he tilted the glass container and held it up. "I can't remember when I had berries last."

No-Chance waved at the young couple and nudged Thunder into motion.

Without the sounds of the reverend's wagon and team, there was a loneliness to their trek. No-Chance and Chickamauga scouted to either side of the narrow trail while Crazy Bear led the sorrel and cart in a steady pace down the overgrown path.

Thunder stretched to reach a patch of pea vines running along a dry creek bed, and No-Chance let him feed. Herbage was scant and, if the reverend was right, would be hidden soon under a layer of snow.

He watched Chickamauga trot out of the gloomy trees toward him. "How does it look that way?"

"Much work to clear a field. Many trees, thick bushes."

"Same in my direction." He snugged his heel into Thunder's rib, and the horse scrambled up an incline and back onto the path. "Say, do you see how much energy this horse has?"

Chickamauga nodded. "He hasn't walked from Old Nation."

"He jumped a ravine. You should have seen it. Took me by surprise. Almost unseated me, what with my leg and all."

"You are fortunate to have such good horse."

"Well, that's the trouble. A horse like Thunder takes someone equally strong to manage him." No-Chance cast a glance at the tall Indian and continued, "Being injured, I'm off my stride. Now that dun of yours, being tired like he is…"

No-Chance stopped mid-sentence at Chickamauga's stare.

"Well, seeing as how Thunder is a horse of, uh, unusual qualities, I thought you might be interested in a trade. Of course, if you are going to let a little thing like an occasional fart put you off."

A piercing *whoop* bounced off trees and surrounded the two riders.

"Osage war party?" No-Chance slid his hand under the flap of his saddlebag.

Another shout echoed through the woodland. The men turned their horses in a circle, searching dark shadows for an unseen foe. Tall leafless oaks, with numerous intertwined branches, sheltered a thick profusion of smaller trees and bushes. Withered grape vines, dangling from limbs, wagged in the chill air.

Chickamauga reined his horse. "Crazy Bear?"

"If so, he is ahead of us." No-Chance nodded down the path. "That way!" He smacked the coiled whip along Thunder's flank and leaned forward, the horse's steady breathing and firm hoof beats loud in his ears.

The forest gave way at the edge of a slight incline. Thunder slid down the soft dirt into a wide creek bed. Ice-crusted ribbons of water crisscrossed around small rocks.

No-Chance jerked back on the reins, causing the horse to rear. A burst of pain traveled from his injured leg and up his spine. He gasped, fighting a wave of nausea.

"Is there trouble?" he yelled at Crazy Bear.

A short distance away, a giant oak leaned across the creek bed. The stout Indian stood beneath its drooping branches. He lifted a skull above his head, leaned back, and let loose another warbling yell.

"It is the great beast!" Crazy Bear called. "A sign from the Maker of Breath. We stop here!"

Angry, No-Chance shouted back, "I thought Osage or Pawnee or some forest demon had attacked."

Chickamauga's gray dun clambered down the incline, dislodging chunks of dirt. No-Chance pointed at Crazy Bear. "Little Brother has found a sign, if it is a sign. A skull of the great beast, if it is the great beast."

"It must be!" Crazy Bear pointed to the short horns positioned low on the broad forehead of the skull. "We stop here."

Chickamauga dismounted and put his hand on Crazy Bear's shoulder. "We cannot build here. When rains come…"

"It is sign." Crazy Bear planted his feet apart and hugged the moss-covered skull. "Spirit of buffalo is here."

No-Chance walked the roan beyond the stubborn Indian. "We build there." He jutted his chin toward a flat plot of land above the creek. "A good place, I think, for a cabin."

"He is right, my husband." Chade slipped out of the cart and hurried up the embankment to look around the peaceful glen. "Let us build here and mount the skull of the great beast above our door."

No-Chance studied Crazy Bear, who was holding the large skull. Flood waters most likely deposited the bone, but it would be useless to argue the point. "Yes, my friend, perhaps it is a good sign."

Chickamauga and Crazy Bear felled trees by the light of a huge campfire while No-Chance nuded the logs of their branches and fed them into the flames.

"To be settled is good," Chade declared, raking unshucked ears of corn from the coals. She poured coffee into two tin cups. No-Chance sipped the hot brew and sucked on the beans that floated into his mouth. Leaning against several logs, he watched Chade kneel next to her husband to examine his torn sleeve.

"I almost forgot." No-Chance felt in the pocket of his saddlebag and pulled out a small folded paper.

"Here, this might help."

Chade took the offered gift, turning toward the fire's light. Her hair fell forward as she leaned to unfold the paper. Smiling, she slid a silver needle free and held it up. "Thank you," she murmured, rolling the needle between two fingers. "Grandmother's sewing basket sat on shelf. I could not reach it when soldiers came. It sits there still, I think."

The men watched as Chade walked, holding a knife, toward the tethered horses. Cooing to each, she ran her hand down their tails and returned with a shank of horsehair.

"We are building a fine shelter," No-Chance declared and opened the jar of blackberries. "This calls for a celebration." He fished several berries out with his fingers and passed the jar to Chickamauga. Each, in turn, popped berries into their mouth, laughing at the grimaces the tart fruit produced.

Despite the ache in his leg, No-Chance felt content. He had not hidden his face in two days. He had ridden like a man. Now, he watched the smoke rise and disappear into the blackness of the night. Light airy flakes of snow drifted from the void above. He held his hand out to catch them in his palm. Maybe there was a place in the world for someone like him.

Chapter 18

Swirls of snow engulfed No-Chance, caking his eyelashes, sliding down his neck, seeping into his moccasins. Freezing air stabbed his lungs, and he turned away from winter's harsh breath.

No sun, no sky, no landmarks—just a gray, white coldness that consumed the earth. Knee-high drifts of snow sucked at his legs, trapping him as surely as the Florida quicksand had many years ago. Exhausted, No-Chance sank down and curled around his bundle of wood until a familiar brogue roused him.

"God thundereth marvelously with His voice. Great things doeth He, which we cannot comprehend."

"Father?" The question echoed in the stillness of a world suspended in ice.

"For He saith to the snow, be thou on the earth; and, by the breath of God, frost is given."

"Father." No-Chance struggled to rise from his frozen coffin. "Where are you?"

"Before ye, Laddie."

Teeth chattering, No-Chance wiped frosty crusts from his eyes and peered into the falling snow at a familiar figure. "Is this the Almighty's punishment? He makes the world disappear and abandons me into nothingness?"

"Nay, 'tis no punishment, but an example of the wondrous things that come from the hand of our Lord."

With numb fingers, No-Chance pulled the strip of blanket protecting his head tighter under his chin. "This wondrous snow swallowed my footprints." Immediately he regretted the sarcasm, but his father's blue eyes remained patient. "The land is foreign. I cannot find my way. Chade and Tampa will be cold without wood."

"Why do ye not ask the Lord's help, John?"

"You, Father, you help me."

Snow settled on his father's head and shoulders, catching in his beard. Smiling, he motioned for No-Chance to follow, turned, and strode through the drifts, disappearing into trees sheeted in snow.

"Wait!" No-Chance scattered clumps of snow searching for his crutch. His injured leg, numb to feeling, no longer responded to his commands. In desperation he inched forward with one arm, pulling bundled branches along with the other.

Throat raw, he called into the stillness, "Wait!" The footprints his father left disappeared like tracks in the sand slowly erased by waves rolling in and out to sea. One was never this cold in Florida, the home of his mother's people. What kind of land punished its inhabitants with such bitterness?

No-Chance watched a shape move through the snowy haze and sank in relief. Strong arms removed the burden of wood and lifted him.

"Thank you, Father, thank you," he whispered.

****

Thistles of pain seared into No-Chance's sleep. He awoke to the smell of smoldering wood and the odor of people too long unwashed. The air's staleness raked his nostrils. An unwilling cough sandpapered his throat.

"He is awake, I think." A voice, warm and gentle,

summoned him, and he struggled onto one elbow.

"Chade?"

"You were gone long time. Chickamauga found you."

"Chickamauga? But…I thought…" No-Chance closed his eyes against the sting of smoke and ran tingling fingers along the rough log wall to convince himself he wasn't dreaming. It had taken a day of furious working to construct the small windowless room before the snow began in earnest. Crazy Bear and Chickamauga fit the logs in place while he removed the largest limbs and helped Chade mud cracks inside and out. A bear skin, hooked on four pegs, covered the small door opening. The vent hole in the sloping roof was barely adequate. Smoke filled the room with each shift of wind.

No-Chance leaned against the wall and watched Chade pat three corn cakes into shape and place them on a flat stone edging the fire.

"You should not have gone for wood, brother." Chickamauga knelt next to No-Chance. "Your leg not strong. We found no game. Crazy Bear set snares for rabbits. Maybe we have meat tomorrow."

"No," a gravelly voice grumbled. "The Maker of Breath is angry. He drops clouds from sky to hide animals and cover us. He no longer wants to see our faces."

"The Maker of Breath is angry?" No-Chance squinted through the haze of smoke.

The fire's glow illuminated the frown on Crazy Bear's face, deepening his scars. "We left land He gave to ancestors. Now *wvcenvlke* desecrate it."

No-Chance sighed at such conviction. It would be

useless to argue. He glanced around the small room. Articles of clothing, leather pouches, bridles and ropes, a bucket, the makings of a crude bow, and a quiver of arrows, hung from branch stubs on the log walls.

Chickamauga leaned against a saddle and poked at the fire, waiting for the edges of a corn cake to brown.

"How did you find me?" No-Chance asked, despite the rawness in his throat. "The snow buried everything. Without the ax, I pulled branches from the trees. Grandfather Sun was lost, and I could not find my way."

"I followed your tracks. I heard you calling," Chickamauga said.

"What tracks? My footprints were gone." No-Chance leaned toward his friend. "The snow filled them up."

Chickamauga shrugged. "Tracks led me to you."

As long as it snowed, no one ventured out of sight of the cabin. In the windowless room, day blended to night. No-Chance pulled his knife from its sheath and flipped it into the dirt floor. *Thlik*. He retrieved it and flipped it again. *Thlik*. It felt cool and perfectly balanced. The blade had been forged of the hardest steel in the days of his ancestors. He imagined his father and grandfather throwing this blade. They that live by the sword, die by the sword. *Thlik*.

"If I had seeds, I could plant in furrow you dig." Chade's voice was as always, soft, not critical.

No-Chance smiled and motioned the others closer to the fire to show them the delicate carving of Celtic knots snaking up the wooden handle.

"This was my father's. He kept it hidden in his boot. No one knew it was there. When word came of his death, I brought his body home to rest next to my mother. But a white man and his wife claimed our house and would not let me in."

No-Chance rubbed his forehead at the vision of the wiry settler with dirty clothes. "The man was chewing tobacco. After he told me the Federal commissioners wanted the Indians off the land, he spit in my face." A cold hatred swept over him at the memory of the thieving squatters.

Crazy Bear and Chickamauga's eyes widened at the insult. A man's spit was powerful medicine.

"He aimed his musket at me. Said no filthy Indian young'un was going to keep him from what he wanted. The white man's aim was poor. Said he hated to waste another bullet on the likes of me. I watched him bite the end off a cartridge and sprinkle powder in the priming pan. When he jammed the ramrod down the barrel, I knew what I had to do." He hesitated, studying the weapon in his hand. "I took this from my father's boot, and my aim was good."

No-Chance flicked the knife into the air, catching it by the blade, and sent it flying into a cloth pouch on the wall. Kernels of dried corn poured from the rip, hitting the dirt floor and shooting in all directions.

"The man's wife came out of the house waving my mother's skillet. Her screams hurt my ears. I would not have killed her, but she grabbed the musket." The ache of memory pounded in his temples, and No-Chance shook his head, muttering, "She grabbed the musket."

Crazy Bear and Chickamauga sat cross-legged, their faces impassive. Chade kept her eyes down, gently rocking with Tampa at her shoulder.

"I buried my father next to my mother and took the

cross from her grave, so no one would know where they rested." No-Chance took a deep breath and continued, "Then, I dragged the white man and his woman in the house they wanted and burned it to the ground."

He stared at the tiny flames that flickered up from glowing coals and remembered the sight of his home in ashes, with columns of smoke spiraling upward and dissolving into a clear blue sky. After the roar of the long-ago fire died away, he heard birds singing and wondered how God could allow anything to be happy in such an unjust world.

It was then that rage was born in his heart.

No-Chance stirred from his memories and looked over at his friends. Crazy Bear nodded. Chade busied herself retrieving the spilled corn.

Chickamauga cleared his throat. "To defend home is good thing. We resisted when tide of *wvcenvlke* sweep in from ocean like great rains that destroy land." He adjusted the blanket around his shoulders. "It is said, in summer before I was born, the prophet, Tecumseh, came to my people. Prophet asked, 'Where are Pequot, Narragansett, Mohican, Pocanet?' They were gone. Our northland brothers vanished with arrival of white man. Tecumseh said Creeks would also disappear if we did not kill intruders. So our fathers fought. They lost."

Chickamauga shook his head. "*Wvcenvlke* took half of our land as punishment. Then, we did not fight, and they took rest of our land. Which was better?"

"But, brother," No-Chance said, "I have killed for much less noble reasons than protecting the land." He rubbed his forehead, longing for the peace that confession might bring. Could brotherhood be based on anything but honesty? Did he dare risk the respect and friendship that suddenly meant so much?

Tampa whimpered, and Chade lifted her blouse to nurse him. The baby's contented sounds broke the tension.

"I sought my mother's people, but the Seminole had fled deep into the marshes. I could not find her clan, so I camped with some Spaniards. One wanted to know what I carried in this bag about my neck and tried to take it." No-Chance opened the blanket exposing his chest. A scar staggered from his right collarbone to his left breast. Once more, he saw the flash, felt the pain of a knife slashing at the leather bag, marking him forever.

"I wore this knife in my boot, like my father. The Spaniard thought I was unarmed. It was easy to kill him. The man's friends scurried away like mice when I challenged them."

He did not tell his companions that he had cut the Spaniard's heart from his chest and stood over the body, screaming his rage—a rage that didn't quell until he watched the body sink slowly into a watery burial of quicksand.

Crazy Bear rose and knelt to look at the jagged scar. "It is like thunderbolt Maker of Breath throws across sky." Touching the scars on his own face, he nodded his approval. "It right a man fights for what is his."

"I have killed others." He looked into Crazy Bear's honest eyes. For his friend, life was simple. "Sometimes there could have been another way. My father's knife never failed me. I accepted all challenges. Finally, I hid among your brethren because I killed a white officer who was drunk. The fool thought to kill me with a broken whiskey bottle."

No-Chance sighed and looked at Chickamauga. "If you wish to take back your offer of brotherhood, I will understand."

"And if you had not killed white officer, where would you be now?"

"In Georgia, maybe Florida."

"I think there was reason officer died." Chickamauga fingered White Cloud's silver necklace around his neck. "I think you were supposed to be on long walk. I think Maker of Breath knew I would need help and sent you. The night my son jumped down, I would have fought soldiers, but you stayed my hand and spoke for me. When one that occupies my heart went away, I wanted to lie down in grave with her." He looked over at Tampa. "You made me think of son."

In relief, No-Chance let out his breath and nodded. He wiggled the knife free of the log wall, studied it, then put it back in its leather sheath and hung it on a peg. Among friends, there was no need to hide cherished weapons.

Chickamauga resumed sharpening a slender length of wood. "My father was master of weapon-making until white man came with guns to trade. Now we must learn again what we knew in ancestor's time." He ran his fingers back and forth along the shaft. "We must understand soul of wood."

Chade handed Tampa to Crazy Bear, who shook his necklace of bear claws over the infant.

"Husband, you scare him." She retrieved the baby, plopped him in No-Chance's lap, and slipped through the door into the blustery night.

Tampa's lower lip pushed into a pout.

No-Chance patted the baby's bottom. "I have something better than an ol' necklace!" He stretched for his saddlebags and fished through them for a small package. As Tampa let out a wail, No-Chance stuck the end of a licorice strip in the infant's mouth.

When Chade ducked back through the door, shivering and stomping her feet, she found the three men bent over Tampa. Black drool ran down the baby's chin. "You see?" No-Chance said. "There's nothing to taking care of a baby. You just have to put something in their mouth." Crazy Bear and Chickamauga nodded, strips of licorice dangling from their lips.

For a while they listened to the ever-present wind whip around the cabin and sucked on the strong candy. It coated their tongues and stuck in their teeth and made them forget their hunger.

"When the wind stops, I'm going bear hunting." Crazy Bear pointed a half-eaten licorice strip at the others. "Roasted bear leg. Umm…good!"

"Never tracked bear." No-Chance studied the coarse fur stretched across the doorway. "How do you hunt them?"

"Build smoke fire at cave entrance. That will force them out. They are dull from their sleep." Crazy Bear crouched with an imaginary spear in his hands. "When they come out, wait until close." He raised his arms, hands spread like claws, and growled through licorice-black teeth.

He resumed his position as the hunter. "Thrust deep into heart and roll away." He dropped to the floor, tumbled over a saddle and into the wall, knocking items from pegs.

No-Chance reached to help Crazy Bear up. "How

is it Brother Bear left its mark on your face?"

The stout Indian grinned and rubbed his cheek. "That is when I learn to roll."

Chickamauga ran his hand down the long curved form of a bow. "I think I will hunt from a distance." He held the newly-crafted bow in front of him and tilted his head to sight along an arrow at the imaginary bear.

****

Every bone in No-Chance's body ached, and the smells of confinement smothered him. He put his face to a hole in the wall's chinking to snatch breaths of pure cold air seeping through to the smoky room. Chade and the baby coughed in their sleep. Despite Crazy Bear's loud snoring, it seemed the incessant wind was but a whisper now.

No-Chance sat and reached for his shirt and tunic, then eased leggings over his swollen foot and ankle, shivering at the touch of chilled buckskin on his body.

"Are we out of wood?" Chickamauga yawned and sat up.

"No, listen. Father Wind is gone. I'm going outside."

A shaft of light cut through the smoky darkness when he lifted the bear skin. He squinted against the unfamiliar glare until his eyes adjusted to the daylight. A blanket of pristine snow covered the ground and sparkled, as the waters of Florida did when the sun glinted from their surface. Glimmering icicles hung from tree branches like jagged teeth from an alligator.

A large black crow settled on a slender limb. Icicles shook and fell, leaving small holes in the snow. The crow cocked its head, let out a loud caw, and left the limb to soar above the trees.

Chickamauga pushed No-Chance out of the narrow doorway, breaking the spell. Crazy Bear, in turn, elbowed them both in his haste to get out of the cabin's dark confines. The men stretched their cramped bodies, filling their lungs with crisp, clean air. Chickamauga shoved snow from the entrance, while No-Chance swept a clearing for a large fire with a forked stick now serving as his crutch.

"Ho, the Maker of Breath has forgiven his people." Crazy Bear yelled, dragging several limbs toward the cabin. "There are many tracks in the fallen clouds. Tonight we have rabbit to fill stomachs. I know their hiding places."

"Good. My stomach rebels at its emptiness." No-Chance broke the branches into small pieces. "Any sign of the horses?"

Frowning, Crazy Bear squatted next to him and shook his head. "A few tracks. Brother Wolf is out this morning."

Chickamauga emerged from the cabin, with live coals balanced on two pieces of wood, and dropped them on the newly arranged logs. "It will be good to hunt again. My bow grows tired of its place in corner."

"Ha! I grow tired of my place in the corner, too!" No-Chance laughed as he fanned the glowing embers and sprinkled dried bark crumbles over them. The wet timber hissed and smoked.

A series of yelps and howls shattered the morning's calm, reverberating through the trees. The hair on the back of No-Chance's neck prickled at the enemy he did not see.

"Quick, get the ax!" He motioned to Chade, and she ducked under the fur hide into the cabin.

The howls seemed to multiply from every direction. Crazy Bear put one hand to his ear, then broke into a trot, following the stream bed into the tangle of ice-brittled bushes.

"Wait, take this!" No-Chance yelled and sent the ax flying through the air, tumbling end-over-end to land directly in front of Crazy Bear. Without breaking stride, the running Indian bent and scooped the weapon from the snow.

"Hurry, they have the scent of our horses!"

Chapter 19

A frightened whinny rose in ripples above the chorus of growls. No-Chance grabbed his whip from Chade's outstretched hand. "Not the horses, not the horses," he chanted to himself, striving to keep pace with Chickamauga. He hobbled through powdery snow, unmindful of the ache the effort stirred in his leg. They would die without horses.

Ahead of them, Crazy Bear bobbed side to side, breaking the trail through shin-deep drifts. He swung the ax in a circle above his head.

"Wait!" No-Chance shouted. Even with an ax, one man is no match for a pack of hungry wolves.

Two horses, ears back, topped a slight rise and galloped toward them. Chickamauga waved his arms, then dove for the protection of a snow-burdened cedar as the horses snorted past, throwing clumps of snow in their wake. Frosted air billowed from their nostrils.

"Whoa!" No-Chance called and pumped the coiled whip in an attempt to slow their panicked flight. He ducked under a large oak to avoid being trampled.

Chickamauga raced on, leaving No-Chance to struggle up an embankment alone. He caught his breath at the sight—five wolves threatened their other two horses, with Crazy Bear charging down the slope into the fray.

The small chestnut, rear haunches burdened with

the weight of two wolves, staggered. Braving the mare's sharp hooves, a gray wolf lunged for her neck and ripped through flesh. Blood spewed onto radiant snow. Eyes wide, the mare shrieked. Excited yelps and howls were lost in the frenzy.

Chickamauga reached over his shoulder, snatched an arrow from his quiver, and notched it into the bowstring. He stiffened his left arm, steadied the weapon, and sighted down the arrow at the pack of snarling animals.

Crazy Bear's guttural whoops joined the menacing growls of the wolves until the sounds of man and animal blended. The wolves broke their stance over the dying horse and turned to meet the charge as he advanced on them, swinging the ax. One wolf yelped, twisted, and dropped with an arrow vibrating from his side.

Chickamauga fit another arrow in his bow.

"Not my horse!" No-Chance yelled and slid down the embankment after Crazy Bear.

Thunder, teeth bared, nipped at a snarling wolf. The large muscles in the roan's flanks bulged as he reared on his hind legs. The wolf lunged for Thunder's exposed stomach. The roan brought his forelegs down and sent the animal rolling.

No-Chance played his whip out and snapped it forward with a loud crack.

The wolf yelped, rolled again, and lurched to his feet. He turned, tail between his legs, and clawed his way through the snow. The whip sliced through the air over and over, biting the fleeing animal's rump until it was out of reach.

Two wolves, fur bristling over their haunches, lips

lifted over bloody fangs, separated to circle Crazy Bear. Roaring mightily, he swung the ax to keep them at bay. One animal ventured close and lunged at his arm.

Crazy Bear staggered, recovered his footing, and cracked the ax against the side of the animal's skull, silencing its vicious growls. Then he sprang at the injured wolf and nearly severed its head with one determined blow.

The largest wolf backed away and crouched, ready to pounce. An arrow thudded into the snow inches from him. He turned and raced for the trees.

A small wolf, female by size, tore at the downed pony's flesh. Another arrow zinged through the air, pierced her paw, and anchored it to the carcass. With a yelp, she ripped free and limped away, trailing a ribbon of blood.

Chickamauga trotted up next to No-Chance, stretched the bow string taut and prepared to shoot his last arrow.

The fleeing wolf stopped and looked back, yellow eyes glittering.

For a moment Chickamauga studied her, then, lowered his bow.

As quickly as it had begun, the sounds that shook the morning ceased.

"Why didn't you shoot?" No-Chance panted as he watched the animals disappear into the gray woodland. Crimson splotches marked their retreat.

"Brother Wolf is hungry, too," Chickamauga answered.

Crazy Bear raised an arm and let out a victory chant.

The musky scent of wolf and blood and fear hung

strong in the air.

"Forgive me, Brother Wolf," Chickamauga said, voice low, as he knelt and pulled his arrow from the dead animal.

No-Chance nudged the wolf with the butt of the whip handle. He buried his fingers in the black-tipped coat of fur. Whatever the value of such a pelt, it couldn't make up for the loss of the gentle pony.

Thunder snorted great clouds of breath and shook his head. His muscles trembled as he pawed the trampled snow. No-Chance approached the agitated horse.

"Steady, steady," he cooed, running his hand down the horse's neck to calm him. He smiled. "I knew you were brave the first time I saw you." No-Chance coiled the whip and turned to study the bloodied chestnut sprawled in the snow. He glanced back toward the distant cabin. Billows of smoke rolled skyward marking its location.

"Have you eaten horse before?" he asked the others.

Chapter 20

Young leaves, glistening in sunlight, laced the trees. Darting through the foliage, birds trailed long grasses in their beaks toward their nests. Fresh breezes carried great promise. It was the time of *Tasahce Rakko*, the Big Spring.

No-Chance paused to watch sparrows chase about, scolding any encroachment from long tails. The cold and hungry time was weeks past. Perhaps now the land would smile on his family.

He took a deep breath, pulled his knife, and cut an "X" into the trunk of an ancient oak. Trees are brothers. It was a shame to mark a brother, but he'd not risk losing the path home in the unfamiliar land.

Urging the roan to motion, he wiped the blade on his buckskin pants and slipped it into the sheath at his waist. His clothing had changed to reflect the new life he'd chosen, and he missed hiding the knife in leather boots.

Wood creaked and groaned as the two-wheeled cart rolled over stones and bounced across holes in the trading path. Sensing the sorrel's sure footing, No-Chance relaxed his grip on the lead rope. A black-tipped wolf pelt rippled atop a mound of skins.

The tight corridor of trees opened to expose Carl Wade's small white-washed house and the lonely framework of a church. The young minister put his hammer down and hurried forward, hand outstretched.

"Praise the Lord! You made it through the winter. We've been praying for you folks."

No-Chance dismounted to accept the offered handshake.

"Welcome." Carl clapped him on the back and pushed him toward the house. "Jerusha will have coffee going. She'll want to know how the baby is." He stopped. "Everything all right? Your leg?"

"It's a torment at times, Reverend, but…"

"The Lord gives us pain to remind us of our sins," Carl admonished. "You folks were scarcely gone a day before the snow commenced. Jerusha and me talked to God regularly for your safekeeping."

A reddish-brown hound crawled from under the porch and set up a howl. Her teats, heavy with milk, nearly dragged the ground. Several puppies on short wobbly legs followed her, yapping and bumping into one another.

"Jerusha, come here," the minister called, taking two steps in one bound.

"Land sakes, Carl, what's wrong?" Jerusha Wade stood in the doorway, wiping flour from her hands onto a calico apron. She brushed a stray lock of golden hair from her forehead and broke into a smile.

"John MacGregor, if this isn't a nice surprise." She held the door open. "Come inside right this minute."

No-Chance allowed himself to be ushered to a chair and sank into its comfort. Jerusha pushed her sleeves up, sprinkled flour on the table, and massaged dough into a mound.

"Get the coffee, Carl. I'll have pie baking sooner than you can say, 'Jehosephat'." A rolling pin clunked on the table as she picked it up and down working the dough into a circle. "So nice to have company. Is Tampa growing?"

No-Chance took the offered china cup, steam rising above a rim of delicate pink flowers. He put one finger through the handle loop and pulled it out again.

"Tampa is fine. Laughs when you tickle his cheek. Barely raised the cabin before we got buried in snow. We lost one of our horses, but Crazy Bear's arm is healed from the wolf fight. Got a scar from here to here." He ran his finger from elbow to wrist. "I got lost and 'bout froze to death in the snow."

Carl sat, mouth open, coffee cup poised in midair.

"Oh." No-Chance wiggled his foot. "My leg works most of the time. Unless it rains."

Carl put his cup down. "Well, our prayers were answered. Seems the good Lord looked after you folks."

No-Chance bit back a reply. The way he saw it, the Lord mistook them for Job and sent a handful of tribulations their way.

Jerusha set a pan down with a thud. "I thought I had problems with two babies and no women folk around." She gently lifted the rolled pastry into the pan and spooned dried apples and sugar into the pie shell. "Poor Chade! How is she?" She plopped another round of dough over the apples, crimping the edges with her fingers.

"She's fine. Wants me to purchase squash and pumpkin seeds when I get seed corn for planting. Hope to get a plow at the blacksmith's."

A sputtering wail interrupted the conversation. Another cry joined the first, louder, more demanding.

Jerusha sighed, slid the pie into the cast-iron stove, and closed the oven door with a towel-wrapped hand.

"When one cries, they both cry." Carl poured more coffee. "And when one is hungry, they're both hungry. I'd take it kindly if you'd pick up my mail and some supplies in Ft. Gibson. I have an account at the general store." The minister ran fingers through his auburn hair. "Don't want to leave Jerusha and the girls alone. Otherwise, I'd have been down the trail to hold services for you folks. One's soul needs to sup often from the healing words of the Good Book."

"Well, Laney, meet our neighbor, Mr. John MacGregor." Jerusha deposited a plump fair-haired baby in No-Chance's arms.

"And this is Leah, our noisy daughter." She handed the other sniffling child to her husband. The aroma of cooking apples filled the room as Jerusha bustled about setting plates and forks on the table. They talked of the terrible winter and wondered how the tribe fared. Carl had seen Indians hunting as far as his place, but none stopped to get acquainted. No-Chance didn't tell him that Upper Creeks might never stop to visit with a white man, especially one that didn't speak the language.

The sun sat high when No-Chance guided the reverend's wagon onto the rough road leading to the fort. He settled back in the seat, a knapsack of bread and smoked ham slices next to him. The visit cost a few hours of travel, but the rare slice of apple pie and a swap of wagons seemed worth the delay.

The next afternoon smoke from hundreds of campfires announced the sprawling fort an hour before his arrival. The sight made his shoulders tense, his eyes narrow. Nothing to fear from the Indians, but there'd be

160

soldiers, bored and looking for distraction. And, of course, Black Storm.

No-Chance slowed the wagon when the encampment came into sight. Sticks, tied with fluttering ribbons and scraggly feathers, marked numerous dirt mounds. A tiny bow and arrow, suspended from a sapling, twisted in the breeze.

Graves, too numerous to count, filled the clearing between the road and the edge of the woods. Closer to the fort, Indians sat huddled at campfires. Women picked their way around ruts deep enough to hold scummy water as they carried bundles of wood or held the hand of a crying child.

Spring had failed to blossom here.

"*Hensci!*" No-Chance greeted a hobbling old woman, a checkered bundle over her shoulder, as the wagon forced her from the road. The hem of her skirt swung in frayed tatters. She nodded, eyes dull as slate and lips pulled so tight they disappeared.

Glancing about for the grandfather among the mean and ram-shackle shelters, No-Chance found the old man's lean-to, the cloth cover in shreds.

Inside the fort, soldiers briskly went about their duties, averting their eyes from the hollow-faced children watching them.

No-Chance pulled his hat low and slouched in the seat. Attempt at concealment was unnecessary. Soldiers paid little attention to yet another Indian crossing the parade yard. He followed the ring of hammer and anvil and halted the wagon at the blacksmith's barn.

Unable to move, he buried his face in his hands. Smoked ham, savored earlier, rested like stones in his stomach. How could he boast at surviving when so many had not?

"You all right, mister?"

No-Chance looked down at the large blacksmith. He stood scratching his bushy beard until his brows, heavy and wild, went up with recognition.

"Say, ain't you that feller what traded me the emperor's ruby?"

No-Chance frowned as he swung down from the wagon. "Now, Edward, I never said—"

"That little gem saved my hide. I'd plumb fergot it was my Minnie's birthday." The blacksmith put a muscular arm across No-Chance's shoulder. The unmistakable odor of garlic wafted in the air with the next sentence. "Her eyes lit up like little twinkly stars when I showed it to her."

"Glad she was taken with it." No-Chance glanced through the double doors. "Would you have a plow and couple of shovels for sale?"

"Well, les'see. There's an old plow I been meanin' to fix, seein' as how it's nigh on to plantin' time." Edward turned toward the barn and shook one leg as he shifted about in his overalls. "Come on in."

No-Chance followed Edward into the shadowy barn, air alive with the stench of sour hay and manure.

"Yes, sir, Minnie keeps her emperor's jewel in her granny's sugar bowl. Keeps at me to have it fixed into a brooch or somethin'. Nobody 'round here does that sort of work."

An Indian boy looked up from brushing a horse as they walked past.

No-Chance stopped to greet him. "*Hensci.*"

The boy, peering through a curtain of black hair, nodded, and moved to the other side of the horse.

"Aw, I caught the little rascal trying to steal my lunch. I couldn't whup him for bein' hungry, so I put him to work. He's been showin' up nigh on to a couple of months. Minnie packs extra boiled eggs for him. Guess you see'd the shape them people is in?"

The blacksmith bent over and grunted as he hefted a plow out of an empty stall.

"I've seen them. We thought there'd be tools waiting when we got here, but there weren't. Guess you're gonna tell me there wasn't food either."

"Yep, there was food." Edward ran the back of his hand across his nose. "Just not enough, and game is hunted out here 'bouts. The major sends a detail of men every mornin' to bury thems that died in the night."

He reached down and patted the rusty plow. "This here blade broke at the tip. But I can angle it back like this." He ran his finger along the metal. "Won't dig the furrow as deep as normal, but it'll turn the dirt right enough. I could fix it up for, say, 'bout four dollars."

"Seems a mite high." No-Chance took his hat off and scratched his head. Maybe he should have stopped first at the general store to see what the pelts would bring.

"Well, metal's hard to come by."

Outside, a cow bawled. No-Chance walked to the back door and studied the animal—acorn-colored hide with white stockings and a star in the middle of her forehead. Pretty thing, with a calf pestering her, trying to feed.

"Say, how would you like to have another sparkly ruby for Minnie? You know you could put them into little rings that dangle from her ears." He held his thumb and forefinger together at the side of his face.

"That would be something."

Edward scratched his head and looked at the cow. "I don't know. Done told you, don't nobody at the fort make jewelry."

"Isn't Minnie gonna have another birthday?"

"Not till next winter."

"Oh, a man doesn't need a reason for getting his wife something pretty. In fact, no reason makes the gift more special."

"Well…."

"Look, some of the best jewelry-makers are Creeks. You've seen the bracelets at the general store?"

"Uh-huh."

"What if I could find a jewelry maker out there? He'd probably trade his skill for food."

"Well, maybe—"

"We got a deal then? I find a jewelry maker, and you'll trade the cow, her calf, a couple of shovels and the plow for a"—No-Chance paused and swallowed— "…a king's ruby!"

"Only got one shovel."

"Done!" No-Chance took the blacksmith's hand and shook it. "How long to fix the plow?"

Chapter 21

No-Chance leaned against the fence and studied the gentle-eyed cow dangling long stalks of hay from her mouth. He remembered the cattle his father brought home after a preaching trip and imagined his booming voice, so full of Scotland, in the ring of Edward's hammer on anvil.

"Aye and a bunch of sissy animals these be," his father would say. "Not like the great cattle of the Highland with their shaggy hair and enormous horns. Ye should'a seen 'em, John, me boy—great beasts that could run all day."

The star-kissed cow was no great beast, but she was the start of a herd. No-Chance smiled at the unexpected trade and turned back into the darkness of the barn. A horseshoe hissed as the blacksmith plunged it into a barrel of water. The young Indian led a big draft horse forward and tied the reins to a post.

"Good," Edward said, nestling his ample body next to the large animal. He lifted its rear leg and positioned it between his knees. "Hold 'er tight, like this. Let 'er know you're the boss."

The boy stood, head tilted, arms folded across his frayed shirt. It was obvious that he would learn only as long as the goodhearted blacksmith fed him. No-Chance sighed and climbed into the wagon. He pulled his hat low and made his way to the general store, pretending an interest in the floorboard when soldiers glanced his way.

Inside the store, rich smells of coffee and spices, tobacco and soap, spoke of abundance for anyone with money. Tables boasted stacks of folded blankets, spun cotton shirts, and pantaloons. A large clock hung behind the counter, its pendulum swinging back and forth with soft clicks.

Two young women, faces pale as moonlight, examined material samples, tossing them onto the counter when they were done. The proprietor stood behind them, refolding abandoned fabric as the women moved to another selection. One whispered to the other, causing a cascade of shrill laughter.

No-Chance cleared his throat. "I have skins to sell. Fox, beaver, wolf."

The women turned to look at him. One pushed blonde curls under her bonnet and rolled her eyes. Her companion produced a lace handkerchief and dabbed at her pointed nose.

The proprietor hurried over. "Say, didn't you come with that bunch in December?" He straightened his bow tie. "Yes, sir, I remember now. You was the scout or translator for 'em."

"Come, I have them in the wagon." Without correcting the man, No-Chance took him by the arm and hustled him outside. "These are fine skins. Stretched and tanned." He positioned a reddish fox hide on the wagon's tailgate and ran his hand through the long silky winter coat. The sun gave the fur a rich golden highlight. "I've got four fox, all prime."

The proprietor turned the fur over to examine it.

"Look here." No-Chance tugged at a heavy five-foot long pelt, letting it hang off the end of the wagon. The black-tinged gray fur rippled in the breeze, and he parted the dense coat with his fingers.

"They're beautiful all right." The storekeeper ran the wolf's tail through his hand. "But gotta be honest, you'd get a better price at Edwards' Trading Post down on the Canadian. He deals mostly in furs."

"You'll do," No-Chance said.

The man smiled and held his hand out. "I'm Sampson. Sampson Pearson. Bring the furs. We'll put you on the books, Mister, uh, I didn't catch your name."

"It's John MacGregor," No-Chance said, huffing with the weight of the wolf skins hoisted over his shoulder. He remounted the steps behind Sampson.

The storekeeper leaned on the counter to cipher a total. "Twenty-five cents for each fox, thirty-one cents for each wolf, seventy-five for each beaver. That'll make it one point aught for the fox hides," he muttered, his pencil scratching across a ledger.

The chatter of the women rose and fell. No-Chance watched them continue their search through bolts of cloth. Frilly petticoats peeped below the hem of their waist-fitting dresses as they lifted lengths of fabric.

The Indian woman he'd greeted along the road entered the store and pulled two small grass baskets from her bundle. Gray hair, tied back with a strip of rawhide, framed a withered face.

"*Hensci*," he greeted her.

She looked at him and frowned.

No-Chance knew she questioned his blue eyes and smiled to soften her heart.

"No, no." Sampson hurried around the counter. "I still have many…" He pointed to a cluster of little baskets, then cupped his hands around hers and shook his head. "Not today."

Her shoulders sagged. Three more women entered the store, salting the air with their chatter. The old mother shrank from their presence and disappeared.

Sampson shook his head. "I've been giving her a handful of beans or rice for her baskets. Truth is, I got more under the counter. The agent's been sayin' nigh on to six weeks more supplies are on the way. Now, back to my cypherin'."

"Sampson," No-Chance interrupted, eyeing the noisy newcomers. "Here's Reverend Wade's list of needs. I'll be back in the morning to pick 'em up. His mail, too." He grabbed a cloth sack off the counter and filled it with dried beans from a barrel. "Put this on my bill. We'll settle up tomorrow." He pulled the drawstring closed and backed toward the door. "I'll want coffee, tobacco, beans, flour, salt, a mite of licorice, and planting seeds—corn, squash, and the like."

The sharp-nosed woman stood in the doorway holding a length of blue-flowered calico to the daylight. She turned, bumped into him, and his measure of beans tumbled to the floor with a thud.

"Oh." The woman sniffed and clutched the fabric to her chest.

"Beg pardon," No-Chance muttered and bent to retrieve the bag, managing to catch the hem of her dress in his haste.

She let out a squeal, and he dropped the bag again. This time, a handful of beans rolled loose. The woman pulled her skirt tight around her legs.

"Mr. Pearsoooon!" Her voice rose to an alarming

note.

No-Chance abandoned his attempt to gather the scattered beans, grabbed the bag, and backed out the door, glancing about for soldiers.

Pounding hoofs and creaking leather announced the arrival of a squad through the open gates of the fort. No-Chance stepped from the boardwalk and ducked behind the wagon to watch the blue-clad men trot past. Unease swept over him. Numerous mixed-bloods among the Lower Creeks came to trade. With his braids and long calico shirt, he would be taken for one of them most likely, but fear of discovery still lived in his heart.

A sergeant yelled directions to a group of men at drill. No-Chance busied himself securing the tailgate of the wagon, while he scanned the parade ground. Indians leaned against buildings or stood in groups watching the activity in the fort. The old woman with the checkered bundle was gone.

Anxious to be away, No-Chance guided the wagon through the gate toward the settlement of Indians. Crude shelters, erected when they arrived, were now falling apart. Men sat at their campfires talking. Without weapons, they could not hunt. Without tools, they could not build shelters or break ground. Several boys, furious in their play, kicked a hide ball back and forth.

A loud caw drew No-Chance's attention to the top of a spreading oak. The crow sat on an uppermost branch preening its feathers. At the base of the tree, the old woman from the general store, sat cross-legged, head drooped. No-Chance reined the horses, slipped from the wagon seat, and knelt in the grass. The tightly-woven little baskets in her lap reminded him of those his mother used to store beads and brass buttons.

The old woman's fingers would have deftly woven the dried stems in and out, stopping occasionally to shape the basket into its finished form. No-Chance reached to pick one up when she opened her eyes.

He raised his voice for the old one. "I am No-Chance, blood brother to Chickamauga, who is son-in-law to Black Storm."

A slight breeze moved a wisp of gray hair across the woman's forehead. She sat motionless, so unblinking that he glanced at her chest to make sure she still breathed.

"It would please me to trade with you, for I have never seen such fine work. I have need of such baskets."

They sat in silence for long minutes. The murmur of the encampment of people grew louder with the clang of cooking pots and passing horses. He shifted uncomfortably. Had she not heard his words?

"I am Stands-in-Water of the Beaver Clan. What is it you wish to trade?" she asked.

He loosened the strings of the cloth bag and poured a handful of beans in her lap.

The old woman nodded in unspoken appreciation and handed the baskets to him.

"Stands-in-Water, the long walk has been hard. How is it with your family?"

Puddles of flesh bagged her neck in layers. Her chin dropped. "I was the wife of Ellecukpe. He died trying to push white man from his fields. I was sad, but my children needed me. My son died in cold white rain that came from clouds. I was sad, but my daughter needed me." She closed her eyes, her voice wavering,

"My daughter died, her skin hot as summer sun. Sadness lives in my heart. Now no one needs Stands-in-Water."

She took a deep breath. "I ask Maker of Breath why he does not take Stands-in-Water to be with those who need her."

No-Chance sat back on his heels. Were there not enough people in his life? Had he not shared his food? Still, he felt rooted to the ground, unable to leave, and finally sighed.

"The Maker of Breath does not take one who is still needed. If you will leave camp with me tomorrow, there is a way Stands-in-Water can be of help."

The old woman pursed her lips, hollowing her cheeks. She looked across the road at the burials and then nodded.

"It is good. Gather your things and wait at the general store early tomorrow." He rose and walked to the wagon. "Search among the people for a maker of ornaments. Bring him. I have need for such a person."

The sun had begun its westward descent as No-Chance guided the wagon through abandoned campsites toward Black Storm's tent. Sprigs of new grass poked through the ground in feeble clumps. He halted the horses and left them to nose the sparse growth.

"Get on 'bout yourself," Stvluste's voice rumbled as he wagged a finger at a half-grown boy. "And don't be too long bringin' dat wood back, you hear?" The large Negro pushed the boy away, knelt next to a smoldering fire, poking the embers and mumbling to himself. "What he mean, be tellin' me ain't no easy wood here 'bouts. Lazy good fo' nothin'!"

"If I'd known it was wood you'd be wanting,

instead of beans, that's what I'd have brought."

Stvluste looked up and broke into a lopsided grin as he struggled to stand. "If'n it ain't Knife Man come back from the dead!" He hiked up his baggy buckskins and put a large hand on No-Chance's shoulder. "I speck you done be froze and bones picked clean by buzzards long 'go."

Stvluste's broken-toothed smile was welcoming. "Come on over here. Just wait 'til Chief knows you be alive. He be here soon enough." The giant looked over No-Chance's head. "Massah Chick'maga and baby be here, too?"

"No, but they're fine. We survived the big snow. I see many didn't."

Stvluste shook his head, long kinky hair bouncing. "Never see'd so much sickness. The Chief, he say land no good. One mornin' Nick just don't wake up. He be with Chief longer than me." He bent close, eyes wide as coins. "I think, one by one, we just won't wake up. Then ever'body be spirits."

"You're talking nonsense, Stvluste." No-Chance pulled away. "Nick was old and tired. It was his time."

Stvluste shook his head again. He straightened and nodded toward the fort. No-Chance turned to watch Black Storm, head down, shoulders sagging, pick his way around mud puddles. He paused to talk with a couple at their cooking fire and then continued down the path. The tail on his catamount purse swung back and forth, flapping against his leg.

Black Storm entered the campsite, looked up, and stopped. The afternoon sun illuminated the chief's tattoos. A flicker of recognition flashed in the old man's eyes before he folded his arms and stood motionless.

His formidable presence filled the campsite and sent a chill down No-Chance's back.

Stvluste reached for the offered bag of beans.

"It is good to see Black Storm, Chief of the Wind Clan, is well." No-Chance straightened to stand tall. "Our hearts were heavy with worry for the grandfather of Tampa."

Beans plopped nosily into the pot of simmering water, and Stvluste bent to poke at the sputtering fire. "Where be that boy?" he mumbled.

"Why have you returned?" Black Storm glowered, voice rumbling like rolling thunder. "Is it not enough you turn heart of son-in-law away from his tribe? Or have you come to steal a woman?"

Heat crept up No-Chance's neck. His jaw tightened, and he took a step backward. Winter had not softened this ancient one. A dozen crows took sudden flight from the surrounding trees, cawing loudly, dipping and swooping into the distance. The interruption gave No-Chance a moment to swallow his anger. If the winter had been hard on him, it had been harder on Black Storm and the tribe.

"I wish to take nothing from the people. I have come to tell you of the new land. Chickamauga and Crazy Bear clear a field for planting. Tampa grows fat at Chade's breast. He will be big and strong and make his grandfather proud."

Black Storm breathed deeply, looking down at the kettle and the tumble of beans layered in the bottom. A breeze stirred a feather tied in a plait of the chief's hair and played at the fringe on his tunic. Stvluste spread a blanket on the ground. When the chief spoke, there was no fury, just the sad drone of an old man.

"I was angry when you left, taking my son-in-law and grandson. But now I know Maker of Breath meant for them to go with you. It is hard for heart to accept this." The chief looked around at the blanket and sat down. He motioned for No-Chance to do the same. "Many of our seed died in camp of death. Our shaman has no potions to banish fever that brings spirits to scare the sick. Medicine maker has no herbs to still cough that lives in the weak. My heart rejoices grandson is well. It is good he was not here during the time of dying. For this, I thank you."

There it was—an acknowledgement. No-Chance squatted, resting a tired knee on the ground. "Chickamauga found game where I did not think any existed, and Crazy Bear's strength kept us safe. Chade sings to Tampa as if he were her own."

"Tampa grows fat?"

"Yes. And he laughs."

"Laughs?" Black Storm leaned forward.

No-Chance nodded and continued, "The land is rocky. Lots of streams. Some places, trees are so thick a man can scarcely push through." He found once his tongue loosened, thoughts tumbled over each other. Perhaps giving hope was better than a bag of beans. "And we've killed deer and foxes. Some beaver. We built our cabin west of here, two suns travel. I come to trade for a plow."

Stvluste hummed as he broke stems of wild onions and dropped the bulbs into the pot. No-Chance took his pipe from a pouch and tapped the last bit of tobacco into the bowl. A glowing twig brought the tobacco to life. Smoke snaked up in slender columns. He waved his hand above the pipe, breathed in the fragrant smell, and handed it to the chief.

"We've cleared a trail past Reverend Wade's place. I marked the path with an '*X*' carved into trees. Chade found blackberry vines and persimmons." With the burnt end of a stick, No-Chance drew a map in the dirt, using stones to locate the fort, the reverend's house, and the cabin. Aware others gathered in the evening shadows to stand silently and listen, he launched into the encounter with wolves.

Chapter 22

"Whoa, whoa!" No-Chance leaned back in the wooden seat, keeping a steady pull on the reins. Snorting at the pressure of the bit, the horses jerked against the confining harness. The brake-shoe ground against the wagon wheel as it rolled to a halt.

"Whoa!" he shouted again as Stands-In-Water put her feet on the front wall of the wagon. No-Chance set the brake, wrapped the reins around the lever, and jumped to the ground.

An old Indian and an officer, arguing in front of the infirmary, paused and turned to watch him bound up the two steps to the boardwalk.

"Poca! Stvmen vyvhanskv? Grandfather! Where are you going?" No-Chance stared at the limp figure in the old man's arms.

The officer cleared his throat. "You know this man?"

"Yes."

"Well, I can't make him understand. Tell him this child is sick and needs care."

"Cesse?" No-Chance touched her flushed cheeks. A liquid cough tortured her body. Without a flicker of recognition, she stared at him through sunken eyes.

"What's wrong?"

"I'm the camp doctor." The officer cleaned his spectacles with a handkerchief before guiding the wire frame over his ears. For a moment he studied the child. "What's wrong with most of the children? Croup, pneumonia, malnutrition."

In Creek, No-Chance pleaded the doctor's case with the grandfather. Frowning, the old man shook his head, his voice cracking in a rush of explanation as he hugged the child close.

No-Chance turned to the doctor. "He says Cesse is dying."

The doctor tapped the face of his pocket watch and held it to his ear.

"Well, is she?"

"Maybe. I know she'll die without shelter, without care."

No-Chance followed the young man's glance back through the open door of his clinic. A single window at the back bathed the room in hazy light. Shadowy figures, lumped beds, and scattered floor pallets crowded the small room. A constant murmur, punctuated by the rack of uncontrolled coughing, rose and fell.

"When I don't have a soldier needing a bed, I do what I can for these people, mostly the children. Exposure, poor nutrition, unsanitary conditions, that's what gets 'em."

Cesse's labored breathing bubbled and popped. She whimpered and broke into a rolling cough.

The old Indian clutched the child against his chest, tucking her faded red blanket around her. He huffed a few words in Creek, turned, and stepped off the porch.

No-Chance put both hands up. "Thank you for your help, Doctor. But grandfather says he does not wish for her to die in the white man's house." He paused before retreating back to the wagon. "Don't you have something you could give her?"

The doctor shook his head, dropped his watch back into a vest pocket, and turned to enter the clinic.

"Wait. I can pay."

"Beyond hot tea and honey and a warm bed, there's nothing," the doctor mumbled. "I wish there were."

No-Chance watched the grandfather, shoulders sagging, walk toward the gates of the fort. To argue with the old man would be useless. The child's captivating smile had been the only friendly face in a sea of hostile ones.

"*Hvtetci, Poca.* Wait, Grandfather," he called and hurried to catch the old man. No-Chance scooped Cesse into his arms, nodding toward the wagon. "Come with me. I know someone who has good medicine." *At least*, he thought, *I hope so*.

Crowded into a corner behind the driver's seat, Poca and Stands-In-Water hovered over the sick child. Her cough rose above the wagon's groan as it bumped and rattled over the twin-rutted road, shifting sacks of supplies and the plow with each lurch.

When the framework of Reverend Wade's church loomed ahead, No-Chance felt a tinge of relief. Surely, these good folks would know what to do. A hound emerged from under the house porch and welcomed the wagon with a deep howl.

Carl Wade hurried around the corner, wringing water from a shirt. "Hello! Good to see you back." He smiled at No-Chance trying not to step on the puppies that followed the mother dog into the yard.

"Quiet, Sheba." He snapped the wet shirt at her,

splattering drops of water over the dog. "Sorry. She does set up a racket, doesn't she? Did you get your plow?"

The puppies pounced on No-Chance's feet, biting into his moccasins.

"Reverend, I've got a problem."

"So I see." The reverend laughed and gave the puppies a forceful shove with his boot.

No-Chance motioned toward the wagon. "Back here." He untied the mother cow from the tailgate, swatted her away, and pulled the canvas open.

Carl peered into the wagon. Stands-in-Water sat stiff and unblinking, hands folded in her lap. Desperation lined the grandfather's face as he looked from the reverend back to the child in his arms. Laboring to breathe, Cesse's chest rose and fell.

"Oh, Lord, what do you have here?"

"One of God's children. I think she's dying." No-Chance motioned to the old woman and helped her to the ground. "This is *Hueres-Ofv-Owv*. In English she's called, Stands-in-Water."

The young minister shifted the damp shirt. "Pleased to meet you."

Stands-in-Water stepped back, fists to her chest.

"Is she afraid?" Carl wiped a damp hand on his pants.

"Probably. She has no family left."

No-Chance turned and reached into the wagon. Cradling the child in his lap, the grandfather carefully shifted her into No-Chance's arms before clambering out.

Carl put his hand to Cesse's face. "Merciful heavens, the child is burning up." He motioned toward the back of the house. "Bring her. My wife's doing wash." They rounded the corner, where strips of white muslin hung over branches and porch railings. Several shirts were spread, arms outstretched, on bushes to dry.

"Jerusha! John brought a sick child." Carl shook out the dripping shirt and threw it over a bush.

With a long stick, Jerusha lifted a mound of clothes from a steaming cauldron and transferred them to a bucket. Wood sizzled and smoked as soapy water splashed down the sides of the pot.

She squinted through the rising steam. "What did you say, Carl?"

Carl took the stick from her and pointed toward No-Chance, who shifted the wheezing child in his arms. The old grandfather stood next to him, clutching Cesse's red blanket. Stands-In-Water peeked from behind both men.

"I said the Lord sends us His sheep to tend. I think He tests us sorely, for John has brought a very ill child with him."

Jerusha's smile vanished as she reached to touch Cesse with soap-reddened hands. "You'd better bring her inside." She turned toward the house and lifted her skirt to step over the mud puddles. "What's wrong?"

"The doctor at the fort says croup," No-Chance answered. Poca took hold of his arm before he could follow Jerusha. "Sorry, ma'am, the little girl's grandfather doesn't want me to take her inside."

"Well, for heaven's sake, why not?"

No-Chance cleared his throat, "Please understand. I saved Cesse's life once. I reckon that's why Poca even allowed her to ride in the wagon."

Jerusha frowned and stepped off the porch. "Of

course, if the Lord sends us a test, He wouldn't make it easy, would He? All right." She sighed. "Over there, in the shade."

Poca spread Cesse's blanket under a large hickory which stood a few feet from the back porch. Cesse coughed again as No-Chance knelt to ease her onto the ground. She struggled to breathe, wheezing with each expulsion of air.

Jerusha knelt next to No-Chance and bent over to rest her ear on the little girl's chest. The pungent smell of lye soap assailed his nostrils when she sat back up and leaned close.

"I fear it's a sight more serious than just the croup." She lowered her voice. "Her chest is filling with poison. You hear that bubbling when she breathes?" She raised her eyebrows. "We've got to do something right away or," leaning so close her soft hair brushed his cheek, she whispered, "the child will die!"

Poca sat on the other side of Cesse, stroking her face, and stopped to stare at them.

"No need to whisper, Jerusha. They don't understand English." No-Chance picked up the child's limp hand. "Isn't there anything we can do?"

"What would Granny do?" Jerusha mused, sitting back on her heels. "First, we have to pull that poison out before it strangles her. We need a poultice."

"Poultice?"

"Carl, empty the wash water." Ignoring his question, she pushed past her husband and Stands-In-Water. "We're going to need the pot again."

She dropped to her knees and reached under the porch to retrieve a heavy basket. Squatting next to her, No-Chance grabbed the other side of the basket and yanked, causing it to tip. Yellow onions spilled onto the ground.

She nodded toward her husband, who was lifting the now-empty pot back over the smoldering campfire. "Put the basket there. I'll get a knife."

"Is she going to make a stew?" No-Chance asked, dragging the basket across the yard, gathering loose onions as he went. "Now?"

Carl shrugged as he poked fresh wood under the kettle. "Don't know. I've learned to get out of the way and let her lead when it comes to caring for the body. My specialty is the soul."

The door slammed. "Carl, the girls are awake." Jerusha hurried down the stairs, clutching a kitchen knife, and reached for Stands-In-Water. "You peel. I'll cut."

The old woman pulled away.

"She doesn't understand. Let me help." No-Chance pulled his knife from its sheath, picked up an onion, and balanced it in his hand. "How is this going to help Cesse?"

Jerusha squatted and in a few quick motions peeled away the paper skins and cut an onion into large chunks. "We'll cook these to a mush. Then cover the little girl's chest with the paste. When it cools and dries, it will pull the poison right out. I've seen it happen before." She dropped chunks over the side of the pot and grabbed another onion. "Granny mos'ly made bread and milk poultices. But she did it with onions once."

Jerusha wiped her eyes with the sleeve of her dress. The onions sizzled softly, sending up a delicious aroma. No-Chance quickly cut another onion, holding it at arm's length in a futile attempt to escape the fumes.

Carl, bouncing a fussy baby on his hip, stepped from the house onto the porch. "Isn't it time for them to eat, Jerusha?"

Blinking back tears, she shook her head without looking up. "They'll have to wait."

A plaintive wail floated through the open door. Frustrated, the minister shifted the baby to the other hip and returned inside.

Stands-In-Water shuffled to the porch and craned to peer through the open door. The young father emerged with both daughters squirming in his arms.

Eyes wide, she held up two fingers. "*Hila! Pipuce hokkolen!*"

"Yes, two babies." No-Chance lowered his knife and studied the old woman transfixed by the sight of the fussing infants. "Reverend, see if she will hold one."

The minister smiled and stepped off the porch. Stands-in-Water returned a timid smile and reached for his offering. Cuddling the plump infant to her chest, she clucked softly and allowed the young father to take her arm and guide her up the steps to a rocking chair on the porch.

By the time the onions had cooked to a mush, the overpowering aroma had gone from delicious to stomach lurching. No-Chance set the steaming kettle next to Cesse. The grandfather scrambled to his feet, warning them away with trembling hands.

No-Chance waved Jerusha back and spoke in the Creek language. "Grandfather, I brought you far from the fort. If it is your wish, Cesse can join the ancestors here, under this big tree."

The old man put his arms down.

183

"Just as the onion gives life to the taste of food, so it can give life to Cesse," No-Chance continued. "We have nothing else to try."

Poca frowned, peering into the pot. He turned away from fumes drifting up from the steaming mush.

"You see." No-Chance caught his breath. "The spirit of the onion will chase away bad spirits."

Cesse began a new spasm of coughing. The old man squatted beside her, looked up, and nodded.

Jerusha stripped the ragged dress from Cesse, exposing her rib-thin body. She covered the girl's chest with a clean rag snatched from a bush and spooned handfuls of warm mush into a thick layer on it. Gasping for breath, the child cried and tried to sit up.

The heat of the poultice penetrated No-Chance's hands as he held it in place. Unable to escape the powerful vapors, tears sprang to his eyes.

Renewed coughing caused Cesse to choke and spit a thick string of mucus.

"That's good, honey. Get it all up." Unmindful of her own tears, Jerusha turned Cesse's head to the side, blotting her face with the corner of a wet rag.

Sitting cross-legged, the grandfather closed his eyes to the child's suffering and chanted in a low voice. Quills sewn to his tunic clicked softly as he rocked back and forth.

Head bowed and hands clasped around a small Bible, Carl knelt next to the old man and prayed. "The Lord is my shepherd; I shall not want. He maketh me to lie down in green pastures; He leadth me beside the still waters. He restoreth my soul…"

Grandfather didn't open his eyes but continued to rock, his chant growing louder.

"You're going to be all right," Jerusha crooned, running a finger inside the child's mouth to extract a blob of mucus. "You're going to be all right."

Carl raised his voice, "Yea, though I walk through the valley of the shadow of death, I will fear no evil for thou art with me."

No-Chance wiped his nose along the sleeve of his shirt. He studied the two men, each fervent in their pleading, and wondered if God heard both prayers equally.

Chapter 23

Pink tinged the tops of newly-leafed trees, in the narrow line between night and day, before even the sparrows resumed their harried activity. Wrapped in a blanket, No-Chance leaned against the wooden wheel of the reverend's wagon, watching the dark sky slowly warm to a soft blush. Five planting days lost waiting for the child's cough to ease. Why, after many years of being alone, was he collecting outcast people?

At the edge of the clearing, just past the skeleton of the church, bushes shuddered. A mourning dove cooed in the distance. No-Chance sat forward. Strange, the dove called before dawn. Squinting to peer through wisps of fog hugging the ground, he glanced at the low shelter where Poca and Cesse slept, then back to the reverend's house.

The horses snorted, circling the fenced corral. Closer, a dove called again. A crouched form moved away from the corral toward the house. Memory of painted Comanche lived in his bones, and No-Chance reached under the wagon for his knife. Glancing around, he wondered if other horse-stealers hid in the shadows.

He shrugged away the blanket and squatted on his heels. To his frustration, the quarrelsome hound, Sheba, set up a howl. The skulking figure paused and rose to full height, one shoulder slightly lower than the other.

No-Chance blinked. "What is he doing here?"

Carl stepped onto the porch, holding a lantern, its soft glow filtering through the mist. "Who's out there? John, what's the matter?" He lifted the lantern aloft to broaden the circle of light, as Sheba met him at the bottom of the steps and resumed her baleful howl.

"No need for alarm, Reverend." No-Chance stood and pointed the knife at the intruder. "You remember my brother?"

"Ahh, yes. So it is. Tell me, does he always visit before dawn?" Not waiting for an answer, Carl shook his head. "I suggest we go back to bed."

Jerusha moved through the door, clutching a long shawl around her nightgown with one hand and a rolling pin in another. An abundance of blonde curls curtained her shoulders. Stands-In-Water peeked from behind her.

The minister handed the lantern to No-Chance and stepped onto the porch. "Good Lord, woman, what were you going to do with that rolling pin?" Frowning, Stands-In-Water looked at No-Chance before being hustled inside.

"A few days in white man's world, and you forget Indian ways," Chickamauga chided.

No-Chance set the lantern down, reached under the porch for dry wood, and dropped the kindling into the campfire's circle of stones. "What are you talking about?" he asked, switching easily to the Creek language.

"When I found your horse in corral, I called. You no answer."

"That was you?" The lantern globe squeaked as he lifted it and stuck a twig into the flame. "I didn't think anyone friendly would come before dawn." No-Chance touched the blazing twig to several pieces of wood. "Is everything all right?"

Chickamauga settled cross-legged in front of the struggling fire. "Soldiers came after you left. They forced their way into cabin. We could not understand them."

A chill shot through No-Chance. "Do you remember their words?"

Light from the sputtering fire cast patterns across Chickamauga's smooth face as he shook his head. "No words we knew. Grandfather Sun has shone his face eight times since you left. We feared for your safety."

No-Chance stopped poking at the logs and sat back. "No need to worry about me." He shrugged. "If I can't out talk a man, I can put him down before he blinks."

Chickamauga ignored the boast. "Some of Roley McIntosh's people passed on way to Edwards' Trading Post. A group is forming to go west and hunt great beasts as soon as fields are planted."

No-Chance shook his braids out and ran his fingers through his hair. "I suppose Crazy Bear wants to go?" He parted a section of hair and worked the strands into a loose braid.

"He work like wild man clearing rocks, trees. He waits to plant and join buffalo hunters."

"We will have more mouths to feed this winter." No-Chance tied a leather strip at the end of the braid and flipped it behind his back. Gathering the rest of his hair, he plaited it through his fingers.

Chickamauga glanced at the house. "Any with strong back?"

No-Chance sighed. He reached for his tobacco pouch as he launched into the events of the past few days. They were sharing the pipe when Jerusha brought a pot of coffee, cups, and a basket of hot biscuits out.

"It is good to see you again, Chickamauga. I trust there is no trouble at home."

No-Chance translated her greeting and reached into the basket. He juggled a hot biscuit between his hands. "Soldiers came to the cabin."

"I don't think it's anything to worry about." Jerusha gathered her skirt and knelt next to him. "They're only making certain no white folks settle in Indian Territory."

"Just the same, the child is better, thanks to you. We need to plant." No-Chance flipped a hot biscuit to Chickamauga.

"Well, I know Carl has been mighty proud for your help with the church-raising this past week." Sighing, Jerusha stood. "And I will miss having another woman around."

"A comfort, I'm sure," No-Chance said.

Jerusha turned back toward the steps.

Wiping his mouth, No-Chance asked, "Notice how little Laney takes to the old woman?"

With one foot on the bottom step, Jerusha stopped. "You don't reckon…oh, well, prob'ly not." She stepped to the porch landing as a wail floated through the open door, followed by the husky crooning of a Creek lullaby.

No-Chance tried to sound casual. "Sounds like Stands-in-Water is attached to them, too."

Carl opened the back door. "Jerusha, the girls are awake."

"I can hear, Carl." The young mother pushed past her husband and disappeared into the house.

"You certainly gave us a bit of excitement earlier." The minister bounded down the stairs, pulled his handkerchief out, and grabbed the handle of the coffeepot. He nodded to Chickamauga and poured steaming coffee into a cup. "I pray there's no trouble."

"Just soldiers poking around. They didn't have an interpreter. There's always a chance for trouble without one." No-Chance tossed a biscuit toward the minister, who caught it and dunked it in his coffee.

"Yes, I suppose there is. God's curse on humanity when He struck the tongue of those building a tower to heaven." He munched on the biscuit, dusting his mustache with crumbles.

Cesse and Poca emerged from the tent. The little girl, a tumble of hair in her face, sank next to No-Chance and leaned against his arm, her squeak of labored breathing audible.

He tweaked her nose and handed her a biscuit. "Reverend, seems you need to learn the Creek's talk. How else can you minister to them?"

"I've been praying about that. Suppose you could stay awhile?"

"I'd stay if I could. But don't reckon to spend another winter like the last. We need to plant and"—he looked down at Cesse—"build a bigger cabin."

The door slammed, and Stands-In-Water shuffled onto the porch, holding one of the twins. The old rocker groaned when she settled into it, and for a few moments, the men listened to the rhythmic creak of the floorboards.

"You know, Reverend, the Lord's provided you

with an answer, and it's not me."

Carl twisted around to study the old woman cuddling his daughter.

"You could teach her English, and she could teach you Creek. She'll make a good interpreter." No-Chance continued, "Besides, Jerusha needs help with the babies."

"Why, she could be my first convert to Christianity. What a triumph for God it would be to bring a lost soul into God's everlasting embrace." The young minister rubbed the beard stubble on his chin with the back of his hand. "Yes, I'll speak with Jerusha right away!"

Glowing embers sizzled as Carl stood and tossed the last of his coffee into the campfire. "We'll have to give her a good Christian name to symbolize leaving off her heathen beliefs. Ruth, that's it! The woman who followed her mother-in-law into a strange land and made her home."

Convert? Change her name? A twinge of regret squeezed No-Chance's chest.

Chapter 24

"Cesse!" No-Chance bellowed as he stomped his feet to discourage the determined puppy attacking his moccasins. "Cesse! Get your dog before I feed him to the Little People!"

Cesse dropped her bucket and scampered up from the stream separating the plowed cornfield from the cabin. She strained to pick up the floppy-eared dog the reverend insisted on presenting to her when they left his house weeks earlier.

No-Chance settled saddle bags and a bedroll over the back of his roan and turned to watch the child and dog tussle on the ground. Laughing, he pulled the little girl to her feet and brushed away the paw prints dirtying her calico dress.

"You feed Dog to Little People?" Cesse asked with a hint of breathlessness, large eyes shiny as polished leather.

"Not if he quits biting my feet!" No-Chance admonished in a half-hearted attempt at sternness. Nourished on cow's milk and wild honey, rabbit stew, and fresh air, void of civilization's stink, the child's cheeks dimpled as she grinned.

"Poca, there you are," he called to Cesse's grandfather, who limped from the tangle of saplings and trees shading the cabin. "Do you have a song for a good hunt?"

A slight breeze stirred the grandfather's long, graying hair. Clad in only a breechclout, his thin torso gave evidence of the hungry winter. He lifted a cupped hand to reveal a deep brown and white feather in his palm.

"I have something more. Eagle came to feed at river that I might kill him. He knew we need his mighty spirit. I made medicine over Eagle's feathers. Now you have his eyes to find great beasts in far-away country."

When the old man disappeared each morning, No-Chance thought he simply explored the countryside. Unfit for a long trip, Poca had been doing what he could to ensure a good hunt. He would have bled the feather and recited a litany of ancient chants meant to make the quill sacred.

"It pleases me, Poca, to have your medicine to guide us. I will call on the eagle's spirit to give vision to my eyes. We will find the buffalo and see our enemies before they see us."

No-Chance tied the quill onto the silver band around his black hat. The morning breeze gave life to the feather, making it twist and dance at the end of the rawhide strip.

"Your medicine is good," he said, brushing smudges from the brim before settling the hat on his head.

Poca's solemn face wrinkled into a smile.

With Tampa clutched in one arm, Chickamauga led his gray dun into the circle. He dropped the reins and held the wiggling child out, studying him for a moment. "The spirit of his gone-away mother is with him sometimes…when he laughs." He shifted Tampa for others to see the resemblance.

No-Chance tilted his head and watched drool bubble over the child's lower lip and down his chin. He reached and ruffled the child's abundance of black hair. "Sometimes," he agreed, unable to clearly fix White Cloud's face in his mind.

Crazy Bear grabbed Tampa and lifted the naked child skyward. "He grows heavy, I think. Maybe he will be a bear hunter, too." As if judging the weight of a sack of flour, the stout Indian bounced Tampa, eliciting delighted squeals.

A golden stream of urine arced out, hitting Crazy Bear in the chest. Laughing, No-Chance and Chickamauga dashed for safety as Crazy Bear swung Tampa's aim in their direction. Poca grabbed the giggling Cesse by the arm and hustled her from the circle.

"Chade!" Crazy Bear roared and held the baby at arm's length.

The young woman appeared at the cabin's door and strolled toward the group. She stopped in front of No-Chance and handed him a small bundle.

"You will need this when your stomach begins to think of home." Long hair tied at the nape of her neck, Chade looked small and fragile. For days, she had argued against their venture into an unknown land to hunt a strange animal. If they did not return, she reminded them, there would be hunger and uncertainty in the winter to come for her and the children.

Accustomed to Chade's gentle smile and laughter, her quiet anger sobered the men, and they looked at each other. She reached for the baby and turned back to the cabin.

Crazy Bear grabbed her by the arm. His coarse

whisper broke the tense silence. "I will bring you robe from great beast, soft as white man's silk."

"And if his medicine is stronger than yours, who will keep me warm when earth goes to sleep? What will we eat when only wolf comes out of den? I will cry in night for children that will not come, because seed of great Crazy Bear is gone."

"My wife, I have always returned from hunt."

Chade touched the scars that ran down her husband's face. She studied his necklace for a moment and ran a finger across the yellowed bear claws, causing them to click softly. "You've always known spirit of enemy before."

Poca led Cesse away from the gathering, and Chickamauga busied himself with the pack horse in the awkward stillness.

No-Chance cleared his throat. "I will stand next to my brother and watch his back. He'll never be alone."

Large tears rimmed Chade's dark eyes and rolled down her checks.

"One buffalo cow will feed a hundred people," No-Chance added. Surely the woman saw the importance of this hunting trip. "We will not be hungry all winter."

Chade nodded. With one solemn glance at them all, she turned and walked toward the cabin, Tampa perched on one hip. Crazy Bear swung onto his horse. His guttural roar split the air as he kneed the horse into a gallop. Chickamauga mounted and followed, spurring his horse across the stream and through the sprouting cornfield.

High spirits of the morning vanished, No-Chance settled into the saddle and urged Thunder onto the path. He shifted to look back at the small cabin with the buffalo skull hanging above the door. Chade did not turn to watch them but disappeared into the darkness of the windowless dwelling. Poca, Cesse at his side, prodded the cow and her calf, with a stick, toward a patch of grass.

No-Chance relaxed into the rhythm of the roan's trot. Often he'd awake from his dreams in the dark hours of night, feeling smothered. The urge to steal away crowded his thoughts, but when morning came, he stayed—the pull of family strong. Today, his spirit soared with the once familiar sense of freedom.

Like salt in a wound, Chade's words stung his spirit, causing doubt. What if they did not return as she feared? He whipped the roan around and raced back down the path, jumped the stream, and reined in at the cabin, sending up puffs of dust.

Chade sat in the doorway, nursing Tampa. No-Chance slid from the saddle, loosened the leather bag at his neck, and poured the remaining stones into his hand. He picked out a light-colored sapphire and returned the others to the pouch.

"Here," he said, holding it between his thumb and forefinger.

Chade smiled and allowed the sapphire to roll around her palm. "It is blue, like your eyes. I will think of you when I look at it." She closed her fingers around the jewel and shifted the baby to the other side of her body.

"It has value." No-Chance stood and spread his hands. "This is not to save. It is to trade if…"

Chade glanced up, moist eyes betraying a fear that bored into his soul.

Instantly, he regretted his words. "I mean, if we are

late. Maybe winter will come, and we can't return until spring. Maybe one of the children will get sick. You will have something to trade."

A stray lock of hair hung to Chade's shoulder, and Tampa's pudgy hand grabbed at it as he nursed.

"For three nights I dreamed," she said. "In darkness, I am standing at edge of field. Stalks have grown tall. They are wailing in sadness. When corn parts, only two men ride toward me, each leading horses. Grandmother Moon is bright, but I cannot see who comes. Their faces are dark."

No-Chance stared at the single tear that slid down her smooth cheek. Words of comfort stuck in his throat. He knelt again. "As sure as Grandfather Sun begins his journey in the east each morning, I'll bring the one who occupies your heart back. I promise."

Chade sniffed and looked down at Tampa while he nursed. No-Chance grabbed a hank of Thunder's mane and remounted. "If you need help, Poca can take you to Reverend Wade's place. I marked the trees to show the path. Stands-In-Water is there and will translate."

No-Chance backed the roan away from the cabin, wheeled, and crossed the creek. "It is only a dream," he called over his shoulder and spurred the big horse to a gallop.

For three days, the three men pushed south, light-hearted with the adventure, meandering right and left of the trading path to inspect thickets of blackjack and oak, following rough streams, or pausing on a rise to view the foreign countryside.

At night, around the campfire, No-Chance brooded on Chade's vision, but this, he kept to himself. After all, women were always afraid.

197

Chapter 25

No-Chance stared. So this was it! This was the great beast with a shaggy mane covering half its body. The massive head with small, unblinking eyes mesmerized him. For an instant he could imagine the curved horns driven by a thousand pounds of fury slashing at everything in its path.

"He's a big'un, ain't he?"

No-Chance looked at James Edwards, the slender man standing next to him, and nodded.

Crazy Bear stepped forward and ran his hand across the rump. With its legs pegged out against the logs, the giant hide covered half the back wall of Edwards' Trading Post.

No-Chance took a deep breath. If the buffalo was this imposing in death, what would it be like on the open range?

"Yes, sir. If'n you boys had been a mite earlier, you could'a hitched up with about twenty fellas headin' out for them shaggies. A big herd was sighted west of the Washita pushin' up from the Red River." Edwards leaned in front of No-Chance to spit a wad of tobacco into a pottery jar and wiped his mouth along his sleeve. "Any more in your group?"

No-Chance shook his head.

"Oh. Well, reckon you'll wanna wait for the next bunch to come through. The others been gone most of three days now. With the Comanch' and Kiowa out and about, best to go with a group." The trader smiled, exposing tobacco-stained teeth. "You're welcome to camp yonder in the willers." The musty smell of hides, sorted into piles along one wall, reeked in the confines of the small trading post.

No-Chance took his hat off and fingered the eagle feather lying on the brim. Outside, the ramshackle collection of log huts, called Fort Holmes, was almost deserted. Even so, spending time in an area with only a few soldiers was unsettling.

"Which direction is the Washita?"

Edwards stepped behind a barrel and finger-sketched a map in the dust covering the lid. "Out back is the Little River. Follow it, maybe three miles. It'll marry up with the Canadian. On the other side is a Shawnee trail that heads south and crosses the Washita." He rubbed his thumb and forefinger together before running his hand through a mop of stringy hair. "That sighting was a couple weeks ago. Them shaggies might be a hundred miles farther west by now."

"Thanks." No-Chance motioned to the others. It could be days before another hunting party appeared, and he wasn't inclined to wait.

The men rode single file along the channel carved by the muddy Little River until it spilled into an expanse of equally muddy water. The three men studied the slow-running Canadian and the plainly marked Shawnee path on the other side.

"Twenty hunters will leave a clear trail," No-Chance said.

"This is true," Chickamauga said. "Still, three days will be hard to make up."

In the afternoon stillness, mosquitoes buzzed about the horses. They snorted, swishing their tails to rid themselves of torment.

No-Chance removed his hat and wiped sweat from his forehead. "The life will be sucked from us if we stand here much longer." He slapped at an insect as it landed on his arm and urged Thunder into the water.

The hilly countryside unfolded into pleasant rolling land, making tracking easy. It was the month of *Kvcohvse*, the blackberry, and the earth was alive with budding flowers and lush foliage.

At noon, the fourth day of tracking, Chickamauga pulled a stick from a dying campfire and knocked the blackened bark away to reveal a glowing ember. "Hunters broke camp late." He tossed the stick back and studied the churned hoof prints of horses. "Maybe scouts sight the great beasts. They hurry."

Crazy Bear led the way, following the tracks into a broad valley. Wind rippled young prairie grass into long rolling waves. Heavy clouds, gray and threatening, cast deep shadows across the landscape. An eagle screeched and soared high over their heads.

"Grandfather's medicine was good." No-Chance pointed toward the eagle gliding down the center of the valley. It settled on a gnarled and twisted tree that stood alone in the meadow. Leafless, it seemed out of place in the midst of lush grasses. Crazy Bear urged his horse to a gallop and rode into the valley. A dull roar resounded in the distance as lightning flashed, ripping through the bank of fast-moving clouds.

"Easy, Thunder," No-Chance cautioned as the roan pranced and whinnied, unwilling to advance forward.

"We camp there, out of valley." Chickamauga

jutted his chin toward a copse of trees on the far side of the ridge.

No-Chance shook his head, "If the rain is heavy, we'll lose the trail."

Crazy Bear, perched on a branch of the old tree, waved at them. No-Chance nudged the reluctant roan into motion. The wind carried a chill, and he shivered. There was something dismal and unfriendly about this land.

"It is sign," Crazy Bear roared as they approached. "They come back here." A dozen painted buffalo skulls nested in the forks of an ancient sycamore. The eerie bones glared at the intruders.

Lightning forked through the darkening sky, followed by a clap of thunder. The ground grumbled in response. Reins dangling, Crazy Bear's sorrel reared and galloped down the valley. Chickamauga wheeled his mount and chased after the frightened horse.

Crazy Bear shifted from branch to branch in his descent.

No-Chance dismounted and bent to study recent hoof prints around the tree.

The heavens roared again. Unburdened, Thunder shot forward.

Still gripping the reins, No-Chance struggled to dig his heels into the slippery grass. Pain shot through his weak ankle, and he stumbled, allowing the reins to slice through his hands.

Freed, Thunder raced away.

Sprawled facedown, No-Chance clenched his bloodied fist and pounded the ground. Why couldn't Crazy Bear stay put? Why was he always dashing off? The ground shivered under No-Chance, and he sat up.

Huffing, Crazy Bear dropped to his knees. "Why you let horse go? Now we walk."

No-Chance hurled against the sturdy Indian, driving him backwards. They tumbled over and over, thrashing through great clumps of grass.

Another peal of thunder muted their shouting.

No-Chance looked back to see a blue-painted skull fall from the shuddering tree. A dark mass moved over the ridge at the southern end of the valley and spread like molasses oozing down the side of a barrel.

In disbelief, No-Chance staggered to his feet as the ground shook. He whirled around.

Chickamauga and the horses—gone.

The mass became a blur of animals coming toward them.

Crazy Bear pulled his knife and planted his feet apart, ready for the onslaught of an unstoppable avalanche.

"The tree! Get to the tree!" No-Chance grabbed his friend to pull him along. The tree was their only hope.

Crazy Bear jumped for a fat limb and pulled himself up with powerful arms. No-Chance reached for the next branch. It cracked with his weight. Pain shot through his raw hands, and he dropped to the ground.

Several buffalo shot past the sycamore, and No-Chance lunged for the thick trunk. In seconds, they were surrounded by a sea of the dark beasts shaking their great manes and rushing around the obstacle in their path. A hand slipped under his armpit and pulled him skyward. Knocking skulls to the ground, the two men scrambled as high as they dared on the aging limbs.

The herd continued to pour without end over the

ridge in the distance. Dust and debris swirled, filling the air.

No-Chance labored to breathe. He grimaced and scrunched his eyes against the dirt's sting. The vision of a tearful Chade flashed through his mind.

Huge beasts grunted and bellowed as they crashed against the sycamore. The tree groaned, jerking back and forth.

No-Chance and Crazy Bear struggled to maintain their footing. With a loud crack, thick roots surrendered their hold to the ground, and the sycamore toppled.

Branches crashed over the top of stampeding buffaloes. They lowered their heads, slashing free of the tangle.

No-Chance fought through the web of branches to pull himself onto the fallen trunk, frantic screams for Crazy Bear lost in the deafening roar of massive animals charging past. Tears welled in his eyes. Mother Earth consumed them. He tried to blink his vision clear in the dense cloud and pulled the neck of his tunic over his nose. The warm air pocket soothed his breathing. His own pungent odor flooded his senses.

Straddling the trunk, No-Chance stretched forward to feel along its rough surface. A hand touched his outstretched fingers. Energized, he grabbed it, pulling first the wrist, then the elbow, inching more and more of his friend through the maze of broken limbs and onto the trunk.

Heaving and choking, Crazy Bear collapsed in No-Chance's arms, and they clung to each other.

The upturned base of the old tree, its great quivering roots flailing out, momentarily parted the frenzied animals. With their stubby tails straight up and bulging eyes, they rumbled past, shattering branches in their path. Within minutes the buffer of debris was gone, and the animals surged back toward the length of the trunk.

The two men scrambled to reach the protection of the base. No-Chance attempted to stand on the sloping trunk and hooked his arm around a root tentacle. Next to him, Crazy Bear steadied himself, slipped his breechclout off and snapped it at the maddened beasts as they lurched toward them. The fluttering cloth shied the animals, and they veered away. No-Chance waved his own breechclout. The fabric caught on the horns of a passing buffalo and ripped from his grasp. In an instant, it was gone.

The last of the frenzied animals roared past, leaving a stifling cloud in their wake.

Both men clung to the tree, gasping for breath, afraid to leave the security of the large trunk. As the roar of the stampede receded to a dull throb, No-Chance's legs quivered, and he collapsed to the trampled ground.

He peered through the dust at Crazy Bear sprawled next to him and laughed—a nervous, exhausted laugh. "I think maybe Grandfather's medicine was too good."

The stout Indian grunted and rolled over to bury his head in his arms.

No-Chance closed aching eyes. Chade's fears were only a dream. His knotted muscles relaxed. It was only a dream, a woman's dream.

A thud of hoof beats pierced his thoughts. Stragglers, there must be stragglers. No-Chance shook Crazy Bear. Then he heard the wonderful, musical whinny of a horse.

Voice raspy, he called into the semi-darkness, "Brother! Here we are!"

The passing shadows stopped.

"Chickamauga?"

Branches crunched beneath hooves of approaching horses. How many horses? Three, four, more? Hair bristled at the back of No-Chance's neck as shadows advanced through the cloud of dust to become figures that haunted his nightmares.

Chapter 26

No-Chance stirred awake, a dull headache reminding him of the injury that put an end to a useless struggle after the stampede. For all the ranting, the rain clouds did little more than leave him drenched and chilled. He blinked at the campfire beyond, again straining at rawhide ropes holding his outstretched arms tight to the trunk of the fallen sycamore. The downed tree that once offered sanctuary now held him captive.

Exhausted, No-Chance shifted his bare butt in the mud and pulled his knees up, plastering his wet shirt to his chest. He felt a slight movement and knew Crazy Bear, tied to the other side, struggled as well.

Shoulders aching, No-Chance studied the pale blue sky heralding a clear day. *We survived cold and hunger on the long walk. Now, we die on a beautiful day. Chade's dream was right.* The thought churned in No-Chance's stomach as he peered at his captors dozing under flimsy shelters. Everyone knew Comanche tortured their prisoners.

Wisps of smoke in the dying campfire curled upward. A young Indian, red face-paint smudged, stood and stretched. The action made the dark curly scalp at his waist wiggle like a small furry animal. The Indian looked over and grinned.

Hoping to disguise the shiver of fear crawling up his spine, No-Chance glared back. Two other warriors stirred and joined their companion in the morning's ritual of scratching. One wore a black silk vest with a dangling watch fob. The other tugged at the brim of a sweat-stained derby, pulling it low over his forehead. Silver loops outlined the edges of ears large as oak leaves. He shook another man awake. Retrieving their lances and rifles, the four Indians strode off toward tethered horses, jostling each other and laughing.

No-Chance watched them ride over the ridge that spilled buffalo into the valley the day before. He studied the remaining three Comanche. One grunted and shifted his position on the ground. The other two, wrapped in blankets, did not move. If he and Bear were to escape unharmed, it had to be before the early risers returned.

The thought spurred fresh attempts to maneuver his hands out of the rawhide ropes. No-Chance ignored the ache radiating from his wrists. He pulled and relaxed, pulled and relaxed, hoping to stretch the binding enough to wiggle one hand loose.

In the space of a heartbeat, a short Comanche bolted up and dealt a sharp kick to No-Chance's leg. The smirk on the Indian's yellow-painted face revealed a row of crooked teeth. Long, beaded rawhide strips, tied at the waist of his deerskin breechclout, swung in the air. He jumped from side to side delivering powerful kicks.

Mud churned as No-Chance pumped his legs to avoid the blows. The need for survival flooded his brain, burying a welling sense of panic. He focused on the brave's sturdy body. A muscle on the outer right thigh bulged. In that instant, when weight was on the right leg and the left leg pulled back, No-Chance struck out with both feet. His tormentor crashed backward into the campfire. He scrambled up with a yell, brushing embers from his body. His two companions stirred from under the shelter and laughed, jeering his clumsiness.

The look of amusement fled the Comanche's yellow-painted face. No-Chance met the cold glare, his mind racing. Don't show fear. Cowardice would bring a slow lingering death. Bravery might save him.

Snarling, the Indian held a knife by its blade and waved it back and forth in a slow, deliberate taunt. Familiar carved Celtic knots adorned the weapon's handle. No-Chance clenched his fist. The knife was part of his history. He knew its feel and, in his hands, it never failed.

"*Tejano*! Texan!" The Comanche spit the word out.

No-Chance pushed back against the tree trunk as he sought to escape the Indian's reach. He caught a brief flash of the blade before its edge penetrated his flesh. Spirals of pain shot along his scalp line and radiated down his forehead, through his eye sockets.

"Seminoli! Seminoli!" he shrieked, "No Texan!"

"Iseeo," another Comanche shouted, and the attacker released his hold and turned to look at the shelter.

No-Chance slumped against the trunk and took a deep breath, repeating, "*Unet Seminoli.* I am Seminole." Liquid warmth oozed down his forehead, snaking a path off the bridge of his nose, down his cheeks. He shook his head, knowing blue eyes belied the purity of his race. "*Mvnks Tejano*! No Texan!" Blood dripped onto his calico shirt.

A tall warrior moved in the smooth fluid motions of a panther, skirting the campfire. Long braids, rolled in beaver skins, fell forward as he knelt and bent close. No-Chance lifted his chin, attempting to return the searching stare. Light reflecting off twisted silver wires in the Indian's ears stirred a memory.

The Panther snatched the Celtic knife from Iseeo. Every muscle in No-Chance's body tightened when the blade ripped through his shirt exposing the leather pouch. He shrank from the hand that lifted it free.

The ancestor stones flashed as they rolled about in the Comanche's palm. He nodded, letting the jewels tumble through his fingers, back into the pouch.

"*Puha*," the Panther said. Leaning close, he patted a tiny decorated bag dangling among the feathers and shells that hung around his neck.

"*Puha*?" Desperate, No-Chance struggled to understand the word's meaning. A dull ache occupied his head. He grimaced at the taste of fresh blood gathering in the corners of his mouth.

The Comanche fished his own leather bag from among strands of shells. They clicked softly as he pushed two fingers into the pouch and withdrew a small deep-red ruby. He held the jewel up and slowly rotated it between his fingertips.

For a moment, No-Chance was lost in a flight of images: being pursued by soldiers, his dying horse, the terror of waiting for an arrow to end his life, and finally his act of kindness to an enemy. His father's ruby had not built a kingdom, but on this day maybe it had bought his life.

With a few words and a wave of his hand, the Panther dismissed the angry warrior intent upon owning another scalp.

The tormentor jerked a blanket off the ground,

limped to a pony, and rode south.

Relief flooded No-Chance's senses as the Panther hacked loose his rawhide bindings. He spent the last of his energy calming Crazy Bear. They may not be bound captives, but without their weapons, they were not free either.

Sitting next to Crazy Bear, in front of the campfire, No-Chance fought a feeling of dizziness. It was important to stay alert while their two captors puffed away on a pipe. The older Indian's features were broad, not as defined or regal as the Panther's. Feathers sprouted from his hair. Morning sun glinted off a long string of large brass buttons—the kind which adorn a military officer's dress jacket.

No-Chance stretched to take the offered pipe with a grateful sigh and took a long steady draw from the stem. Tension drained from his muscles when he exhaled, allowing the smoke to escape his lips. It wasn't likely Comanches would kill someone sharing their tobacco. The throb in his head eased, and he handed the pipe to Crazy Bear.

The older Indian cleared his throat, "Espanola?"

No-Chance shrugged. "A little."

"Eng-glash?"

No-Chance nodded and repeated, "Eng-glash."

A broad smile crawled across the Indian's face. "Ahhh, I good Eng-glash." He rose and stood over No-Chance to examine his wound. Dozens of crow feathers, tied to small plaits of hair, fluttered with the motion.

"I tell you, Parlin-wah-pit make thank you, for gift of…" The old Indian hesitated, fingering the buttons on his necklace. "For gift of *puha*…power." He patted the warrior on his shoulder. "Him blood good now. Much strong with Seminoli medicine stone. Now you make medicine with more pretty stones. Head be much good again."

No-Chance's head throbbed anew when he touched the sticky wound at his scalp line. He stared at the blood on his hand. These Comanche expected him to heal himself. He took a deep breath. It wouldn't be the first time he bluffed his way out of trouble.

He patted a smooth circle on the moist ground, scooped gray ashes from the edge of the fire, and sprinkled them over the circle. How much did he dare? He stared across the smoldering fire and pointed at the Celtic knife now at the warrior's waist.

Parlin-wah-pit ran his hands down the beaver skin covering his braid and stared back. Burning wood crackled softly, crumbling to smother feeble flames. It seemed an eternity before the Indian relinquished the weapon.

Jaws clenched, No-Chance pulled the point of the blade through the layer of ash, drawing a pattern of Celtic knots. He knew the design by heart. Satisfied, he held the knife in one hand and the bag of jewels in the other.

"*Puha*!" He tapped his chest with them. "My *puha*, my power!" One man's medicine was no good in the hands of another unless given freely. It would be wise to remind them of this.

No-Chance drove the knife blade into the ground and fished a ruby from the pouch. He held the gem to the sun and chanted, "Great Spirit, Maker and Taker of Breath, One who knows good and evil. I hold a drop of blood from a prick in your finger. You know your child's suffering. Send your power to heal and renew my strength."

With fluid hand motions, the feather-headed Indian translated the prayer. Parlin-wah-pit nodded, touching the small decorated bag at his own chest.

No-Chance closed his leather pouch and slipped it over his head. He'd need to stop the bleeding, if they were to believe him. He ripped a wide strip off the bottom of his long shirt and tied it around his forehead.

The old Indian smiled. "I am Good-Talker. You eat." He laid a skin of water and fat roll of pemmican on the ground. "Parlin-wah-pit wants know name of Seminole that gives his power away. Why come Comancheria land?"

"I am called No-Chance, and this is Crazy Bear of the Mvskoke. He has a brave heart and has killed many bears." No-Chance reached with blood-crusted fingers to touch the heavy necklace on his friend's broad chest. "We come to hunt the great beast, the buffalo. The soldiers drove us from our home many rivers away in the East. Our stomachs were empty for a long time."

Good-Talker turned to translate to Parlin-wah-pit. No-Chance cut a slice of pemmican and bit into the greasy wedge. The taste of blueberries and nuts eased his hunger, and he handed a slice to Crazy Bear.

With a shake of his feathered head, the old Indian cleared his throat. "Parlin-wah-pit send Iseeo, bring our people here. We hunt buffalo. You hunt buffalo with us. Maybe, yes?"

Hesitating for a minute, No-Chance nodded. It would not be wise to refuse an invitation.

Satisfied, Good-Talker continued, "Many come now to *Numunah* land, Comanche land. Yesterday find much hide-hunters. Make Comanche heart hot. They no more kill buffalo."

No-Chance froze. The hunters from Edwards' Trading Post? The last mouthful of pemmican stuck in his throat.

The old Indian grunted as he reached for the partial roll of pemmican and continued, "Iseeo heart still hot. That why want Seminole scalp. Other tribes come. Our enemies, the Utes. Tonkawas come, eat Comanche flesh. *Tejanos* with long guns come. It no good. The People watch after buffalo. Great Spirit glad. You be Comanche friend. You stay. We learn you hunt good."

"It will be an honor to hunt with The People," No-Chance said, blueberries souring in his mouth.

Good-Talker scratched his mass of hair and feathers. "Long time ago, before this man's memory, The People hunt without horses. Much hard to do."

"Oh, we had horses," No-Chance said. "The buffalo surprised us. Our horses ran before the herd. My brother, Chickamauga, chased them."

He turned to look down the valley, once lush prairie grass trampled and churned. A new fear took form. Maybe Chickamauga had been the one missing in Chade's dream.

Chapter 27

Steam lifted from puddles that hadn't been sucked into dry ground, gumming the air and encouraging a chorus of insects. Here and there, grass tufts struggled to straighten in the aftermath of the stampede. No-Chance watched Parlin-wah-pit guide his brown and white pony over the ridge back to the dead-tree camp.

"A watched pot never boils," No-Chance muttered with one more glance at the horizon. "Let's go back. Until we get horses, we're going to have to hope Chickamauga finds his way here." He kicked a rock from the path they'd worn in their pacing and winced. His newly-healed leg ached with the battering of Iseeo's well-placed kicks.

"He will miss buffalo hunt," Crazy Bear said as he kept pace with No-Chance's halting stride back into camp.

"I doubt he missed the buffalo," No-Chance answered, tugging at the makeshift breechclout fashioned from the lower half of his calico shirt. His wardrobe suffered in this newfound life. Still he fared better than Crazy Bear, who chafed at a strip of wool blanket between his legs.

"We eat," Good-Talker said, holding up a fat skunk.

Parlin-wah-pit led his horse into the shade of the hill. Black tattoo lines radiated like spokes around a wheel hub from a puckered scar in his broad back.

"I'd have done a better job of cutting that arrow out of his hide if I'd known it would be prettied up," No-Chance said, settling against the trunk.

Crazy Bear squatted on his heels, arms around his knees.

Good-Talker looked up from the task of skinning the skunk. "Much honor in such a wound." He grinned, lifting one eyebrow. "Woman like strong man." The old man skillfully ran the knife blade between the skin and muscle of the animal, inching the carcass free of the pelt. He plopped the pale glistening body on the ground and carved the flesh into long strips.

"When Parlin-wah-pit maybe eight summers old, him make long walk to save village. Much sickness, white man's sickness. Every lodge, bad spirits. Many die. Medicine Man no have cedar to burn and chase away bad spirits."

The old man continued as he threaded the meat onto a sharpened stick. "Him walk alone three days, much distance, to Little Raven Valley, where best medicine cedars grow. Cut ten branches. Carry back to village. Cedar smoke fill every lodge, make air pure again. Soon, no more die. Now him called Parlin-wah-pit. Means Ten Cedars, our language. No forget bravery of boy."

Good-Talker pushed the end of the stick into the ground and leaned it across the fork of an upright branch suspending the meat above the fire. He licked the juice from his fingers and reached for another stick.

The sun slipped behind the hills, throwing the valley into afternoon shadows. No-Chance shaded his eyes, watching the horizon for the hundredth time. If

Chickamauga caught their horses, he would have waited until daylight to return. That is, if he hadn't run into other Comanche…or maybe Kiowa or Osage…or been overtaken by the stampeding buffalo.

"Tomorrow, village comes. I give you horse to look for brother." Good-Talker stood, holding an armful of painted buffalo skulls. "I have fine herd," he boasted and set the bones on the ground. No-Chance watched him retrieve several more from the jumble of broken limbs and build a pyramid of cracked and broken skulls.

"I will be grateful," No-Chance answered. "Together, my brother and I have a son."

Brows raised, Good-Talker questioned, "This is so? How can this be?"

No-Chance smiled. "It is a long story, one for when the wind howls and blows the snow from the north." He pointed toward the fire. "Now, my stomach talks to me."

Grease dripped from roasting meat, flaring the flames. No-Chance pulled a browned strip from the offered stick and nibbled at the skunk-meat. The taste was strong, almost sweet. He glanced at Crazy Bear devouring his portion.

As night darkened, Good-Talker switched easily between the language of his tribe and English, translating for Parlin-wah-pit. No-Chance, in turn, translated from English to Creek the stories of the Comanche for Crazy Bear.

Stretching, No-Chance scanned the black sky for the North Star. Good-Talker pointed to the shelter. "You sleep now."

"Brother Bear has the snore of ten bears," No-

Chance answered. "I have grown used to the noise, but it would not be kind to disturb our hosts. We will sleep over there."

He walked from the campfire's light, cleared a spot free of shattered branches, and stretched out on the ground. The ache in his head reminded him of Comanche savagery. It would be safer with a few yards between them.

A distant coyote howled his presence. Farther away, another one answered. Just as the moon's brilliance began to wane, a soft crack stirred him. He shifted his position. Another snap. No-Chance opened his eyes and leaned on one elbow to peer across Crazy Bear toward the dying campfire. In his slumber, Parlin-wah-pit scratched his leg and turned over.

A breeze chilled the settling dew. Listening to the whisperings of the wind, No-Chance hugged his arms to his chest. At that instant, a hand clasped over his mouth.

"Brother!" Chickamauga's hair brushed No-Chance's face as he bent to quietly question, "You are not held captive?"

No-Chance shook his head. Chickamauga released his hold.

"My heart is glad to see you," No-Chance whispered, as he sat up and grabbed Chickamauga's arm to make sure he was not dreaming. "What took you so long?"

Chickamauga leaned forward. "After I caught horses, great beasts scattered them again." He reached to touch the bloody bandage on No-Chance's forehead. "You hurt?"

"Almost scalped!"

Chickamauga drew back and looked toward the shelter.

No-Chance nodded. "Comanche."

"Why you not prisoner?"

"Remember the Comanche scout that Coache shot? That's him. He recognized me as the one who patched him up." In a barely audible voice, No-Chance added, "Else you'd be looking at a dead man. Most likely, the hunters from Edwards' Post are dead."

Both men studied the sleeping figures on the other side of the smoldering campfire. Decorated lances leaned against the brush shelter. Hanging from the end of one weapon, a blond hank of hair stirred to life with a fresh breeze. The scalp shuddered, then hung lifeless again when the air stilled.

"The horses are beyond." Chickamauga nodded into the darkness. "Let us be away before they wake."

No-Chance put his hand on Chickamauga's shoulder. "They want us to hunt buffalo."

"Do you trust them?"

Did he trust them? No-Chance shivered at the gruesome stories exploding in his mind. The Comanche had ways of killing a man, piece by tiny piece. They were excitable, unpredictable, just plain uncivilized. Did he trust them?

"No," he whispered. "Not all, anyway."

Crazy Bear stirred and sat up, yawning.

Chickamauga scrambled to prevent his sleepy friend from making noise by putting both hands over his open mouth. Crazy Bear struggled free. No-Chance shook his head and put one finger to his lips.

Their attempts at silence were futile. Bear's coarse whisper was like the rough grating of a bare limb against a cabin roof.

"Chickamauga! You gone long time."

"Shush," No-Chance hissed under his breath and looked over at the shelter. "Chickamauga found the horses. We leave now."

"No!" Crazy Bear scowled. A deep bruise below his left eye puffed, making it smaller than the right eye. "We hunt great beast soon."

Good-Talker's brass buttons clicked as he sat up to stare across the flickering campfire. Parlin-wah-pit stood and shouted into the darkness. Lance raised, he leapt over smoldering coals with a bone-chilling shriek.

Chapter 28

The fierce cry shattered pre-dawn calm and echoed in the narrow valley. No-Chance bounded up, words tumbling from his mouth, as he sought to block Parlin-wah-pit's advance.

"No! This is my brother!"

The tall Comanche hesitated but did not lower his lance. Intent on capturing Parlin-wah-pit's full attention, No-Chance moved forward. He forced himself to smile.

"Tell him, Good-Talker. It is my brother." He could hear the hollow clattering of the heavy button necklace as the old Indian moved toward them. "Tell him my brother who was lost is now found." He put his hand on the lance. Parlin-wah-pit resisted lowering the weapon, until Good-Talker translated.

No-Chance studied the stern expression on the warrior's face and repeated, "We must celebrate!" He diverted his attention to Good-Talker. "Tell him, I send my brothers for our horses. We have coffee and tobacco." Nodding, No-Chance walked backward. "It is a good day when a man's brother is found. We will have a fine smoke and celebrate."

The mask of gaiety dropped when he turned toward Crazy Bear and Chickamauga. With a loud laugh, he clasped both on the shoulder and spoke in the Creek language. "Hurry, before dawn brightens the sky. I told them you go for our horses. Yesterday, we had no choice. Today we do."

"You not come with us?" Chickamauga's eyes narrowed.

No-Chance shook his head. "I am a guest of scalp-takers. They are not the civilized brothers we are used to. It may stir their blood to refuse the hunt. If I am successful, we will have full bellies this winter."

"I not run from fight." Crazy Bear barreled his chest, hands on his hips.

Chickamauga straightened his shoulders. "I stay with you."

"Listen! The tall one owes a debt to me." The memory of the yellow-faced warrior was fresh, and No-Chance hesitated. "I will be safe. Besides, my brother, you have a son without a mother. And you"—he turned to Crazy Bear with a slight smile—"have a wife who would take my scalp if you do not return."

He glanced over his shoulder. Good-Talker stood arms crossed, head tilted, intent upon catching their conversation. Parlin-wah-pit rested the long lance in the crook of his arm. Behind them, threads of light laced a gray horizon.

No-Chance forced another laugh and smiled at the two Comanche before turning his attention to Chickamauga. "Go now."

He gave them a shove, turned away, and called in a cheery voice. "Beans, we've got beans, too." No-Chance strode toward the shelter, picking up several branches as he went past Parlin-wah-pit.

The old Indian returned to the campfire and watched No-Chance push coals back to life with a branch. "Why brother sneak like snake that slithers through grass?"

No-Chance reached for a strip of dried skunk meat. "The country is strange to us. The hills are many. In the dark, my brother was unsure if we were friend or foe."

Good-Talker squinted one eye, "And if you prisoner?"

"We would not be going on a buffalo hunt tomorrow!" No-Chance shrugged.

Twigs crunched under foot, and he turned. The stone that settled in his stomach vanished as Crazy Bear squatted and dropped an armful of sticks. No-Chance sighed. For his friend, the promise of a hunt outweighed safety.

Parlin-wah-pit paced the campsite. No-Chance pondered how to explain Chickamauga's long absence, while pretending an interest in Good-Talker's incessant blabber.

A horse whinnied in the distance, and the old Indian looked up. "Ahh, we have feast now," he said, rubbing his hands together.

No-Chance watched Chickamauga descend the hill. Didn't anyone listen to him? Early morning sun glanced off the metal trappings on the horses.

"*Hensci*!" Chickamauga shouted in greeting.

A lump swelled in No-Chance's throat.

Clad only in a breechclout, Chickamauga slid from the saddle, dark eyes alert, and held out three jackrabbits. By the time warm air stirred insects to activity in the meadow, Good-Talker had set the pot to bubbling. The promise of a feast settled uneasy nerves.

No-Chance massaged his leather smoke pouch. The rich aroma of fine Tennessee tobacco from the trading post wafted in the air. Sharing smoke was a sign of friendship and peace among any Indian tribe he'd ever known. Never had he felt the need of that assurance more than with these Comanche. He ran a greasy finger around the inside of the pipe bowl, then tapped shreds of tobacco into it.

Parlin-wah-pit reached for a smoldering brand with an air of authority. No-Chance relinquished the pipe. He didn't like another man taking the first draw but forced a nod.

A few puffs brought life to the tobacco. Parlin-wah-pit waved the smoke into his face. As the cloud lifted, so did his scowl.

No-Chance relaxed and leaned against the fallen tree.

The sides of the valley shimmered in the soft green of tender grasses. An ugly scar of torn and churned dirt marred the ground. He followed the swath up the far ridge and blinked. Shading his eyes, he studied a distant movement. Where buffalo earlier poured over the ridge, a group of riders appeared. They descended the hill, whooping and shouting, thundering toward the camp.

Passing moments seemed an eternity as the advancing riders took the form of near-naked Indians painted in brilliant reds and yellows, with silver ornaments throwing bright flashes of light from the horde. Hundreds of feathers fluttered from man and horse alike.

The men steadied their mounts, mesmerized by the avalanche of riders flooding the valley. Good-Talker jumped up and down, waving his arms.

With pounding hooves, the painted horses charged around the campsite raising a cloud of dirt. The race over, twenty mounted warriors trotted their winded ponies back to surround the newcomers.

No-Chance fanned the air and side-stepped a lathered appaloosa. Irritated, he looked up through the settling dust at a yellow-faced warrior.

The familiar rider pointed to a dirty blond shank of hair hanging from the horse's bridle. A slow crooked-tooth grin snaked across the Indian's face.

Scalp bristling, No-Chance reached for his knife at the unspoken threat.

"Iseeo win again. Always win race." Good-Talker pushed his way through the dismounting men to stroke the muzzle of Iseeo's horse.

The din of shouts and laughter melted as, one by one, the riders studied the visitors. No-Chance squared his shoulders and glanced at his brothers. Both stood grim-faced. Barely daring to breathe, he ran his thumb up and down the carved handle of his knife.

He studied the solemn warriors, young and muscular with long, black braids. One was smeared in red paint, his chest heaving. Another stood, arms folded, agate-black eyes glittering through a mask of white. Several ran feathered quirts through their hands. Only the prancing and snorting of horses broke the silence.

Parlin-wah-pit shouted a command. As if released from a spell, the Indians nodded and grunted, before turning their attention to boastful conversation. No longer an object of curiosity, No-Chance looked at Good-Talker.

The old Indian smiled. "Parlin-wah-pit say, you friend, save life."

When a young Comanche discovered the bubbling pot, the riders surged past, eager to taste the celebration stew. Laughing and talking, the men jostled one another as they dipped into the pot with a buffalo horn each carried dangling from their waist.

Good-Talker hurried toward the campfire. "You eat. Women, children, come soon."

Stomach knotted, No-Chance waved him on and retrieved his Celtic pipe from the ground. He cupped the warm bowl in the palm of his hand. He'd be damned if he'd share tobacco with the whole parcel of banshee-wailing scalp-takers.

Iseeo, the only Indian still astride his horse, stared. Streaked yellow paint didn't conceal the hatred in his eyes. The warrior wheeled his horse and proceeded down the valley.

Chapter 29

Flames licked at mounds of dead limbs, sending a shower of bright red embers into the night sky. A young warrior paused in his dance to throw his head back and howl. Sweat streaked the red paint on his pulsing body. Plaits of black and brown hair, sewn to his wristbands, swung as the Indian threw his arms out and swirled.

Bells heralding the arrival of Parlin-wah-pit's band of people earlier, now rang with the cadence of drums and rattles, whoops and hollers. Bathed in a golden glow, decorated Comanche pranced around the fire, thrusting lances into imaginary buffaloes.

"You and brothers dance, too? Have good hunt. Many hides."

No-Chance looked up at Good-Talker. Next to him, a plump woman with red circles painted on her checks, lowered a basket of steaming deer meat and hurried away, giggling.

The old Indian settled himself and smiled. "She good wife. Give me sons." He nodded toward two boys in breechclouts, who were crouching and jumping in wild movements in imitation of older warriors.

No-Chance felt Crazy Bear nudge him. "My brother wishes to know when we see the great beasts."

Good-Talker laughed. Shreds of meat dangled from his teeth. "It good thing to be eager. Great Spirit send hot fire in sky. Scare buffalo. They much tired. Easy hunt." He held up a grimy finger. "Iseeo say one day away. Many buffalo. Tomorrow, we walk with silent feet."

"Silent feet?" No-Chance wiped grease from his mouth. "All these people?"

Good-Talker's eyes widened. "Only hear Comanche when he want you hear!"

No-Chance surveyed the milling people, talking in small groups and watching the dancers. Naked children chased one another and rolled in the dirt, their laughter lost in the ruckus. A woman holding a water skin sauntered out of the shadows. Deep fringe at the bottom of her skirt swayed in soft movements with each step.

No-Chance accepted a buffalo horn from the woman and looked up as she bent to pour water into the container. Black hair fell in thick strands across her face.

"Thank you, I…" The rest of his sentence faltered. The tip of the woman's nose was cut off, a badge of unfaithfulness. It was said the same punishment was practiced by the old ones back in Georgia, but he had never actually witnessed it.

"This Maria." Good-Talker patted the woman's bent form, leaving a grimy smear across her skirt. He reached for a hunk of roasted meat. "Now, she good wife, too."

Good-Talker rose and began a rhythmic motion before the fire. In the haze of flames, it was difficult to distinguish where the mass of crow feathers ended and hair began. He bobbed to the beat of drums. Light reflected off the button necklace as the old Indian moved among the dancers.

No-Chance jumped at a heavy hand on his

shoulder. Parlin-wah-pit knelt and smiled, crinkling painted white lines down his cheeks. With a dull clunk, four lances rolled from the warrior's arms onto the ground. Smiling again, Parlin-wah-pit picked up one of the weapons and nodded toward the bonfire.

"I think we've been invited to dance," No-Chance said.

Crazy Bear grabbed a lance and bounded into the midst of celebrating Comanche. His guttural roar spilled forth with such emotion dancers stopped to watch. The stout Indian held the weapon out level to the ground. With a short run, he somersaulted over the lance.

Onlookers erupted into cheers as Crazy Bear distorted his marred face with a growl. Parlin-wah-pit motioned to No-Chance and strode into the orange light of the fire, holding his weapon high.

"Are you going to join them?" No-Chance asked Chickamauga, who shook his head.

"I wait until I know heart of buffalo first." He picked up a lance and examined the large flint bound to the shaft with thin rawhide strips.

No-Chance rose and walked into the world of spirits. The roaring crackle of flames blended into shushing of rattles and muted drumbeats. Sweat rolled down his face and sides as his heels lifted and fell in measured steps around the fire. He looked into the black sky at stars, distorted by heat waves, and closed his eyes against the sting of smoke.

Moving faster, swirling and dipping, he felt the curtain of civility slip away. Fury, born in the depths of past despair, surged through his veins, pushing him forward. His head throbbed with each hypnotic beat of the drum. He put his hands over his ears to stop the noise.

A sudden shove sent him stumbling toward the fire. He regained his balance and swung around to confront a yellow-faced warrior. Iseeo! The Indian sneered, before disappearing among the dancers. No-Chance clenched his fist and followed.

Red, black, and white-painted faces blurred into gruesome feathered objects bobbing this way and that. One after the other, warriors startled from their own trances, backed away from his frenzied search for Iseeo. Howls became screams of rage as strength oozed from his body leaving him rooted in one spot. No-Chance grimaced and rubbed the still-raw cut across his forehead. His hands, sticky with fresh blood, trembled.

Above the shrieks, a familiar voice from his childhood rumbled. "Remember laddie, ye that live by the sword, die by the sword." Brilliant orange flames consumed branches until they crumbled into thousands of smaller flames. He could see his father's house burning again and knew the scream of rage was his own.

****

Sharp prickles of pain pierced his dark dreams and No-Chance struggled to sit up. "*Por favor, senor,*" pleaded a woman's voice.

"Maria?" He focused on the form above him

"*Si.*" She peered down at him with one hand covering her lower face. Thick lashes fluttered above large brown eyes. She dabbed at his forehead with a wet cloth.

"Stop…"

"*Por favor.*" She resisted his protests, holding the

229

rag in place. "You fall. Open wound. It bleeds."

"You're not Comanche?" Curiosity replaced spent anger.

"No. The *Numunah* raided Papa's rancho long time back." Her voice dropped to a whisper. "I wish go my *casa*, but Papa not want me now."

Maria straightened at a dull metallic clicking noise. No-Chance knew, without turning, that Good-Talker sat next to him. Instead, he watched Maria untie her cloth belt with one hand. He closed his eyes when she dropped the other hand from her face to bind his forehead.

"You had a vision from the night spirits?"

No-Chance turned toward the old Indian. "What?'

"When dance, what spirit tell you?"

"That when a man kills another man, he will be killed also."

Good-Talker cocked his head. "Spirit not tell of buffalo?"

The camp was quiet, except for an occasional murmur of voices or the bark of a dog.

"No, the spirit did not tell me about the buffalo."

Chapter 30

Soft grunts and snorts, carried by the wind, promised the nearness of buffalo. Their smell, strong and musty, had been in the air for some time. The hunters walked their horses through meadows grazed short by the great beasts, and streams fouled by urine, before stopping at the base of a gentle hill.

No-Chance readjusted the borrowed quiver of arrows on his back and fingered the knife handle at his waist. It would be useless in this hunt. Parlin-wah-pit had forbidden the use of a rifle. The sound would stampede the herd. Stripped of ornaments or shells or any noise-maker, the hunters barely breathed. Meadow larks and buzzing insects serenaded their wait.

Thirty Comanche shifted in their saddles to glare at Crazy Bear when he slapped at a mosquito. No-Chance stifled a grin, though over-eagerness on his brother's part was worrisome. Would he remember Good-Talker's instructions to match his speed to the buffalo, approach on the right, and aim for a spot behind the last rib to pierce the animal's lung? Most of all, would he remember that plunging into the herd before the given signal was a punishable offense?

Chickamauga sat rigid, moving only to wave an insect away. Up and down the line, painted Comanche waited for the herd to complete their morning grazing. Dyed turkey feathers fluttered in horses' manes.

Designs meant to give them speed decorated their flanks.

No-Chance caught Iseeo staring at him. He glared back and felt for his knife once more.

Horses snorted and pawed the ground. Parlin-wah-pit passed, spacing the hunters so as to give each a fair start.

No-Chance declined Good-Talker's offer of a trained buffalo pony, preferring his large steady roan. Thunder hadn't run from the pack of wolves and wouldn't falter now. He knew that as surely as he knew Grandfather Sun followed Grandmother Moon in never-ending pursuit.

Parlin-wah-pit urged his mount to the top of the ridge, looked back, and nodded. In silence, the hunters moved upward. A welcome breeze met them at the top.

Hundreds of buffalo grazed casually along the valley's length. Some wallowed in dirt pits, raising clouds of dust. Tawny calves frolicked or suckled at their mothers' side. Two large bulls at the far end grunted and pawed the ground in confrontation.

The specter of being caught up again in the rampage of shaggy beasts swept over No-Chance—the terror, the helplessness, the choking, blinding dust from pounding hooves of maddened animals.

Crazy Bear's nudge jolted No-Chance from his memories. Eyes dancing with excitement, the stout Indian held up two fingers. He poked his lance at an imaginary bull and grinned, wrinkling the scars down the side of his face.

Next to him, Chickamauga pulled two arrows from his quiver and fit the nock of one into the string of his bow, allowing the other to rest between his thumb and forefinger. No-Chance swallowed the lump in his throat and reached over his shoulder for an arrow. One buffalo would feed a hundred people.

Parlin-wah-pit raised a hand above his head. Instantly, the Comanche bent low and spurred their horses to a gallop. Without urging, Thunder followed suit. No-Chance fumbled, dropped an arrow, and retrieved another from his quiver.

The wave of riders reached the animals before they could mill about in confusion. Each hunter picked his target and whipped his pony to full speed.

No-Chance watched Parlin-wah-pit loosen an arrow with such force that it disappeared completely into the side of a large bull. The buffalo staggered to his knees and collapsed with an audible grunt. As soon as the arrow left the bowstring, Parlin-wah-pit's horse leapt away from the dying animal's horns and into the herd toward another prey.

All around him, No-Chance heard the whistle of spent arrows as the herd fled. Frightened calves, unable to find their mothers in the stampede, bawled. He spurred the roan toward the nearest cow.

His first and second arrow failed to penetrate the mass of matted fur and flapped harmlessly. Behind the ribs, he told himself. The third arrow struck the cow's right flank, and she bellowed in pain, turning to attack. No-Chance jerked the reins to avoid her slashing horns and, pulling his knees tighter, leaned forward when the roan reared.

Blood from the injured buffalo steamed in the crisp air. With a rocking gallop, she plowed on, swinging her head from side to side.

No-Chance willed his body into the stride of the

roan as he raced to catch the fleeing cow and took aim. Suddenly, there it was! The slightest hint of the rib cage. In that instant, he pulled the bowstring to its limit and let the arrow fly.

The shaggy beast stumbled, attempting to maintain her footing. Her right flank sagged as she staggered forward.

No-Chance slowed his horse, careful to stay clear of her reach. The cow, eyes bulging, swung her head around. Blood flowed from her nose. With a mighty shudder, her legs buckled, and she collapsed, plowing into the ground.

No-Chance lowered his bow and stared at the massive animal. Thunder pranced and whinnied.

A golden calf trotted up to the downed animal and bawled. This time, despite the stampeding, he fought a sense of urgency and took careful aim. The calf dropped, and No-Chance wheeled his horse into the rush of buffalo.

Above the rising dust, he caught a glimpse of Chickamauga racing alongside a large bull. Two arrows, loosened one after the other, dropped the lumbering beast to its knees. Chickamauga raced on.

Exhilarated, No-Chance spurred Thunder toward another target. Ahead, a wounded bull charged a spotted pony, unseating its rider. Head down, the enraged beast gored the rearing horse in the belly. With the weight of the flailing horse firmly impaled on its horns, the bull plowed head first into the ground.

The fallen warrior scrambled clear of the struggling animals and ran limping into a cloud of dust. The herd surged together, making escape to the outer fringes impossible.

No-Chance veered from his quarry, urging Thunder toward the injured man. He shifted his weight forward, as the roan sailed over the dying creatures and back to the center, to absorb the jar of the ground's impact. With long powerful strides, the roan overtook the fleeing Comanche. At the last moment, the hunter looked over his shoulder and reached to accept No-Chance's outstretched arm.

With the sudden added weight, the horse slowed before regaining momentum. No-Chance squinted to peer through the swirling dust, in a desperate search for an opening in the stampede. Grunting, snorting, buffalo slammed into each other and bounced away without slowing. The roan's hooves tore clods of trampled ground with sharp pivots and turns. No-Chance and the rescued Comanche shifted their bodies in concert as the horse wove through the maze of deadly horns.

Dirt filled No-Chance's nostrils. As he felt it fill his lungs, too, they broke clear of the solid mass of animals and trotted up a gentle embankment. The Indian slid off Thunder's rump and bent double to catch his breath. No-Chance blew his nose between two fingers to clear his head. He was right to refuse one of Good-Talker's horses and patted the roan's lathered neck.

The Comanche caught hold of the bridle and scratched the horse's muzzle. Excitement trembled in his voice as he spoke to the animal.

No-Chance studied the lean, young man. Tiny red beads sparkled in his thick black braids. Wordless, the Indian clasped No-Chance's forearm in a tight grip.

The roar of hundreds of thundering animals receded as the majority of the herd disappeared over a rise. A familiar guttural, "*Ahi, ahiiii,*" rose above the multitude of excited yells. No-Chance twisted in the saddle to see Crazy Bear with his lance high in the air, motioning to him through the thinning dust.

Dozens of buffalo, strung along the valley, galloped around carcasses in their effort to rejoin the main body of fleeing animals. Some wandered in an aimless daze.

Crazy Bear charged after a trotting cow.

No-Chance laughed. Their bellies would be full this winter. He nudged the roan down the hill, falling into a familiar rhythm as they raced back into the meadow.

Yips and yells rose above tortured bellows as animals thudded to the ground. Several warriors dashed alongside No-Chance, all intent on one last kill before their horses played out. The roan pulled ahead of the others.

No-Chance fit the nock of an arrow into the bowstring. A strange buffalo, large and black, ran at the rear of the herd. He focused on the bull, urging his mount closer. The rib cage should be just behind the dark massive coat.

This time it will take only one arrow, he told himself.

Chapter 31

Later, No-Chance wondered which came first, the sharp pain that burned across his leg or the roan's horrible squeal of agony. Now, the world was white, devoid of sound and feeling. Was this what death was like? No heaven, no hell. Nothing.

Nothing? For when the soul hath departed, the body shall be as nothing. No more than a lump of clay that crumbles into dust beneath the feet of...of what?

A soft breeze brought the smell of dirt and grass and sweating bodies. Faint buzzing teased at his consciousness until it became a clamor of murmurs rising and falling. And something else, something annoying, insistent. Something demanding his attention. Then he knew—the caw of the crow! Of course, his father announced his arrival home.

"Father?"

No-Chance opened his eyes to intense sunlight. Quickly, he squeezed them shut. No! His father was buried! Home was nothing but ashes, long ago melted into Georgian soil.

Still the crow called.

He squinted again. A man's dark form blocked the offending brilliance. Maybe his father was calling him home to heaven.

"Father?"

The fuzzy image became sharper as it bent over

him. "My brother will not join ancestors on this day."

"Chickamauga?" No-Chance pushed to his elbows and grimaced at the aches that came alive. "What happened?"

Crows fussed, dogs barked, and in the distance, children shouted and laughed. No-Chance shielded his eyes to stare at the people surrounding him. Body paint smeared and braids unraveled, the hunters shifted their stance or leaned forward on their mounts.

"Drink." Kneeling, Chickamauga tipped a skin of water to his lips.

The water tasted of leather. With each swallow, No-Chance's mind cleared. He sat up. "Where's my horse?"

"Thunder runs where grass always green." Chickamauga nodded, and several warriors stepped back, opening the circle.

A few yards away, the roan's smooth shiny coat glistened golden red in the sun, his head in an awkward twist. A yellow-shafted arrow with black feathers protruded from his shoulder.

Pain radiated down No-Chance's leg as he struggled to stand. Blood oozed from a shallow gash across his thigh. Was the arrow that grazed his leg meant for him or the horse? He limped to the roan. Dried blood coursed a path across the horse's shoulder and down its breast to congeal on the ground. He jerked the arrow free and held it up.

"Whose is it?" He spun around. "What son-of-a-coyote, what dung heap, what belly crawling snake did this?"

The gathered warriors looked at each other. Some backed away.

His voice rose as he snapped the arrow shaft in two pieces. "What slug of a man hides behind a hunt to strike another man?"

The Comanche greeted his rage with silence.

No-Chance searched the solemn-painted faces of the warriors for some sign they recognized the arrow. Was it shame he read in their eyes? Yes. Here, where the buffalo meant survival, a good horse was valued over a wife. These warriors might not understand his words, but they would understand his actions. He held the yellow shaft up, cleared his throat, and spit. A rope of glistening spit dripped from the feathers.

As if hypnotized, the circle of men stood motionless and watched the breeze stretch the saliva to mere threads before breaking.

Approaching riders broke the spell. Crazy Bear led Parlin-wah-pit and Good Talker toward the gathering.

"I sent Little Brother for Good-Talker," Chickamauga said. "Do not let anger blind your eyes." Strands of black hair, loosened from the single braid down his back, stuck to his face. "We are guests in this nation. Their ways are strange to us."

Chickamauga was right. He was always right. No-Chance clenched his teeth and waited for Parlin-wah-pit to slide from his horse. Good-Talker's brass buttons clattered as he dismounted and bent to run his hand down the roan's neck.

Voice even, No-Chance swallowed the rage threatening to choke him. "Whose arrow?" The feathered end of the broken shaft twirled between his fingers before he dropped it at Parlin-wah-pit's feet.

"What black-hearted dog did this thing?" No-Chance shouted into the crowd as he scanned the solemn faces. The snicker of horses multiplied as the crowd grew. They knew. They all knew.

Good-Talker translated the demand.

Frowning, Parlin-wah-pit fingered the medicine bag hanging from his neck with one hand. "*Pac* Iseeo."

"What did he say?" No-Chance looked at Good-Talker. "Is this Iseeo's arrow?"

Purple-black feathers bobbed in the old man's hair as he nodded.

"Tell Iseeo only a coward shoots a man's horse from under him and hopes the fall will do his dirty work." No-Chance searched the crowd of painted Indians for his yellow-faced opponent. "Tell him if he wants to fight like a man, I'm ready."

Good-Talker's voice was calm, steady, and No-Chance wondered if the old man's translation was word for word. A murmur fluttered through the ring of Indians. Several riders sidestepped their ponies allowing Iseeo to pass into the circle.

The Indian's yellow face paint streaked in the heat like drips from a tallow candle. He reined his appaloosa in front of No-Chance. Scalps attached to the bridle danced in the hot breeze.

"Does the great Iseeo always battle horses or only men with their hands tied behind their backs?" No-Chance crossed his arms and stared at the leering Comanche while Good-Talker translated.

A smile snaked up one side of Iseeo's face revealing teeth the color of sun-parched prairie grass. With a forced laugh, he addressed the other mounted warriors.

The foreign words had hardly been spoken, before Good-Talker repeated, "Iseeo say black buffalo his.

You run horse in front of arrow."

"It's a weasel-hearted lie." No-Chance sputtered. "A lie!"

Iseeo continued his taunting laugh, head high, boasting to other warriors.

Good-Talker pursed his lips and turned to No-Chance. "Iseeo say, not afraid of man who comes into Comancheria land."

"And I say it's a woman-hearted coward that sits atop his horse bragging." No-Chance rested his hand on the knife at his waist.

Before Good-Talker could repeat the threat, a voice rang out. Everyone turned to watch a young man slide off the back of a spotted pony, his ankle swollen large as a gourd, beaded braids draping his shoulders. He talked in short rapid sentences, sweeping his hand from the hill to the dead roan.

Parlin-wah-pit and Good-Talker interrupted the speaker several times to ask questions.

No-Chance resisted the urge to smile. Of course, who had a better view of the hunt than the injured Comanche he rescued and left on the hillside.

Iseeo's eyes narrowed as he slid from his horse.

Good-Talker turned from the argument. "Stone Bird say you have brave heart. Grab him when fall. Big horse fearless, like bear. Fly like eagle in chase for black buffalo."

The old Indian continued to nod and listen to Parlin-wah-pit argue with Iseeo.

No-Chance glanced at Crazy Bear and Chickamauga standing, weapons in hand. He'd encouraged the hunt, been glad they'd stayed. Now he'd loosened his tongue and put them in danger.

"Parlin-wah-pit say blood of guests not spill in camp. Hear women wail. Sing death song. No have fight." Good-Talker scratched his head. "Aim poor. Iseeo give you his horse."

Eyes narrowing, Iseeo threw the appaloosa's reins to the ground.

No-Chance crossed his arms again. "Tell him my roan was worth a dozen of his ponies."

Good-Talker relayed the demand.

Iseeo glared, nostrils flaring, and stomped, rawhide strips swinging at his legs, to another rider and mounted behind him.

The circle of Comanche drifted away. Good-Talker and Parlin-wah-pit helped strip the roan of its bridle and trappings. Crazy Bear and Chickamauga gathered branches to build a funeral pyre.

No-Chance retrieved the reins of Iseeo's buffalo horse and scratched its muzzle. His heart felt as black as the thick smoke that spiraled into the afternoon sky.

Chapter 32

"Aaragh!" The cords on Crazy Bear's neck bulged as he strained to push a huge bull onto its belly. The movement of hundreds of pounds of flesh forced evacuation of the animal's bowels. The three men groaned at the stink.

"We should have brought Chade," Crazy Bear gasped. "Women don't mind this sort of thing."

"How can this be woman's work?" No-Chance muttered as he wrestled the heavy head to upright the horns. He dug through the deep mat of fur and cut around the neck to meet the incision made across the brisket. "Chickamauga, are you sure this is right? I never skinned a deer like this."

Chickamauga straddled the hump of the buffalo. "You see a deer this big?" Nettles and burrs, caught in the shaggy mane, scratched his arms as he dug his hands into the incision. "Bear, we pull. No-Chance, release the hide."

Blood and juices oozed and squirted with each slice of the knife. Slick to his elbows, No-Chance hacked the forelegs off at the joints. His long braids dipped into seeping fluids.

"We must hurry." Chickamauga wiped sweat from his eyes with his forearm and glanced up at the afternoon sun. He grunted with the effort to split the hide down the middle of the spine. "With my two bulls...Bear's two...your one, we have much to trade at Edwards' Post."

No-Chance tossed his head, flipping his braids back, slinging droplets of blood into the air. "What do you mean, my one? I got two!"

Chickamauga smiled, wiped his face, and struggled to strip the hide on one side. "I do not count calf. We keep for Tampa."

"Yes. The best for Tampa." No-Chance ran his blade under the hide on the other side and peeled it back. Blood dripped from the knife as he pointed to the animal's rump. "Take the tail, Bear. You will be the only Creek in Black Storm's village with a buffalo fly swatter."

Crazy Bear batted at several of the buzzing insects annoying them. He walked to the back of the glistening carcass and slipped in the manure pile.

Several boys, watching from their ponies laughed and held their noses.

With a rolling growl, Crazy Bear sprang toward the riders, waving his arms over his head. The horses shied at the sudden threat, eliciting another peel of laughter from the youngsters. They wheeled about and galloped down the valley.

Dead buffalo littered the meadow like giant lumps of dirt. Women straightened from their work to scold and wag their fingers at dust stirred by the fleeing riders.

Crazy Bear huffed back. "It not good for spirit of man to be mocked by skinny-legged pups!" He pounded his bare chest and shouted after the long-gone boys. "I have killed twenty bears!" He threw his head back and roared.

"Twenty bears?" No-Chance lifted one eyebrow.

The stocky Indian glared.

"Sometimes what man does to feed family does not require courage," Chickamauga said. "Those boys…no more than nits on head of old women."

A whiff of foul air burped through an incision as No-Chance drove his knife into the flank of the skinned buffalo. He wrinkled his nose and continued slicing until the side completely opened.

Slick and shiny, the intestines slipped through the opening, sliding onto his knees. He tried to ignore the warm fluids that bubbled out as he cut away the flank. Freed, the entrails continued to unfold like a tangle of worms disturbed in a spade of dirt. No-Chance scooted back out of the bloody pool. The odorous mountain of gut, organs and stomach pouch advanced toward him.

He jumped up and slapped at the flies drawn to the blood coating his arms. Warm juices ran down his leg into his moccasins as he turned and hobbled off.

Chickamauga stopped pegging the hide onto the ground. "Where you go?"

No-Chance glanced back at his two brothers. Their hair hung in limp strands. Gore dripped from their fingers. Sweat glistened on their bare chests.

"To get us some women."

****

With a final hack of his knife, Chickamauga broke the last rib steak away from the spine of his large bull and handed it to Crazy Bear. He put his hands on his lower back and stretched. The once-glistening mass of the great beast's entrails had lost its rich color. Any fresh breeze entering the valley became tainted with the stench of bloody carnage.

Hundreds of wooden frames, erected beside the numerous carcasses, were strung with strips of meat drying in the sun. Dogs growled and fought over scraps thrown their way. Joyful voices of playing children could be heard above the buzz of those that worked.

Leading a group of women, No-Chance stopped at one bull with legs splayed out. He put his foot on the rump and removed the feathered lance that marked the buffalo as Chickamauga's. Several women fell to work with their knives. He continued limping toward another animal and extracted two arrows. Two more women fell to work.

"Ho, brothers!" No-Chance grinned as he marched at the head of his band of skinners. "I told you I'd bring us some women!"

Chickamauga wiped his blade through the grass and studied the four women. Only Maria, with her hand covering her nose, looked to be less than twenty summers.

"Experience is good," he said. "These old mothers are sorry for us?"

"No. They are without husbands, without sons. Maria came to translate." No-Chance watched gray-haired women pick over bones with bits of flesh clinging to them. "They will help us for a share of meat." He handed the retrieved arrows to Chickamauga. "And they will share one of the hides."

Crazy Bear stood. "It is good. We should do man's work, not crawl on knees. Give them two hides. The trail of the great beast is wide."

Frowning and clucking her disapproval, one woman pushed Chickamauga away from the carcass and drew her knife. She pointed at the large woolly head severed from the body. With a few quick slashes, she removed the fat tongue and held it up. Blood dripped down a thin arm covered with numerous scars attesting to the grief she'd inflicted upon herself.

"Cut tongue first," Maria said. "Leave heart for buffalo spirit."

No-Chance nodded and repeated her instructions. "Bear, you take these two and go find your other bull. Chickamauga, you need to build racks for drying. I will take Maria and this old mother." He put his hand on the shoulder of an elderly woman with strips of colored fabric fluttering from her hair. "We'll find my cow and its calf."

Soon, the heady smell of burning buffalo chips and roasting meat mingled with the stench of death and hung like a low cloud over the valley. Exhausted, No-Chance surveyed the rickety drying rack he'd constructed. It would have to do.

The old woman, Walks-With-A-Limp, muttered to herself as she shaved thin strips of meat from a large slab and hung them along the rack's crooked branches.

No-Chance stretched his sore leg out and watched Maria scrape bits of skin from the cow's pegged hide. She didn't grease her hair like the rest of the women, and it danced in the breeze, curling and unfurling about her head.

Maria glanced at him, covering her face with one hand. She got up and walked around the hide so her back was to him, knelt, and resumed working. The motion had a rhythm to it, as she rocked back and forth. He sighed. Might as well ask the question nagging to be answered.

"Maria, why were you punished?"

She stopped, arm stretched across the hide. For a few moments she didn't move. Finally, she sat back, head bent, hair curtained forward.

"I foolish woman. I believe trader come from Santa Fe. He say, take me to Papa if I lay with him." She sniffed. "What else I have? Night before he leave…I go to him."

She wiped her eyes with one arm. "I foolish, but he stupid. He mount me like coyote and howl pleasure to moon." Maria turned. Dark eyes defiant, she pushed her hair back, shielding her face with one hand. "We discovered. I lost tip of nose to betrayal. Trader lost more."

Chapter 33

The spotted mare from the North Country banished flies from her flanks with a lazy swish of her tail and side-stepped an attempt to harness her. No-Chance dropped his bridle with the silver disks. For now, a rope would have to do. He ran his hand down the horse's arched neck, combing fingers through the long black mane, and continued his inspection—narrow withers, straight legs not splayed or knock-kneed, hooves in line with the first joint.

"Iseeo's blue horse not like taste of metal." Chickamauga stood, balancing a bow in need of repair on one shoulder. Wind stirred strands of hair about his face.

"No, but she will." No-Chance retrieved the discarded bridle and stepped back to survey his new possession. The horse bore a deep blue coat that shimmered in the sun and faded to a blue-spotted gray on her rump and flanks. "She does not belong to Iseeo now. I hope he remembers that fact." They surveyed the herd of ponies, some grazing or rolling in dust circles, none taller than the blue horse.

"Old men say Iseeo travel many suns for this Palouse. He will not forget her," Chickamauga said, following No-Chance toward the hunting camp. The smell of roasting corn and meat, honeyed pecan bread, and stewing grapes greeted them as they wove their way around drying-racks and scattered tents.

Chickamauga paused at a circle of old men, in the process of repairing a variety of weapons, and held up the cracked bow. Several nodded, shifting to make room for him. In their midst, a small kettle of hoofs simmered above a fire. Waving away the smoke and fumes, No-Chance squatted to watch Chickamauga dip into the pot with a wad of buffalo hair and spread a layer of hot glue along a thin split in the bow.

"In a few sleeps, the women will finish their work on the hides. The tribe will move on to another hunt." No-Chance fingered the bundles of dogwood shafts waiting to be fitted with arrow points and feathers. "Bear will want to follow the hunt. Even now, he practices with boys wanting to be warriors."

"We have much meat. Bear should think of home." Chickamauga held the bow securely on either side of the repaired crack and blew wisps of steam away.

"Our brother thinks only of the hunt." No-Chance stood, glancing at a knot of Comanche men, heads together, jeering each other while playing a game with bone pieces. "I will find Good-Talker. Tell him we go home when the hides are finished."

Chickamauga nodded. "It is good. I am missing our son."

"Walks-with-a-Limp makes baskets for the meat." No-Chance looked down at the bridle in his hands and sighed. "It seems the old mother likes silver disks." He turned and followed the meandering path toward their campsite, past men relaxing with pipes or gathered in conversation. Some looked up and nodded. Others looked away. Always, he kept watch for Iseeo. The man had been missing for several days. Only a fool loses track of an enemy.

Their campsite, filled with the chatter of women working hides, hummed with activity. Grinning, Walks-with-a-Limp struggled to her feet and motioned No-Chance forward to see her handiwork. Hands mapped with dozens of tiny cuts, she lifted a large flat-sided basket and tucked the end of a broad stem back into the loose weave.

"Walks-with-a-Limp does good work," No-Chance said, knowing the woman would not understand his compliment. It did not matter. The old woman cackled with delight as he worked four disks along the leather reins. One for each basket.

He turned his attention to Maria and watched her wrap the scraped hide of the calf around a slender tree and pull on each side, stretching the leather into shape. The breeze played with her loose hair, fanning it into a thousand strands.

One disk left on the bridle. He fingered it for a moment, then slid it free and touched Maria on the shoulder. "Here," he said.

Maria released the pelt, allowing it to sag to the ground. She turned the disk in her palm, finally lifting it between her thumb and forefinger and held it over the spot where the tip of her nose should be. She laughed then, and No-Chance realized he'd never heard joy in her voice or seen her smile.

He would miss the silver ornaments. Little by little, pieces of his past disappeared into the hands of others. He wished bad memories would disappear as well.

"Ahh." Good-Talker beamed when No-Chance found the old man's tent. "Is good day. Scouts find many buffalo two rides west. When snows come, cooking pots full. Today, I learn you kill like Comanche."

"Today?" No-Chance frowned. "I came to tell Good-Talker that to hunt with him has been a great honor. We have much meat. My family will not be hungry this winter. I am thinking, my brothers and I—"

Good-Talker thrust a lance at No-Chance. "We go make horses ready. Scouts find old bull and two cows in canyon of little springs. Brother of No-Chance and my sons go find. They practice kill." Good-Talker pointed toward the herd of horses. "Come, we go, too."

"Bear is gone?" No-Chance grabbed the lance. "I'll get my saddle and meet you."

****

Leather creaked as No-Chance shifted his weight to lean forward and stroke the Palouse's neck. The blue horse seemed nervous, throwing her head, snorting, but she tolerated his weight. After a few tries, she'd even accepted the bridle. Without the disks, it was lighter, without music. Maybe that was a good thing.

He and Good-Talker rested atop their horses on a treeless rise. In the valley below, Crazy Bear and the old man's two sons raced with a group of other boys, separating two cows from a lone bull with piercing yells and flapping blankets. Circling the confused beasts and turning them from one direction to another, the riders herded the cows toward the springs at the back of the canyon where there could be no escape.

"To make kill, ride behind, right side of buffalo." Good-Talker dismounted and squatted to draw a humped animal in the dirt. "Here, this spot, weapon must go deep, rob buffalo of breath." He stabbed the end of his stick into the proper location. "Back here," his bony finger tapped the rump of the sketch, "no good."

Shrill voices, not yet mature, shrieked in imitation of their elder's whoops. Good-Talker laughed and pointed. "See, they not afraid."

No-Chance watched the would-be warriors ride up to the old bull and poke at him with their lances or loosen an arrow. At each fresh wound, the black beast bellowed and hooked his horns toward his attacker. Nimble ponies darted away, carrying their riders to safety.

"Some woman will be doing a heap of mending on that poor hide," No-Chance muttered.

Good-Talker smiled and scratched his head, sending the feathers into a frenzy of movement. "That one most honored. With him, boys learn spirit of buffalo. Be brave when close. Feel hot breath, smell anger. Buffalo is life of Comanche. Must respect, not fear life."

The Palouse's mane rippled down the length of her neck. She snorted and pawed at the ground. No-Chance pulled the reins tight, forcing the mare's head up and scratched behind her ear.

Good Talker continued, "See, boys circle and strike from behind. Remember, no can kill from front."

Crazy Bear's strong howl of delight was clearly audible above the younger boys' voices. He grew nearer and nearer the enraged animal with each taunting pass. A deep uneasiness settled over No-Chance as he watched the stout Indian's growing confidence.

Blood streamed down the sides and hind legs of the large animal. He swung his massive head from side to side. Crazy Bear circled to the rear of the beast, stood in the stirrups and roared.

No-Chance's muscles tensed as he watched his brother spur his horse. This charge was different. Even Good-Talker felt it and stood to watch.

Crazy Bear bent to the left, and the horse followed his lead, throwing dirt clods as he raced in next to the lumbering beast. Crazy Bear hurled his lance forward into the buffalo's withers and yanked his horse away from the slashing horns.

Staggering, the beast faltered and collapsed onto his knees. Crazy Bear trotted his pony back and reached to retract his weapon.

Good-Talker shouted something in Comanche and turned toward his pony. "Not dead!" He shook his head, "Not dead!"

No-Chance jerked his attention back to the meadow and nudged the Palouse down the incline.

Holding his lance, Crazy Bear sat atop his horse, pumping his arm up and down, roaring his victory.

The bull pushed his hindquarters up, then struggled onto his front legs as his massive body trembled.

"No!" No-Chance's shout echoed in his ears, resounded throughout the canyon, bouncing off the sides, and multiplied into a hundred warnings. In horror, he watched Crazy Bear's horse rear at the buffalo's sudden lunge.

Unseated, Crazy Bear scrambled to face his attacker.

"Run!" No-Chance shouted, whipping the reins from side to side.

Crazy Bear stood his ground.

Long strings of bloody spittle swung from the beast's mouth. Head down, he plunged forward.

As Crazy Bear leaped up and over the animal's large head, a horn hooked his thigh, nearly tossing him to the ground. He struggled to stay astride the animal's hump.

The old buffalo lurched from side to side.

Crazy Bear fell, rolling beneath the buffalo's hooves.

Good-Talker's young son charged his horse at the buffalo to distract him. The horse shied, and the boy tumbled backwards. For what seemed an eternity, the huge animal trembled. With a loud bellow, he gathered strength and began a faltering charge. The boy scrambled to his feet and ran a zigzag path toward the hill.

Good-Talker's words rang in No-Chance's ears, "Remember, no can kill from front." Without taking his eyes off the thundering animal, his fingers fumbled with the thin rawhide that held the black snake whip to his saddle horn. With powerful strides, the mare closed the distance between them and the thundering avalanche. No-Chance stood in the stirrups, played the whip out behind him, and snapped his wrist.

The buffalo lowered his head at the boy's back. The whip sliced through the air and wrapped around a weathered horn. No-Chance jerked back on the reins, causing the mare to rear and dig her heels in the ground.

The whip handle tore from No-Chance's hand and sailed forward smacking the charging animal in the eye. The weakened buffalo faltered, falling on one knee, before rolling headfirst into the ground.

Good-Talker raced past and snatched his son out of the path of the animal's tumble.

With loud moans, the old buffalo lay in a bloody

mass. Half a dozen arrows thudded into the great heaving body. Good-Talker lowered his son, walked his pony back, and circled the beast. He thrust his lance deep into the animal's side, behind the last rib, and ended its misery.

"There." He looked at the panting boys and commanded, "There is where you kill buffalo."

The ominous vision No-Chance had secretly harbored for the past month filled his head and seized his chest in a tight grip as he trotted back to his brother's crumpled form. Why had he let Crazy Bear out of his sight?

Blood poured from a gaping tear in Crazy Bear's thigh. He clutched his ribs, gasping for breath.

No-Chance dropped to his knees and pressed on the wound. Blood oozed, warm and sticky, between his fingers.

"Why? Why didn't you run?"

Crazy Bear coughed, splattering droplets of blood. Voice raspy, he grimaced. "A man looks his death in the eye."

Chapter 34

Inside the lodge, a small fire made heat oppressive. Walks-With-A-Limp rocked back and forth as she squatted next to Crazy Bear's prone body. Her cheeks bulged with a hunk of chewed pouip root. She nodded at No-Chance, and he lifted a soiled rag from the deep wound in Crazy Bear's thigh. Blood oozed with the release of pressure and seeped over purple ridges of torn skin.

Crazy Bear gasped when the old woman leaned forward and spit a mouthful of juice inside the gaping injury. With a loud hacking noise, she discarded the chewed wad onto the dirt floor and began the process again.

Sweat trickled down No-Chance's forehead as he knelt and stanched the flow of blood. He wiped his face in the crook of his arm and glanced at Chickamauga, cradling Crazy Bear's head in his lap. They had been here before, the two of them, hoping to stay death from a loved one.

A shaft of light cut through the haze of smoke in the lodge as Parlin-wah-pit opened the entrance flap and peered inside. The tall Comanche bent to enter, his arms full of green foliage. He laid a cedar branch on the smoldering fire, causing it to sputter and crackle. Within minutes, the lodge filled with a clean fragrance. Parlin-wah-pit hummed while he waved white smoke over each of them, purifying the air of evil beings.

A fresh round of coughing caused Crazy Bear to clutch his ribs. Bloody froth bubbled between his lips.

No-Chance knew that one or more of the long curved bones protecting the heart and lungs had been broken. That alone would not kill a man. There were other injuries that could not be seen. He lifted the bloodied rag to let Walks-With-A-Limp deposit another mouthful of pouip juice into the wound.

Good-Talker sat outside, chanting a medicine song and shaking a gourd full of buffalo teeth. Buffalo magic was powerful. Crazy Bear had been brave and faced the great beast. Such a man would not die, Good-Talker assured them.

A simple belief. No-Chance knew better. Brave men died all the time.

He studied the amulets and bundles of feathers and bones that old men brought to the tent throughout the afternoon. They sat with Good-Talker, each one confident that their medicine would help—a basket of whippoorwill feathers to fool the night spirits, an eagle talon for strength, a bag of deer hooves to chase away fever.

A stuffed crow hung from a pole in the center of the lodge. The bird stirred any time the tent flap lifted allowing fresh air to circulate. Black onyx replaced its eyes.

No-Chance shivered at the cold stare the dead crow fixed on him.

"Father, I failed," he whispered. "I promised to take care of Bear. Surely you have the ear of our Lord. Plead for the life of this simple servant."

A shaft of light and air intruded, moving the bird

and breaking the trance. Maria entered carrying a basket of prickly pear leaves.

Walks-With-A-Limp nudged No-Chance with her elbow and leaned into him with her ample body, pushing him away.

Maria put a hand on his shoulder. "You can do no more for your brother. Walks-with-a-Limp is a healer and knows many cures."

No-Chance sagged back on his heels. He had not been able to save his mother. He had not saved White Cloud, Tampa's mother. He nodded and joined Parlin-wah-pit at the back of the lodge.

Walks-With-A-Limp sorted through the basket for the largest prickly pear leaf and split it lengthwise, laying it open. Thick juices glistened across the cut surface. The old woman positioned the raw sides of the leaf over the wound.

Maria tore the end off a faded blanket and helped wrap the woolen strip around Crazy Bear's swollen leg. She looked over her shoulder at No-Chance. The silver disk, held in place over her nose with a leather strip threaded through the holes on either side and tied at the back of her head, glinted dully in the soft light.

"*Suvate*. It is finished," she said. "We wait."

No-Chance closed his eyes and leaned back against the tightly-stretched tent hide. Good-Talker had grown hoarse singing the monotonous chant. Words from an ancient age, when spirits had form and sat shoulder to shoulder with mortals. Words for which the meanings had been lost in the passage of time. No one doubted their strength.

The soft clatter of shells and bones interrupted his thoughts, and he opened his eyes to Parlin-wah-pit's pensive stare. The Comanche sat cross-legged, fingering the beaded bag hanging among the feathers and bones on his necklace. No-Chance touched his own leather sack containing the glittering jewels. He would give them all for Crazy Bear's life. How could he explain that these stones didn't really have any power? At least not the kind Parlin-wah-pit thought.

"They have no power at all," he murmured aloud.

The old woman paused in the process of bathing Crazy Bear's flushed face and looked up.

Parlin-wah-pit frowned in his attempt to understand.

No-Chance cleared his throat. "My brother's power comes from the bear." He formed his hands into claws and growled. "Power. *Puha*, from the bear." He stretched forward and lifted the claw necklace. It clunked heavily in his hand, wicked reminders of Crazy Bear's bravery.

In that instant, despair smothered No-Chance, and he bolted from the tent.

Outside, the horizon flared a faint orange with the setting sun. Several elderly men joined Good-Talker in his continuous chant, accompanied now by the soft thuds of a deer hide drum. A slow, measured cadence marked the passing time.

Lodges, illuminated by interior campfires, glowed softly. The aroma of boiling pots of stew and corncakes heating on flat stones, wafted in the breeze. The village was quiet, waiting. They waited to see which spirit was strongest—bear or buffalo.

Chickamauga stepped from the tent and hunched his shoulders. He shook his head. "The night will be long."

No-Chance rubbed his face and took a deep breath. "My soul grew weary and wished for the excitement of a hunt. I promised the safety of our careless brother. Chade warned me. She had a vision that only two men would return. We should have stayed home."

"A vision?" Chickamauga crossed his arms and took a deep breath. "Our brother would come searching for buffalo alone. You could not hold him behind a plow."

No-Chance shook his head. "It is more than that. I fear death follows me. I lost one family. I don't want to lose another."

Chickamauga studied the dark sky. Tiny pinpricks of light fluttered through a thin veil of clouds. "Only the rocks live forever," he said with a sigh and led the way back into the lodge.

In the darkest hour of the night, when the moon descended in the sky, No-Chance arched his back to relieve aching muscles. He sat next to Crazy Bear, ready to do battle with the specter of death, the thief that came on silent feet. This time, the unwelcome intruder would be cheated of his prize.

Crazy Bear coughed, bringing up a mouthful of bloody spit. No-Chance dipped a rag into a bowl of sage-scented water and wiped his brother's scarred face. Two purple-rimmed hoof prints danced on Bear's heaving chest as he gasped for air.

Store of medicines exhausted, Walks-With-A-Limp and Maria abandoned the vigil, promising to return with first light. Good-Talker and Parlin-wah-pit dozed outside, wrapped in their buffalo robes. Drums and whistles were still. Even the night singers, wolves and coyotes, kept silent counsel. It was as if the whole world was listening to the ragged breathing that filled the lodge.

Chickamauga fed twigs into the smoldering coals. Sputtering flames bathed his face in a golden light. The renewed fire gave life to the shadows that hugged the edges of darkness.

No-Chance tensed as he watched dark forms dance along the sides of the hide wall. Was this how death came creeping in? Vague images that rose in victory, only to fall again, writhing about in the flames.

Bear groaned as he struggled up on one elbow. "Help Chade," he rasped, and then collapsed in a fit of coughing. Bright red blood tinged his teeth, and he wallowed his tongue trying to spit.

"Yes. Chade will laugh when you tell her how you danced with the buffalo." No-Chance slipped an arm under Crazy Bear's back and lifted, cradling him against one shoulder. "Here, drink this," he said, dipping a buffalo horn into a tea of boiled mullein roots. "Old mother says it will ease the cough. Then, you sleep."

Bear shook his head and whispered, "I must see owl spirit when he comes for me." His breath, rancid with the stink of fever and blood, filled the air. No-Chance dropped the horn and wrapped both arms around him. Spilled tea sizzled against hot stones surrounding the campfire, sending up puffs of steam.

"The owl spirit will not find you. I will pluck out his eyes. It is not time to die."

"I do not die." Crazy Bear's gravelly voice held a touch of reproach, "I travel…to another land." Tears pooled along the rims of his glassy eyes as he forced out each word. "I go…hunt with father…and father before him. My gone-away son…waits." He stretched his neck, turtle-like, and whispered, "One day…we hunt together…again."

No-Chance buried his face in Crazy Bear's matted hair. "Yes," he whispered, "yes, we will hunt together again." He hugged the man that had become a brother and rocked back and forth.

A gust of wind lifted the tent flap, and the fire bore new life, sending a wisp of smoke spiraling upward. No-Chance felt the body in his arms relax, grow limp. His skin bristled as a chill washed over him.

The sudden silence was deafening.

Chickamauga pulled a blanket over his head and chanted until emotion choked him into silence.

Outside, Good-Talker took up the chant. His voice floated out into the pre-dawn darkness, announcing the death of a brave warrior. In the distance, a wolf answered with a lonely howl.

Chapter 35

"…in their deaths they were swifter than eagles, they were stronger than lions." Remembering one of his father's favorite Biblical verses, No-Chance buried his head in his hands and slumped forward, elbows on his knees. Crazy Bear had not feared death, had gone bravely into the dark land. Yet, it was senseless. The old bull was not an enemy, not even needed for food.

"It would be honor for bones of brother to rest with Comanche ancestors."

No-Chance looked up at Good-Talker, who stood with the early morning sun behind him. In the light, shiny feathers in the old man's hair shimmered in hues of blue and purple.

"No, we will take our brother home." No-Chance stood and reached a hand to help Chickamauga up. "I promised…" Voice cracking, he swallowed the lump in his throat. "I promised we would all return."

Good-Talker nodded. "Spirit of brother lives in place of death. My woman, wrap body in tent. You take home." He turned and motioned for his number-one wife.

The plump woman hurried forward and wiggled the tent pegs out of the ground with one foot and bent to enter the lodge. Her broad bottom filled the entrance as she backed out pulling one of the long lodge poles through the opening. With a swoosh, the tent collapsed.

Chickamauga helped her fold the edge of the heavy tent back exposing Crazy Bear's body to daylight. An ashen pallor replaced the fevered blush of the previous night, while his bare chest blossomed a rainbow of gruesome bruises.

Chickamauga backed away.

"Go. Bring our horses," No-Chance said and put a hand on Chickamauga's shoulder. "I will make our brother ready for his journey to the dark land. You must make us ready for a different journey."

Chickamauga nodded, and No-Chance watched him walk, head lowered, one shoulder slumped, toward the horse pasture. It would not be right to ask Chickamauga's help. The Creeks believed that unless they were blood-related, death visited those who touched the dead. He had no such belief.

Good-Talker and his wife shooed away several young boys who stopped to stare at the corpse, mouth agape, hands stiffened into claws. Around them the village stirred as women banged cooking pots, collapsed tents, and loaded horses with mountains of buffalo meat. Somewhere in all the activity, an old man chanted his greeting to the new day.

"There is one more thing, I ask," No-Chance said to the couple. "A pot of red paint." He knelt next to the body and tamed Bear's wild unkempt hair down, tucking the ends behind his ears. The three long scars, revered by the Comanche, stood out as puckered ridges.

Good-Talker squatted next to him and held out a clay bowl.

With a deep breath, No-Chance dipped into the bowl with three fingers. A shiver ran down his back as he smoothed a mud-like coat of red paint over Bear's clammy face. Bracing himself, he pulled Bear on top of the canvas tent and folded one side over his friend, forever shutting away the sun.

Good-Talker laid Bear's blood-crusted lance and knife into the fold along with the horns of the black buffalo, and they rolled the tent around the body into a tightly-tied bundle.

Chickamauga returned with their horses and busied himself fashioning a sturdy travois from the long lodge poles. The journey home would be burdened with more than jerky-stuffed baskets.

After leaving offerings of corn cakes, dried berries, and pemmican at the campsite, Walks-with-a-Limp and the old women patted the bundle farewell. One by one, they joined the passing procession.

Parlin-wah-pit reined his horse and dismounted in a single fluid movement. Long twisted silver earrings swung with the motion. The scalps hanging from his belt flapped against his leg as he walked. He studied the loaded travois.

No-Chance cleared his throat and held both hands up, locking two forefingers together in a sign of friendship.

The Panther returned the greeting and tapped the medicine bag suspended about his neck.

"Ho, friend ready go now?" Good-Talker, button necklace flashing in the sun, halted his horse beside Parlin-wah-pit. "See," Good-Talker continued, pointing to a group of four crows startled from scavenging a trash heap. "Buffalo hunt be good. Birds show us way."

The large black birds circled before flying off toward the west. One broke away, circled again, and rounded to the east. Good-Talker turned to watch the lone crow disappear in the glare of the sun. "Maybe buffalo that way, too."

No-Chance shook his head. "That one shows me the way home."

The old Indian scratched his feathered head. "Good-Talker all time remember Seminoli friend. Oldest son tell children how blue-eyed man save him with rope that sings." He grinned. "Son have new name. Him called, Runs-from-Buffalo." He leaned across his horse. "You hunt with Comanche again someday."

Without waiting for a reply, he waved and disappeared into the line of villagers along with Parlin-wah-pit.

Bells jangled on passing horses. Children clad in breechclouts laughed as they darted between riders.

No-Chance kicked at several dogs sniffing the bundle on the travois.

Within minutes the camp was abandoned. Only large dirt rings and blackened campfire sites marked their assembly.

Chickamauga and No-Chance watched the tribe disappear behind rolling hills until the snorting of their own horses, as they swished their tails at nipping insects, was all that kept them company.

No-Chance gathered the lead ropes of the heavily-packed horses.

"Look." Chickamauga jutted his chin in the direction of the Comanche.

On the far ridge, a lone rider pranced his horse back and forth. He held his lance aloft, shaking it. A bone-chilling *whoop* resounded through the empty valley before the rider disappeared.

Chapter 36

The valley of the buffalo stampede, calm and serene in the noonday sun, stretched before Chickamauga and No-Chance. New grasses covered the churned ground. A meadowlark chirruped from a scrubby acacia bush. Only the huge upturned trunk of the dead sycamore tree gave testimony to the violent, panic-stricken flight of the great beasts weeks before.

Chickamauga nudged his horse down the slight incline, leading Crazy Bear's sorrel. The heavy travois supporting their brother's thickly-wrapped body stirred insects as it bumped along the ground. Boat-tailed grackles, disturbed from their feeding, flew up before the advancing horses.

No-Chance fanned the air in frustration. A feeling, persistent and ominous, refused to leave him. He clucked to the string of horses and urged the Palouse around the travois and up beside Chickamauga. They approached the sycamore, each man lost in memories.

A woodpecker, searching for bugs under the crumbling bark, took flight. Long tenuous roots of the upturned tree flayed in the warm breeze as if searching for the ground. A broken buffalo skull had tumbled from the pile stacked by Good-Talker after the stampede.

No-Chance halted the blue horse and slid down. He ran his hand over the rough tree trunk, remembering the mad scramble into the protection of its limbs. Retrieving the skull, he brushed dirt from the faded paint and traced a finger along the maze of cracks. Crazy Bear's laughter at finding the tree of skulls seemed to whistle in the wind.

"Let us go from this valley of thundering hooves."

"Yes." No-Chance glanced up at Chickamauga. "It will be good to be far away before nightfall." He shielded his eyes from the sun and scanned the direction they had traveled. An apprehension that had been growing all afternoon returned.

With a sigh, he replaced the skull atop the stack of bones and mounted. If for no other reason than to retrieve the prized Palouse, Iseeo would follow. The hatred in the surly Indian's manner promised revenge.

Heat waves distorted the dry prairie grass on the rolling plain. Nothing stirred in the oppressive afternoon sun. Saddle leather creaked as No-Chance shifted his weight and wished for the black hat lost to the stampede. Once he glimpsed a young boy wearing his beaten hat, tattered eagle feather twisting in the air, and resisted the urge to claim it. Let the boy experience Grandfather's medicine.

He turned in the saddle again and scanned the low hills. In the far distance a flock of birds flew up, circled, and one by one descended again.

"Chickamauga."

"I see. The crooked-tooth warrior wants your scalp. He will be sorry. It is stringy and smells of buffalo grease."

"Ho, you think yours would look finer at his belt?" No-Chance fingered the handle of his Celtic knife. "I figure two, maybe three, will think to get their buffalo hides the easy way." He looked back at three heavily-packed horses loaded with heaping baskets of dried meat and four fine robes folded into packs.

Chickamauga nodded and jutted his chin toward a thick line of trees on the horizon. "We make stand there. They come on silent feet. Grandmother Moon will be skinny this night."

No-Chance opened the flap of his saddlebag and pulled out an object wrapped in aged buckskin. Good-Talker, thankful his son escaped the black horns of the old bull, had given up his prized war ax. The wood handle was hard, rubbed shiny with the oil of many hands. No-Chance lightly fingered the nicked blade. How many battles had this weapon seen; how many skulls, cracked? He tucked the tomahawk in his belt.

"Brother," he said.

Chickamauga looked over at him.

"Wear something for me." No-Chance slipped the leather bag from his neck and held it out. "When we get deep into the timber, take the horses and keep going."

"No," Chickamauga sputtered. "I do not run from dog-eaters. I do not leave brother to fight alone. Would you make me a hollow man?"

No-Chance smiled and pushed the bag into Chickamauga's hand. "No one will say you are not a man of courage. Listen to me. This time I am the one who speaks wisely. Many mouths depend on us. Grandfather will not seek the help of the white man. When the snows come, they will all perish without one of us. The seed of Chickamauga will be lost forever."

He watched Chickamauga's shoulders slump in resignation and added, "Besides, it is my pretty hair Iseeo wants. I am glad he comes for me. For many sleeps my heart has been hot for his blood."

Twigs crunched beneath the horses' hooves as they entered the thick shelter of hackberry and cottonwood trees. Deep in the stand, a small stream gurgled as it tumbled over stones. The horses whinnied and picked up their pace with the smell of water. He slipped his black snake whip and a lariat over his shoulder, and tied the reins of the lead packhorse to the saddle pommel.

"I will catch up in two days. Before you reach the Canadian." He handed the Palouse's reins to Chickamauga, pulled his feet onto the saddle, and hefted himself into a squat.

"And if my foolish brother does not appear in two days, what do I tell Chade and Grandfather? What do I tell Tampa when he is young man? It would shame me to not know where bones of second father rest."

No-Chance steadied himself. "Tell him sometimes it is harder to listen to reason in one's head than to surrender to the hot desire of one's heart." He searched the canopy of limbs above their heads. "Tell Tampa his second father killed a yellow calf of the great beast for him."

The bark of the cottonwood tree bit into his hands when he grasped an overhanging branch and lifted his feet off the saddle. Leaves rustled as he pulled his body onto the limb and watched the Palouse's gray-spotted rump move away.

No-Chance peered through the foliage at Chickamauga, who shifted in his saddle. Their eyes met in a silent farewell.

The young Indian clasped a fist to his chest, then clucked to the horses, and continued down the trail.

No-Chance settled against the tree trunk to wait.

The change was subtle, almost unnoticed, with the deepening shadows—loud buzzing of locust and crickets replaced the sweet serenade of sparrows and orioles. The long-tailed inhabitants of the tall cottonwood became used to the set of blue eyes that blinked back at them and scurried from branch to branch, unmindful of a new presence.

An owl hooted in a neighboring tree and caused a shiver to run through No-Chance. This time he could not risk chasing the harbinger of death away. Like the owl, he waited for death. Someone's death.

He pushed his back against the trunk and closed his eyes. The gurgling of the brook was tantalizing. His tongue clung to the roof of his mouth. Thirst kept him agitated, alert.

An old coldness crept into his bones. Deep in his soul, he understood Iseeo—understood the anger that pushed the Comanche warrior into a pit of hatred.

The rolling drone of the locust high in the trees grew louder. No-Chance opened his eyes and listened for the missing chirrup of the crickets. Instead, he heard the soft rustle of decaying leaves. He pushed to his feet and inched away from the thick trunk along a branch that stretched over the path. He had chosen well. A dying hackberry allowed enough moonlight through its sparse leaves to make out the painted figure of a man skulking along the forest floor. Maybe ten paces behind, a second man followed.

Fingering the lariat into a loop, No-Chance wrapped its length across his back and allowed the first man to pass. He pushed a piece of bark loose with his toe and let it tumble as the second man stepped directly below. The Indian paused to peer up into the tree, just as the lariat dropped neatly over his head and jerked tight.

No-Chance prepared himself for the weight at the end of the noose, gripped its length with both hands, and stepped off the branch, backwards. The rope cut across his back and into his hands as he swung out and smashed into the body being lifted off the ground. The flailing Comanche's white-painted face distorted into a skeletal mask of agony, mouth open in a mute scream, eyes huge, ready to explode.

For a brief second, they dangled opposite each other. The frantic Indian clawed at the noose, while No-Chance hung with a death grip on the other end of the rope. Then, he opened his hands and dropped to the ground. Gasping, the Comanche collapsed in a heap,

The rope spiraled down on him. No-Chance pulled the Celtic knife and sliced across his opponent's throat. A man can't scream with his throat cut.

The Comanche's eyes blinked and his fingers, bloody, trembling, reached out. No-Chance jerked away, dropping his knife in the process. The hand wavered and fell.

Huffing, No-Chance looked up to see the first Indian turn. The figure froze. A primal cry, shrill and piercing, shattered the night, and Iseeo reared back, tomahawk in hand.

Chapter 37

Rage emanated from the scream and resounded through the grove until it seemed to come from the trees themselves.

No-Chance dove for the protection of the cottonwood.

Iseeo's tomahawk whooshed through the air, landing with a thud in the trunk. An eagle feather tied to the handle quivered at the end of a rawhide string.

No-Chance jerked Good-Talker's war ax from his belt and jumped to meet Iseeo's charge. Without taking his eyes off the madman, he shifted the weapon in his hands finding the right feel.

Face distorted, mouth wide in a loud shriek, Iseeo's body glowed yellow in the dappled moonlight as he advanced, brandishing an upraised knife. No-Chance willed himself to watch the knife and ignore the wailing meant to call forth the evil spirits, the devils from hell.

Just as Iseeo's feet left the ground in a mighty lunge, No-Chance swung the war ax, striking the knife, sending it deep into a thicket. The impact of Iseeo's charge drove No-Chance backward, jarring the ax from his grip. Nose to nose, each grunted with the exertion of battle. No-Chance's hands slipped in the ochre-colored fat smeared over his opponent's body. He struggled for a solid grip and succeeded in pushing their tangled bodies into a roll.

Iseeo kept the momentum of the tumble, remaining on top when they smashed into his dead companion. The Comanche's battle-scarred hands went for No-Chance's neck.

Gasping for breath, No-Chance swung at Iseeo's ribs. Grease deflected the impact of the blows, and his fists slid away. He tore at the vise-like grip on his throat. From the corner of his eye, he saw the carved handle of his knife. It meant dividing his strength to retrieve it, but the Celtic weapon, passed from father to son, had never failed him.

He pummeled Iseeo with punches, then swung one arm out, stretching until his fingers touched the beloved weapon. Once firmly clinched, its energy was powerful.

Iseeo struggled to maintain the upper advantage and abandoned his choking attempt to pin the knife-wielding hand to the ground.

Air filled No-Chance's lungs in great gulps. A growl deep in his throat gained intensity.

Tendons down each side of Iseeo's neck protruded, his biceps bulged as No-Chance summoned the strength of his forefathers and inched the knife closer.

Their eyes locked in mutual loathing—for Iseeo, it was the rage of humiliation, for No-Chance, revenge. Old anger at past injustices rose and fused with renewed fury.

Iseeo's grimace became surprise, then terror, when the blade plunged into his chest. Warm blood gushed with the strike, and he fell limp. Blood mingled in swirls with oily yellow paint.

No-Chance's own heaving roared in his ears until he rolled Iseeo's body off and into the grass. "You think you are a warrior? You think you are a brave man?" No-Chance yelled, his voice strained, unnatural. He rose to his knees and grabbed a hank of hair, lifting the Comanche's head. "You would scalp a man while his hands are tied? You would sneak up on him in the dark of night? "

The edge of his knife scraped along the skull, sawing a circle in the scalp until the handful of hair popped free. "You will go to your ancestors shamed." He wedged Iseeo's clenched teeth open with the blade and pushed the scalp into the dead man's mouth. Thin streams of blood inched down the Indian's forehead, pooled in the rims of vacant eyes, spilling over like scarlet tears.

"Your ancestors will cover their heads in grief." He lifted the tomahawk and brought it down again and again, hacking through skin and bone. "Now, you will never find your way to the dark land."

Panting, No-Chance stood and wiped his face in the crook of his arm, muscles quivering as anger seeped from his soul. He stared at the severed head, black hair sprouting from its mouth. Exhausted, he staggered to the cottonwood, leaned against it, and vomited.

A deathly quiet settled over the bodies and trampled grass. A quiet so deep, so chilling that No-Chance wished to run, yet managed just a single trembly step toward the only sound left—the soft whish of water over rocks. With thirst flaying the back of his throat, he sank to his knees, crawled to the water's edge, and drank.

Later, he lay on his back, eyes closed, in the middle of the stream. In another few weeks, it would succumb to the heat of Grandfather Sun. Only inches deep, the water lapped at his ears, washing the gore of revenge deep into the land of the Comancheria. If he lay long enough, perhaps it would wash away the memories.

One by one, night singers resumed their activities. Two frogs bellowed, while downstream another competed in a deep rolling voice. An owl hooted, then with a flurry of wings, swooped up some poor creature venturing too far from the underbrush. For a moment, its squeals disturbed the singers.

No-Chance sighed and gazed up through an opening in the laced canopy of branches. Grandmother Moon descended in the black sky. He rolled over and pushed to his knees, emotions spent, energy drained. The bodies had to be concealed. All Indians retaliated for lost relatives, especially Comanche.

No-Chance stood and shook his head sending a shower of droplets into the air. He wrung the water from his breechclout. Damp moccasins squished as he picked his way around the carnage that had leaked blood into the soil. Death had loosened Iseeo's bowels and the stench turned No-Chance's already-emptied stomach, but he paused and cut the otter pelt armband from the dead Indian.

Minutes later, he was relieved to be out, running along the timberline. The previous afternoon, he and Chickamauga led their mounts down a ravine a mile or so distant. It was a natural hiding spot and, most likely, where he'd find Iseeo and his companion's horses. The wind blew from the northwest. He circled the swell in the landscape to enter the ravine from the south.

The soft snicker of horses carried by the breeze was sweeter than the chirping of the night creatures. No-Chance smiled and continued to work his way toward the sounds. A gray mottled mare raised her head and snorted when he stepped from the shadows. Behind her, a spotted pinto looked up. Then a third horse, Iseeo's milk-white, decorated with yellow hand prints across its rump, moved into view.

No-Chance froze. He dropped to a squat and scanned the gully, studying each dark shape along the sloping banks. Near the top of the hill, the unmistakable outline of a reclining body took shape.

For the second time that night, he slipped the Celtic knife from its sheath and clamped his teeth along the dull side of the blade. The metallic taste of the century-old weapon filled his mouth.

His limbs felt heavy, unwilling to respond to his reluctant push up the side of the bank.

Almost at the top of the hill, No-Chance heard deep steady breathing. He moved a twig from his path and inched closer. Several feet away rested the sleeping form of a boy, thin shoulders and back not yet those of a man.

No-Chance peered over the hill's crest at a stand of timber in the distance. The boy had fallen asleep waiting for a signal that would never come. Now, he dozed peacefully as if he were in the security of his own lodge, dreaming no doubt of brave deeds and buffalo hunts, of horse raids and counting coup.

Weary, No-Chance removed the knife from his mouth and stared at it. The boy stirred and pulled his knees up. He wore only a breechclout and heavily beaded moccasins; no feathers, no ornaments, no paints, no scalps.

Returning the weapon to its sheath, No-Chance pushed away. He would not cause some Comanche mother to wail and slash her arms in grief over a young son eager to prove himself a warrior.

He held the otter pelt out to the white horse and rubbed it across the animal's muzzle. Before gathering up the reins, he glanced up the bank at the slumbering figure and lifted a water skin from a saddle pommel, resting it atop a large rock.

Minutes later, No-Chance mounted and stretched his body along the white horse's neck. The three ponies trotted across the dark prairie and into the shelter of trees. When they neared the towering cottonwood where the stench of death and blood was strong, the animals balked. He tied their reins to a thick sapling to keep them from bolting.

No-Chance wiggled Iseeo's tomahawk free of its bite into the old cottonwood. Then he searched through the weeds and vines until he retrieved the knife meant to kill him. Like Iseeo, these weapons would fight no more, nor be left for others to find.

Holding his breath, he stripped the bodies of their breechclouts and moccasins, bone necklaces and armbands, feathers and trophy scalps and stuffed them into a leather case strapped to the gray pony. Without these trappings, it would be hard to know whose bones had been found.

A mockingbird warbled a clear-throated song. Daylight would come soon. No-Chance doubted the boy, wishing to be a man, would venture into the thicket once he found himself alone. But if he did, the blood-soaked ground would speak only of a battle. It would name no names or speak of an ambush between enemies. No-Chance shoved the first body across the spotted pony and reached under its belly, pulled the rawhide rope dangling from the dead Indian's neck across and tied the ankles.

He hoisted Iseeo's body over the gray mare and tied the severed head in a blanket. Congealed blood began a sluggish drip from the open neck and marked the path until No-Chance led the ponies into the water, tied and left them to quench their thirst.

One final task remained to ensure the secret he shared with Mother Earth. Beginning at the path's entrance to the timber, No-Chance walked backwards, sweeping the ground back and forth with a leafy branch. Footprints disappeared in the dust. The branch stirred dirt through the pools of blood. Soon, animals would come to sniff out the blood and leave their own tracks behind.

Satisfied, No-Chance continued his backward walk to the edge of the water and mounted the milk-white horse. Instead of continuing across the creek and onto the opposite bank, he turned the ponies upstream, staying in the deepest few inches of water. Their hooves clattered against the stony bed.

Delicate pink fingers of light streaked through an early morning sky when the gully widened and split. No-Chance chose the east fork and kneed the white horse into the faster current. The banks grew steeper, the underbrush thicker, the air alive with the buzzing of insects and bird calls. He knocked a web from an overhanging branch.

Large boulders jutted into the creek bed and lined the high bank. No-Chance halted the horses and listened. The sound was distinctive, unmistakable—the soft whimpering of pups. He scanned the rocks for an opening and smiled at a yellow wolf peering back.

"Ho, mother wolf. I have need of you this day. I

bring you an offering."

He slid off the white horse and splashed through water to untie the body. "This Comanche is brother to the weasel and thought to count coup on one who had been a friend in his village." He climbed halfway up the bank, braced his feet against a rock, and pulled the body onto a ledge.

With an eye on the growling wolf, No-Chance cut the rope and tucked it into his belt. Not even that would be left. He picked his way back down to the horses.

"Old mother, do not forget this favor." He remounted and called up to her, "May this warrior's blood enrich your milk and his flesh make you strong. May your little ones sharpen their teeth on his bones." He kicked the horse to a trot, anxious to be away.

An hour later, he had hidden the clothing, the severed head and a saddle into rock crevices along the deep ravine. He looked back at Iseeo's decapitated body. Hordes of flies and mosquitoes swarmed the corpse. The gray mare snorted, swung her tail, and rippled her mane at the torment. If a suitable hiding place wasn't found soon, they would drive her mad.

No-Chance pushed back a surge of panic at being burdened with this hideous creature of the dead. What if he couldn't locate another cave? He didn't have a tool to dig with, to bury his deed. What if he was destined to have this putrefying thing follow him forever as punishment? Iseeo's final revenge.

Circling above the ravine, frantic crows created a loud racket unnerving the horses. A pair of vultures swooped down to land on an overhanging sapling, bowing it with their weight. Hawks floated high above the commotion.

No-Chance rubbed the back of his neck. He was tired, not thinking clearly. Anyone within five miles could see the rabble following him, and probably hear them, screeching their vigilance to every predator in the area.

Two green flies buzzed his ear. He swatted the air and yelled, "Gol-derned miserable blood suckers! I'm not the one stone cold dead!" His words were lost in the raucous cawing. No-Chance jumped into the stream and splashed to the gray mare.

"Bone is bone." He cut the rope securing Iseeo's body and dragged it onto the bank. "Without a head, nothing will mark this skeleton as Comanche!"

Within minutes, what was left of Iseeo disappeared beneath the assault of dozens of hungry flesh-eaters, jealously defending their chosen spot on the corpse. He knew they would gorge until their bellies were distended and they waddled off, too heavy to take wing.

The spectacle of predators shredding their prey sent a chill through No-Chance, and he scoured the ponies clean of dried blood. He threw handfuls of water over the milk-white's rump. The yellow handprints streaked, washing away the last vestiges of a warrior named Iseeo.

No-Chance removed the bridles from the gray and pinto, herded them up the embankment, out of the ravine, away from the gruesome secrets it held. The fight had come to him unbidden. Now, it was over.

Spreading lantana bushes, awash with tiny red and yellow blooms, scratched his ankles as the horses picked their way out of the scrubby timberland and onto a rolling plain. He urged the milk-white to a gallop, reveling in the freshness of the morning air.

The gray mare and spotted pinto raced alongside before veering westward. No-Chance watched them disappear over a rise. He envied their freedom to run with the wind, to leave behind the burdens of death.

He'd failed his promise to keep Crazy Bear safe. How could he tell Chade her loved one lives only in her dreams? He would rather face a thousand Iseeos.

Chapter 38

A lone eagle hovered over a snarling wolf. Its sharp talons opened to claw at the muzzle of the attacking animal. Another gray wolf bounded out of a white mist surrounding the struggle. The mist swirled as other wolves broke free of the cloud and crowded into the clearing. They clambered atop one another, lips curled above fangs, tearing at the brown tips of the eagle's wing feathers. The bird's shrill cry was drowned in the mounting chorus of howls. Fog pulsed, as if breathing; then, closed over the battle scene, until all that remained were the angry growls of a dozen hungry wolves.

No-Chance awoke from the nightmare with a jolt, chest heaving. He shivered despite the evening's sticky warmth. This same image haunted his dreams the previous night after he succumbed to exhaustion along the banks of the Canadian River. It disturbed his thoughts, making rest impossible as he followed the river east.

A scent of wood smoke lingered in the air. No-Chance sat up and studied the dead campfire. The growing apprehension of something dreadful about to happen churned in his stomach. The dream was a warning, a vision from the spirit world. The weight of its meaning stifled his breath.

Weeks earlier, they had crossed the muddy water

of the Canadian to follow the trading path into the vast Comanche territory. He expected Chickamauga to be waiting at the bend in the river. No sign of him. No deep grooves that marked the passing of a loaded travois. No grass trampled beneath the hooves of a half-dozen horses.

He buried his head in his hands. Blinded to the threat behind them, he had sent Chickamauga off alone. What had he been thinking? This was also the land of the Kiowa, who were as bad as the Comanche. Sometimes even the flesh-eating Tonkawa raided north. As soon as it was daylight, he would head south along the Comanche trail.

No-Chance rose to check on Iseeo's horse, grazing on tufts of grass near the water's edge. The sluggish lap of water along the riverbank deepened his gloom. For years, the songs of Mother Earth had been his solitary companion at night. He missed the steady breathing of Chickamauga, the loud snoring of Crazy Bear, the soft cooing of Chade as she rocked Tampa to sleep—the comforting sounds of family.

The sense of urgency would not leave. No-Chance threw a blanket across the milk-white, grabbed the wooden Comanche saddle and leather bridle from the ground. He would not wait for Grandfather Sun.

In the faint moonlight, the trading path disappeared into the shadows of thickets and scrubby trees. No-Chance ducked under low hanging branches, prodding the horse along. His passage interrupted the sharp chirrup of crickets, altering the night's steady rhythm.

In the distance, a night singer howled. The cry was answered by another and, then, a third. Fevered wails built in crescendo as wolves filled the darkness with their talk. The nightmare was alive, loud and insistent. Again, No-Chance caught the scent of burning wood and kicked the white into a gallop toward the excited yelps.

He leaned forward as the horse topped a low ridge. A dozen points of light twinkled in the dark meadow below. He reined to a halt and studied the flickering movement that was weaving in and out of the soft glow created by a ring of small fires. At the center of the circle, a large bonfire illuminated the figure of a man and six horses. A ball of flames raced out into the darkness. It hit the ground and scattered into tiny dancing flares that sputtered and died.

No-Chance spurred the horse down the slope and across the meadow toward the furious turmoil. Yelling, he stood in the stirrups and arched the blacksnake whip over his head. With a flip of his wrist, he sent it snapping into the pack of wolves. Another burning arrow thudded to the ground, scattering several of the threatening animals.

The milk-white reared when a wolf turned from its attack on the picketed horses and lunged at her legs. No-Chance struggled to maintain his balance as he sent the tightly braided whip cracking over the back of the large animal. With a yelp, the wolf's hind quarters sagged. Blood poured from a gash, soaking its gray fur in crimson. Over and over, the whip lashed out, ripping flesh, sending every new aggressor whimpering to safety.

Two wolves attacked on the far side of the large ring. Frantic horses whinnied and pulled against their restraints. Chickamauga stood in front of the center bonfire, bronze skin glistening with sweat as he loosened flaming arrows.

A wolf darted between the small sentinel fires, toward the horses, followed by the sharp scream of an injured pony. Chickamauga touched the padded end of an arrow to the blaze and sent it streaking into the snarling wolf. The impact hurled the beast backward into the midst of others following his lead.

No-Chance spurred his horse through the circle, past Chickamauga, to run at them. The whip reached out with its dreadful cracking. Tucking their tails, the band retreated deep into the timber, abandoning their scorched, writhing brother.

Knife in hand, Chickamauga dropped to his knees and ended the wolf's misery. He sat back on his heels and looked up as No-Chance slid off the milk-white.

"What kind of song dogs brave Grandfather Fire?"

No-Chance squatted. Despite the tightness in his throat, he managed a reply. "Comanche ones."

The corners of Chickamauga's mouth twitched, black hair hung in wet strands. "My heart feared I would never see my brother again." He lifted the leather pouch from his neck and held it out. "Your medicine is good. It brought you back."

No-Chance balanced the small bag containing the ancient jewels in his palm. He nodded and slipped the rawhide string over his head. It wasn't the power of these sparkling stones, each with its own story, that brought him back.

Thin smoke columns curled from the perimeter of dying campfires in the blush of dawn. No-Chance kicked dirt over the center bonfire. Thick branches of cottonwood trees bowed with the weight of large baskets of dried buffalo jerky. He watched

Chickamauga gather his arrows and bend to examine the dead wolf.

"There's no market for a scorched pelt."

Chickamauga nodded. "Our loudmouthed brothers will not wish to feed at campfires again." He glanced at the brightening sky. "The hungry ones will be back. They have been my companions since yesterday." Chickamauga ran his hand through the wolf's thick fur. "Their wait will be rewarded."

Unbidden, the sight of Iseeo's body disappearing beneath the horde of frantic vultures visited No-Chance's mind. He scuffed the toe of his moccasin through a line of ants disappearing into the folds entombing Crazy Bear. Even numerous layers of the brightly-colored tent could not smother the growing stench.

"We'll need to suspend this litter between two horses when we cross the river." No-Chance backed a yellow dun between the long smooth poles of the travois. He reached under the horse to tighten the wide surcingle that served as a harness for the heavy frame carrying his friend's body.

Chickamauga poured water from a skin onto the ground, creating a puddle. He dipped his fingers into the mud and waved flies off deep gashes oozing blood down the flank of a small pinto. The pony whinnied as the Indian covered its injuries.

"You are lucky my four-legged friend. Your wounds will heal." Chickamauga nodded at the milk-white. "You ride a fine horse, brother."

No-Chance smiled. In true Creek fashion, Chickamauga seldom asked a direct question. An aged branch of a large cottonwood tree creaked as No-

Chance loosened the rope suspending a basket of dried meat and lowered it to the ground.

"Iseeo may have been meaner than a rabid skunk, but he knew horses. He won't need the mare anymore." A small brown and white pinto grunted with the weight of the bundle settled on its back.

No-Chance folded his arms across the pack and leaned forward. "There was a boy. He was asleep guarding the horses down in that draw where we looked for water. Never woke up. I took their horses from under his nose. He will walk through his moccasins by the time he finds the tribe."

Chickamauga's face wrinkled with a smile. "He will have a great story to tell elders. He will say night spirits stole horses to pull Grandfather Sun across sky. Who can stop spirits? Not a boy."

No-Chance lifted another bundle. "Well, I hope he remembers to tell the elders the spirits were friendly and left a bag of water."

He moved toward a bay, which shied away. Chickamauga hurried to steady the horse. "Comanche will search for one of their own."

"They will find nothing." No-Chance wiped sweat from his forehead. The sun wasn't fully up and already the morning felt heavy. He sighed and added, "I let their horses go. I'll have to let Iseeo's mount go, too. If Parlin-wah-pit's people raid our way, they would recognize her."

Chickamauga swung onto his horse and looked back at Crazy Bear's corpse. "First, she will get brother across river."

Chapter 39

No-Chance stepped onto the wide porch of Edwards' Trading Post. He shifted the packages in his arms and studied three men examining the horses he'd left in the dappled shade of a hickory tree. Chickamauga watched them, too, his feet planted wide, one shoulder slumped, and arms tightly folded.

Heat from the hard-packed soil warmed the soles of No-Chance's moccasins as he strolled toward the gathering. The men, intent on their conversation, didn't turn at his approach.

"Injun ponies gots lots of endurance, I hear tell. They feed on 'bout anythin'. Don't need no oats or such." The grizzled man ran a hand down the brown and white pinto's neck. Rings of sweat colored the underarms and back of his faded red shirt.

"Don't know, Art, they look mighty small. I like this white 'un. Mighty fine horse flesh." The man wrapped his hand over the muzzle of Iseeo's horse, forcing long bony fingers under its lip to peer at the incisors. "Why don't ya offer that Injun that pocketful of bungtown coppers ya got. He won't know they're worthless."

The milk-white jerked her head up and shook her mane. Stepping backward, the examiner pulled a wadded handkerchief from the back pocket of blue woolen pantaloons. "Lord Almighty, don't somethin' smell ripe!"

Art, still taken with the paints, moved to the small pinto and brushed at the caked mud on its rump. "Would ya look it this, Lloyd? This one's hurt. Wonder whut happened?"

No-Chance set his packages on the ground. "Clawed by a wolf!"

The men jumped at his voice and turned.

Lloyd wiped his nose. "Whut?" He rammed the wadded rag back into a pocket, pushing his pantaloons low on his hips.

The third man stepped forward, scratching his thick curly beard, and squinted at No-Chance. "Why, it's one of them gone to the blanket, sure enough."

"What's that, ya say, Dickie?" Lloyd leaned forward, cupping ears big as bowls.

Dick nodded toward No-Chance and Chickamauga. "You know, a squaw man, Injun-lover, gone savage." His voice dropped to a hoarse whisper, "Ain't civilized no more."

Art stared. "Yup, don't no Injun have blue eyes." Then, as if conscious of his manners, he held his hand out. "Howdy, mister."

No-Chance nodded and accepted the hand.

Art pulled at the firm clasp holding him. "These my partners, Lloyd and Dickie." He winced and pulled again. "Uhhh, we've been lookin' at buyin' a horse."

No-Chance released his hold and extended his hand toward Dick.

Flexing his fingers, Art backed away.

Dick pretended not to notice the outstretched arm and turned toward the grazing horses. "Don't suppose you'd be of a mind to sell us one of them mounts? We got a mare pulled up lame."

Lloyd hitched his pantaloons, wiped his nose, and grabbed No-Chance's hand with both of his. He pumped furiously. "Well, sir, it's mighty hot in this infernal sun. Why don't we step on over to our wagon for a sip of whiskey brung all the way from the Monongahela?" He turned and pointed at two covered wagons sitting beside the post.

Dick hissed to Lloyd, "Whatcha want to be wastin' good liquor on these two for?"

"Hush," Lloyd spit back. "I know what I'm doin'."

No-Chance motioned for Chickamauga to follow.

Art nodded toward Chickamauga. "He never once answered me when I was bein' sociable. Don't understand no English, do he?"

No-Chance shook his head. "You don't understand Creek, do you?"

Art hurried to keep up with No-Chance's long stride. "Can't say as I do. Hey, does he have any scalps?"

"No, but I almost got my hair lifted." No-Chance bent to show the newly healed scar across his forehead.

Art's mouth dropped open, and he shifted his eyes toward Chickamauga. "He didn't do that, did he?"

No-Chance suppressed a smile. "Let's just say, I wouldn't get him riled."

Lloyd leaned out of the wagon and handed a small wooden cask over the tailgate to Dick, who grunted with the burden of lowering the barrel.

"Hey, Lloyd," Art stammered. "I got somethin' to tell ya,"

"Not now, I'm busy. Just get cups out, would ya?"

Art raised the cover of a side box attached to the

wagon. Tin vessels clinked as he ran his fingers through the handles and lifted five in one hand. Two slipped from his grasp, and he dropped to his knees attempting to catch them. Soon, all five rolled on the ground.

"Aww, jeez, you're 'bout as clumsy as a groom on his weddin' night." Lloyd picked two cups up, blew dirt off their rims, and held them out to Dick.

"Now, sir, I'm ready to bargain for that white horse of yours." Lloyd sat down and motioned for No-Chance and Chickamauga to do the same.

"Well, I wasn't thinking about selling any mounts. And, if I was, don't know as I'd sell the white one. She's one of the best." No-Chance sank down and leaned back on the wagon wheel with Chickamauga beside him.

He lifted a cupped hand to his mouth. "*Cewvnkete?*"

Chickamauga nodded at the offer of fool's water.

No-Chance took both cups from Lloyd. Art wiped the remaining containers with the end of his shirttail and held them out to be filled. A reverent silence fell as each man saluted the other and sampled the beverage.

Gut warmer, wild eye, brave-maker—no matter the name—No-Chance hadn't had a good drink of liquor since slipping in among the Creeks on the removal west. He swirled the deep amber liquid around in the tin cup and raised it to his mouth. Fumes cut a path to his brain before he ever tasted it. With the first swallow, white heat spread down his throat, through his nose, and tickled the back of his eyeballs. The second swallow brought tears to his eyes and swept through his chest to settle in a smoldering puddle in the pit of his stomach. By the time No-Chance drained the cup, his teeth were on fire.

"Good stuff," he croaked and nodded for a refill.

Lloyd smiled. "More for our friend here."

"I...I don't know Lloyd. Maybe we shouldn't..." Art paused, glancing at No-Chance.

"Nonsense, we're conductin' business." Lloyd stuck his empty container out and wiggled it. "Me, too."

Dick frowned, uncorked the small keg again and allowed a sparkling stream to gurgle into everyone's cups. "Don't know why we ain't usin' a bottle from that case of red-eye," he mumbled. "Injuns don't know no difference."

No-Chance frowned at the stingy measure meted out. Just as well. Drinking could blind a soul after a dry spell. He took a long swig and felt the inside of his ears burn.

He leaned against the wagon wheel and closed his eyes. His father's voice laughed with the rustle of leaves in the thick blackjack oaks sheltering the trading post. "Mind ye, me boy, many a man fell under the spell of the devil's own brew only to find themselves wiggling about in Hell's bath water. Nare taste more'n a thimble full lest ye be askin' the Lord Himself for mercy."

Lloyd cleared his throat. "Mister, I got coppers, blue trade beads, and abalone-shell buttons. I can make a powerful trade for the white horse."

No-Chance rubbed his temples, hoping to chase lingering fumes from his brain. "Got no use for pretty little trifles. Where you going with those wagons?"

The question flummoxed the old man. "Well...well, we're takin' trade goods across the Red River, all the way to San Antone." He narrowed his eyes. "Why?"

No-Chance sat forward and looked at the ruts the wagon had made in the ground. No doubt about it, they were heavy and loaded with more than beads. "Oh, going that far, you'd want a horse with stamina, like one of those pintos."

Art wiped his lips with the back of his hand and brightened. "How about that brown and white one?"

"Hush, I'm handlin' this." Lloyd held his emptied cup out to Dick, who scowled back. "Well now, if'n ya was gonna trade, just what would ya be interested in?" The old man wiggled the cup until it was filled again.

No-Chance drained the last mouthful of whiskey. It coated the roof of his mouth, burned his nose passages clear, and seeped into his eye sockets.

"I couldn't...let the white go...for anything less than a rifle and some powder," he gasped.

"How'd you know we had—" Art stopped in mid-sentence and looked over at his partners.

Dick slammed the keg down on the ground, popping the cork, and splattering the contents. "Them's bound for Texas Rangers. Figure to get forty dollars a piece."

Art scrambled to stop the leak as the powerful smell of whiskey flooded the air.

No-Chance leaned forward. "You gotta get them there first."

"Don't go bustin' a gut now, Dickie. He's right!" Lloyd tipped his cup, swallowed, then shuddered. "Damnation, if a cask of that stuff ain't worth more'n a rifle!" He turned to No-Chance and narrowed his eyes. "For a rifle and some powder, I gotta have the big white horse, else there's no deal."

No-Chance looked at Chickamauga who sat rigid and solemn. "I can see you got your mind made up." He rubbed his chin. "For the white, you'd best throw in a poke of buttons and beads."

"See, I told ya to leave it to me." Lloyd stood. "Come on Dickie, help me get a rifle case open."

Chickamauga rose, steadying himself against the wagon. He stared at Art a moment, then reached and took the cask from the startled man's hands.

"Hey, whatcha doin', mister?"

"Shhh." No-Chance rubbed the scar across his forehead and pointed to Chickamauga. "Best not get him riled!"

Chapter 40

Grandfather Sun, in fiery splendor, blazed across the clear afternoon sky, burning away tiny wisps of clouds. Even Father Wind bowed before the intensity of the sun and deprived the world of his breath. Only crows braved the heat, creating a shrill, unforgiving racket in a clump of cottonwoods.

Reluctant to move so much as an eyelid, No-Chance peered through slits at the haze of large birds fluttering from branch to branch above him. The blinding fires of Hell raged in his brain, and he covered his eyes in an effort to snuff out the flames. If his internals would quit threatening to push the Monongahela back up to scald his tongue, he would put the new gun to use and scatter the tormentors into another world.

Next to him, Chickamauga moaned. No-Chance rolled over and blinked into focus the hunkered form of his brother, who rocked back and forth on his knees, clutching his abdomen. Chickamauga's long hair fell forward and became soaked in the foul liquid that finally erupted, leaving him doubled over.

No-Chance pushed himself into a sitting position. His brain vibrated with the movement, and he clasped both arms across the top of his head. He had been away from the white man's world too long. His stomach had gone soft.

"Get up!" he ordered, touching off spasms of pain behind his eyes. "Oh, Lord, no," he whispered and held his breath. The devil's brew, his father called whiskey. If that was so, then the Lord was the wrong one to beg mercy from.

"Beelzebub...." No-Chance took a deep breath. "Have mercy." He cradled his face in his hands. What was he doing?

With a loud flapping of wings, a giant among crows found the ground and pranced back and forth. He flooded the air with scolding caws. No-Chance wilted under the crow's unblinking stare.

"Father, you don't understand," he whispered. "How can I tell Chade I failed my promise to keep Crazy Bear safe? She will leave." No-Chance closed his eyes, slid to the ground, and curled into a ball. "I don't want her to leave."

Hours later, he cupped his hands to create a dam in the ribbon of water snaking along the creek bed. Headache dulled, he now suffered with a tongue as thick as the mighty buffalo. For the third time, he waited for fine sand to settle in his palms before slurping tepid water.

A few feet away, the small brown and white pinto snorted and relieved himself. A golden stream coursed its way down the slight incline, and converged into the water bubbling over a bed of stone. No-Chance watched the fading cloud of urine move past. He scanned the bushes for sight of the other ponies, for the blue Palouse, for Chickamauga's horse. They were gone, even those loaded with packs. The dun, burdened with Crazy Bear's body, was gone too.

No-Chance sighed, swished his bandanna in the

water, and crawled back up the incline to wring it over Chickamauga's face.

Gasping for breath, Chickamauga sputtered and swung a limp fist in retaliation. With effort, he stood and stumbled down to the creek.

No-Chance retrieved a roll of pemmican from a pouch and squatted next to his brother. He sliced off a portion of the pounded buffalo meat mixed with fat and held it out as a peace offering.

"My stomach…" Chickamauga leaned away with a grimace. "Do not buffaloes…thunder through you… too?"

"It takes a special man to drink fool's water." No-Chance made a flourish of taking a bite he didn't want. "Admit I was out of practice at first. Didn't take long to know what I was doing again."

Chickamauga grunted and sat back.

"I would have let you sleep, but we need to gather the horses before dark. Only one pinto didn't stray," No-Chance said as he scanned the bushes. "Look around. The dun is missing. We were such fools, even the dead hide from us."

He helped Chickamauga up, nodding toward the trail of bent grasses, and trampled bushes. "Bear's spirit grows restless."

On the second night within the Nation's boundaries, a new moon banished darkness, and they did not stop for rest. No-Chance shifted in the saddle to recount the horses they'd nearly lost. Three sturdy ponies, each loaded with buffalo meat, pemmican, hides, and supplies from Edwards' Trading Post, plodded along the narrow path. The knowledge they would not be hungry or naked when winter arrived did not lighten the dread growing with the nearness of home.

The crooked shape of a lightning-savaged tree marked the edge of their field. No-Chance nudged the Palouse into the field and tightened his grip on the dun's lead rope, almost wishing for another swallow of Monongahela courage. The heavy litter caught against corn stalks, bowing them under as they moved through rows of waist-high corn. Grandfather and Chade worked hard in their absence.

No-Chance looked toward the glade of trees hiding the cabin and prayed, "Please, Father, give me the words to tell her."

Alerted, Dog set up a howl. The bothersome puppy had become watchful, a guard against intruders.

"Whistle before Grandfather sends an arrow our way," Chickamauga said.

No-Chance shook his head. "They will know who comes. The odor of death goes before us."

A wail, pitiful and haunting, shattered the night and sent shivers up No-Chance's back. He needed no words. Why had he thought he would? They left the field and crossed the creek to the sound of Chade's deep sobs and Dog's excited barking.

No-Chance slid to the ground. The prayed-for words did not come. He stood mute, fingering the dun's lead rope. A baby's frightened cry sent Chickamauga hurrying to the cabin. He emerged, cradling Tampa, and bent to comfort Cesse. She'd seen enough death in her five summers to know its smell, to know its permanence.

Poca looked older in the moon's bright light. His eyes, sad and knowing, fixed on the dun. He took the rope to lead the horse away.

Chade collapsed across the painted Comanche hide. Her anguished pleas muffled in the huge bundle that continued to bump across the yard.

No-Chance pulled her away from her husband's body. She fought his embrace and turned, beating her fists against his chest.

"You said he would be safe," she screeched. "You said you would watch after him." Her words became daggers slicing his heart. "You said you would bring him back."

"I'm sorry." No-Chance caught her flailing arms and his throat tightened. "I would trade places with Bear, if I could."

"But you cannot," she whispered, eyes clouded with grief, cheeks wet with tears. Tousled black hair framed her thin face. "He is forever gone. I will hear his laughter only in dreams." Fresh tears welled, and her voice wavered. "I will feel warmth of his arms only in heart." She sagged and buried her face in her hands.

Knowing sorrow robbed her strength, No-Chance pulled her close. This time she did not fight as he folded her to him.

Poca unhitched the travois, sat cross-legged next to the body, and chanted to the ancestors of one that journeys to the dark land.

****

Heat from the morning sun stifled the air in the windowless cabin. No-Chance leaned on the shovel and wiped his forehead. "Is it deep enough?"

Chickamauga stopped chopping at the hard dirt with a deer antler, put his hand to his back, and straightened. They stood in a waist-deep hole. A mound of loose earth filled the center of the cabin. He nodded and hoisted himself out of the grave.

Outside, brightness stung the senses. No-Chance shielded his eyes with his hand and breathed deep. The aroma of pristine soil clung to him. He watched the young widow sit motionless in the shade of a tree. Next to her, Tampa pushed to his knees and rocked in place.

"Poca, Chade, it is time."

Chickamauga helped maneuver the heavy body through the narrow door and into the deep hole. Chade stood at the edge of the grave. She grasped a deerskin shirt to her chest. Tiny shells dangled from the hem and clicked softly as she lowered it to rest on the bundle. She lifted a fringed bag from a peg and lowered it also. Poca sprinkled crumbled sage over the items.

No-Chance fingered a parchment-wrapped packet of buffalo jerky and squatted to lay it next to the shirt. Bear would need these things for his journey. Taking up a handful of dirt, No-Chance allowed it to sift through his fingers into the grave, the last handshake he could give a brother.

The soft thud of earth, as it hit the bundle, brought fresh tears to Chade, and she fled the cabin.

"Did you remove his moccasins?" Poca asked.

"Yes, Grandfather. You will not hear him walking when you sleep."

Satisfied, the old man began a new song—low and sorrowful, bidding a brother of the nation good-bye. He continued the chant until the grave was filled and patted smoothed. The three men emerged into the daylight, dripping with sweat. Chade brushed past them, stopping at the door of the cabin and turned, looking at each man.

"I mourn now." She disappeared into the cabin's darkness and lowered the bear skin covering the door.

"What does she mean?" No-Chance asked.

"Chade follows old way. Will stay alone. No bathe, no come out, no speak. In old country, Crazy Bear's family tell when time of grief over." Poca shook his head. "They gone to land of ancestors."

Behind them Tampa's sporadic fussing grew to a constant whimper. The men watched Cesse scamper up from the stream. Her red blanket, tied around her neck, fluttered across her back. Tampa held his arms out to the small girl, and she struggled to lift him.

Chickamauga relieved Cesse of the wiggling baby. "In old country, aunt mourned alone two seasons when husband died." He shifted Tampa in his arms and shrugged. "Then she given new husband."

No-Chance rested his hand on Cesse, who leaned against his legs. He stared at the cabin.

"Without Chade, who will mother the children?"

Chapter 41

"It's true, Grandfather, even the shit of the mighty buffalo is useful." No-Chance reached into a bag, extracted the last dried mound of dung, and shoved it into the sputtering fire.

Squatting, Poca rocked back on his heels and watched curls of smoke wrap around the droppings of the great beast.

"It makes a hot fire. See how the pot bubbles?" No-Chance pulled the tops off a handful of wild onions and dropped the bulbs into the simmering liquid.

Poca peered into the new cast-iron kettle brought from Edwards' Trading Post. The old man smiled and looked across the yard at the cow.

Chickamauga shifted a fretting Tampa in his arms. "There were few trees and buffalo too many to count, Grandfather." He motioned to the thick profusion of scrub oak and hickory. "The Maker of Breath gives us many trees."

Poca continued to stare at the cow. "But He does not cut wood for us."

No-Chance laughed and bent to stir the pot. Chickamauga returned to the task of feeding Tampa and dribbled a stream of cow's milk into the hungry baby's mouth. Tampa's small tongue curled, pushing the creamy liquid back through pursed lips. Milk ran down his chin into the folds of his plump neck.

Frustrated, Chickamauga handed the horn of milk to Cesse and stood to watch No-Chance stir dark chunks of buffalo meat up from the bottom of the bubbling stew.

"Do you think it will work?" he asked, bouncing Tampa on his hip.

"She has been all day without food. It will work." No-Chance sniffed the aroma wafting from the pot. He picked up a folded blanket and fanned the fumes in the direction of the small log building.

The cabin, dull and ominous under the shelter of oaks, looked forlorn. Gloom darkened the doorway, threatening to spill out into the yard. Crazy Bear's good omen, the buffalo skull, glared from its perch above the door.

"Nothing says you have to starve while you mourn." He waved the blanket harder causing flames to lick up around the pot. No-Chance glanced over at Poca. "You've never tasted anything like this buffalo meat, Grandfather. Come, it's ready." Then louder, "Cesse, bring those new tins over."

Standing next to him, the little girl looked up at his loud command.

No-Chance fairly yelled, "Bluffer meat's the best there is. Better than deer, don't you think, brother?"

Chickamauga looked at the cabin. There was no movement. "Richer than squirrel meat," he agreed, raising his voice, too.

Poca ambled over, took a tin plate from Cesse, and dipped it into the stew. Tilting the upturned edge against the inside of the pot, he drained the liquid away, leaving chunks of meat and onions sliding across the shiny surface. He handed the filled plate to

Chickamauga.

"Chade's grief fills stomach," Poca said in a soft voice. "Chade eat when ready. Yelling will not bring woman from cabin."

Chickamauga fished a strip of meat from the plate, blew on it, and touched it to Tampa's lips. The baby sucked at the morsel.

No-Chance reached for the fat infant. "If she won't come out for her own hunger, maybe she will for Tampa."

He spread a blanket a few feet from the door and sat the baby down. Tampa's lower lip puffed out. Tears welled in his dark brown eyes.

The three men sat cross-legged watching the doorway while they ate. Tampa's eyes clamped shut, the corners of his mouth pulled down. Whimpers progressed to cries.

"She will come out. Wait and see." No-Chance hoped he was right.

The cries grew to angry wails. Tampa's plump arms flayed the air as he hiccupped between screams.

Cesse scrambled to rescue the baby. Poca held her back until she, too, cried.

Chickamauga rose to one knee. No-Chance stayed him with his hand. "No, wait! She comes out."

Chade, eyes red and swollen, emerged. A dusting of dirt replaced the shine of her black hair. She tossed a look of irritation toward the group of men and bent to pick up Tampa.

"I told you." No-Chance jumped to his feet and dipped his plate into the stew. "I told you…" The sentence died on his lips when Chade, clutching the sobbing child, re-entered the dark cabin.

"Chade eat when ready," Poca repeated, waving flies from the rim of his plate.

The pot of stew continued its gentle bubble.

Chapter 42

Sitting on the roof of the new cabin, No-Chance stopped work and took a deep breath. A chill breeze heralded the arrival of autumn. It was nearing the end of *Otowoskv Rakko*, the month of the big chestnut. Soon *Ehole*, the month of frost, would visit to banish memories of the grim summer.

From his perch, he looked over at the field filled with the stubble of dried corn stalks. The harvest was only fair. Next year they would need to plow an area twice the size. He fit another rough shingle into place on the sloped roof, then stopped to study the tiny cabin on the other side of the stream.

Grandfather was right. After several days, Chade accepted plates of food set in the doorway. And within a few weeks, she'd weaned Tampa and left him to the care of men and a small girl. It was an unreasonable thing to do. Men were no match for crying children.

No-Chance reached into the small keg for one of the metal nails, which cost dearly at the trading post, and drove it into place with a whack. Chade was proving stronger than he'd thought. He'd pleaded through the log walls that no one would doubt her grief if she came out. He whacked another nail and turned once more to study the dark doorway. Sometimes he imagined Chade watching him.

"Roof is good?"

No-Chance glanced down at Chickamauga. "Another day, it will be finished. Are you leaving now?"

"Come down. We talk."

No-Chance swung from the edge of the roof to the ground.

"It is Creek way to share with tribe." A bundle rested on Chickamauga's shoulder.

No-Chance narrowed his eyes. "You're taking buffalo to Black Storm?"

"There is little corn in the nation." Chickamauga held his gaze. "Few weapons for hunting. To wait for food from white agent makes heart of man small."

"Take what is right." No-Chance bounced the hammer in his hand. "But tell Black Storm that No-Chance shares his kill. Tell him No-Chance works hard to be a son of the tribe."

Chickamauga smiled and patted the bundle. "Black Storm knows grandson grows fat. I will tell of bravery among Comanche."

They turned at the rumbling approach of the small two-wheeled wagon. Grandfather led the horses across the yard. Cesse sat atop the gray dun, her short legs splayed out on its wide back. She grinned and waved to No-Chance.

He dropped the hammer to lift the small girl and deposit her in the wagon beside a napping Tampa. How could he remain cross when morning sunshine smiled back at him?

Chickamauga nestled the offering of dried buffalo next to the children. "We finish corral when I return."

"Stop at the reverend's house. Bring Stands-in-Water back with you." No-Chance helped Poca into the wagon seat and handed him the reins. "Maybe she can talk Chade into ending her mourning."

Grandfather sighed. "Chade know when time right."

The next morning, No-Chance stood, arms crossed, in the center of the finished cabin and inhaled the aroma of aged wood. Thick log walls to hold back the icy breath of Father Wind and a shingled roof to shed the coming rains. Best of all, a rough puncheon floor to lift them from Mother Earth's damp fingers—invisible fingers that crept into a man's body.

A shallow loft across the back of the cabin stored their meager harvest of corn and squash. Baskets of buffalo jerky and a leather pouch of Comanche pemmican leaned against the upper wall. Stalks of rosemary and bundles of gray sage dangled from a ceiling rafter.

Chade would be pleased when she saw the iron kettle resting in the fireplace. He settled his pipe and tobacco pouch on the jagged stone mantel. Finally, he sat cross-legged in front of the fireplace and closed his eyes to better picture the coming winter.

On cold nights, Poca would settle himself before the fire. As the oldest one, to him fell the task of telling and retelling the story of how animals divided night and day, how turtle got his shell shattered, or why skunk had a stripe. In this way, he would teach Cesse and Tampa the things they needed to know about their world.

When Poca's voice grew tired, the old man would goad others into relating tales of the fierce Comanche. No-Chance rubbed the scarred ridge across his forehead. They would not mention Crazy Bear by name. Not because the gone-away one was no longer remembered or loved, but because to do so would be disrespectful.

He imagined Chade bending toward the fire's light while she sewed blue and white trade beads and shell buttons and worthless bungtown coppers across the front of a new tunic or stitched a pair of moccasins.

No-Chance opened his eyes and stared at the kettle. Maybe Chade wouldn't be part of the circle. What if she mourned through the long winter, shut up in the tiny cabin where darkness robbed the eyes of sight and the soul of hope? What if Black Storm found Chade a new husband? He felt empty at the thought of spending the winter without the warmth of her voice, the gentleness of her laughter.

He rose and padded over the wooden floor to the cabin's one small window and stared across the creek. A chill breeze teased the promise of rain. Red and golden oak leaves skittered along the ground. Soon Grandfather Sun would begin hibernation.

How long could someone sleep with ghosts and remain sane? Crazy Bear loved life. He would roar his disapproval at so long a confinement. Even now, Bear's growl could be heard in the sheltering oak's groan of branch against branch, the shudder of dying leaves. No-Chance picked at a splinter of wood in the windowsill. Didn't he owe it to Bear to protect Chade from herself? He looked out at the trembling trees and smiled. Today was a fine day to end her mourning.

Grandfather said Chade would know when the time was right. No-Chance reached into a basket for a piece of lye soap. Chade just needed someone to tell her the right time was now, this very day. He stood on tiptoe to yank a blanket from the loft edge.

Halfway across the yard, No-Chance paused, listening again to the tree's crackling whisper. Determined, he splashed through the creek as cold needles shot up his legs, excited energy pushing him up the incline in two bounding leaps.

"Chade!"

No-Chance ducked and stepped through the doorway into a world of darkness. The dank smell of dirt and mold, urine and sweat, death and sadness took his breath away. He buried his nose in the blanket and waited to adjust to the gloomy interior. Dust specks danced through feeble slivers of light finding their way between missing dabs of chinking.

"Chade?"

No-Chance followed the soft rustle of movement to the far corner. In the shadows, Chade pushed herself against the wall and sank to the ground.

"Give me your hand." No-Chance knelt in front of her. "It is time to leave."

A matted lock of hair fell across her face as she shook her head. "I no longer know day or night. I must mourn the proper time. It would shame memory of..." Her lower lip quivered.

"The wind brought the voice of the gone-away one," No-Chance said. "He no longer wishes for you to share the place of his bones."

Motionless, Chade stared at him, long-ago tears streaking the grime on her face.

"Why didn't wind speak to me?" She lowered her eyes. "No, it is not time."

No-Chance scooped her into his arms. "You did not hear the wind talking because your ears are full of dirt."

Chade, arms and legs flailing, weighed no more than a newborn deer. Surprised at her lightness, he ducked through the doorway into the daylight and fresh air. She stiffened at the sudden immersion into the world of the living and buried her face in his shoulder.

"No, no!" she wailed. "The elders will say Chade shames the gone-away one."

"Stop fighting." No-Chance slid down the embankment into the creek and splashed along its length toward a small pool. "The people know of your love for your husband. You honor him more by staying alive."

"No," Chade screamed, clawing at his hands. "I go back."

Exasperated, No-Chance shouted. "Do you not feel the slow death that has crawled into your body?" His feet numbed as cold water inched to his knees. He opened his arms and dropped the struggling woman in the middle of the pond.

Chade gasped as her backside hit the soft bottom. She attempted to get her footing and fell backwards completely immersed. Stunned and wild-eyed, she struggled into a sitting position. Moisture sparkled in the dull jumble of hair and dripped into the water lapping at her shoulders.

Surprise melted into anger, bringing the first flush of color to her checks. She fought the weight of wet clothing to stand. Her cotton blouse and skirt clung to her body as she put her hands on her hips.

"I…I…how could…" she sputtered and turned to wade out of the pool.

No-Chance tossed the blanket onto the bank and

dived toward Chade knocking her down into the water. He wrapped his legs around her waist to keep her trapped as he rubbed the bar of soap through her tangled hair. Edges of the bar crumbled with the furious scrubbing until a milky froth gathered around them.

Eyes squeezed shut, Chade shrieked as soap ran down her face. She struck out blindly. No-Chance dodged her blows. Her struggle is halfhearted, he thought, and put his hand on top of her head to force it under. Foam swirled in the churning water. He released his hold, and Chade bobbed up, sputtering and gasping.

"You can fight if you wish. But this dirt of sadness is washing away." He attacked her hair again with the soap. She swung at him sending up sprays of water.

Through the suds, he felt the slickness of clean hair. He pushed her head underwater and held it for an eternity, then let go. Gasping, she lurched upward and scrambled to her feet.

No-Chance stood in front of her, fists on his waist. Rivulets of water dribbled from his braids onto his shoulders, down his chest.

Heaving large gulps of air, Chade wiped soap from her face and stared at him. Dripping water created a myriad of small rings that played across the pond.

"Your sadness tortures my sleep." No-Chance held out the bar of soap. "The time of mourning is over. The children need you."

His voice dropped with a sudden realization. "I need you."

Chade stood for long minutes. Slowly, she tugged the clinging blouse and skirt over her head. The wadded garments landed with a thud on the bank. Her wet skin shone in the afternoon sun as she moved toward him to take the offered soap.

A wild energy shot through No-Chance when Chade's hand touched his. He felt rooted in the soft mud oozing around his feet.

Shivering, Chade turned the lathered bar in her hands. She scrubbed along the length of her arms and over her round breasts. A white soapy film slid down her abdomen to glisten in the dark hair of her womanhood. She knelt and lay back in the water washing months of grief away. Her thick hair fanned out on the pool's surface.

No-Chance pulled his feet free of the earth's grip and waded to the bank. Words caught in his throat, and he could not breathe. Chest ready to explode, he reached for the blanket and shook it open.

Chade stood and bent to squeeze water from her hair. A smile played at the corners of her mouth when she looked up. Without speaking, she walked into the blanket and No-Chance's embrace. Her brown eyes searched his face. Water sparkled in her dark lashes as she lowered them and placed the palm of her hand on his chest.

"Chade," No-Chance whispered in relief, "your smile lives in my heart. Your touch warms my soul."

She put her head on his shoulder.

He sighed with relief at her acceptance of him. "I am a nothing-man without you."

Chapter 43

No-Chance shifted his arm under his head to watch the orange glow of burnt wood flicker in the stone fireplace. It was fitting the first fire in the new cabin should witness the beginning of a new life for him. When had hatred left him? Was it when Tampa was born or when he lay helpless and dependent upon Chickamauga's kindness? Was it in the struggle to survive the raw land, or yesterday, when he read acceptance in Chade's face?

He inched away from her warmth and sat up. Wood crumbled in the dying flames. The sense of dread tugging at him had nothing to do with leaving such comfort to steal into the cold and stir the fire.

With a sigh, No-Chance slipped from the covers, broke and laid sticks on the smoldering coals. The woman's nearness numbed his mind and robbed him of the strength to think through his problem. He lifted another blanket from the loft and stood to watch Chade sleep, the aroma of sage she'd used to purify her body still strong.

At the doorway, he slipped into moccasins, draped the blanket around his shoulders, and stepped into the night.

Grandmother Moon was clothed in a soft shroud of clouds. Water lapped against the creek bank. No crickets or locust or frogs sang. It did not matter winter was coming. The family—his family—would be warm. Their stomachs would not rumble in protest when snow covered the ground.

No-Chance sat at the foot of an old oak and leaned against its trunk. A few tattered leaves, still clinging to life, rustled above him. He watched the sluggish arousal of mist as it rose from the water's surface and began a slow creep up the banks. Like crawling fingers, the fog advanced along the ground to swirl at his moccasins. No-Chance hugged his knees.

The mist settled, chilling his bones. He had lost himself to love and, in taking a woman of the tribe, had betrayed his promise to Black Storm. Daylight would bring the harsh reality of his actions. His honor would demand a decision. How could he leave all he ever wanted? How could he stay?

"Trust in the Lord, and a way shall be found, my son."

No-Chance scrambled to his feet. "Father!"

Moonlight caught in Alexander MacGregor's flowing white hair and beard as he strode through the swirling fog. "Aye, and glad is my soul at your turmoil. For 'tis proof your heart has turned from man's sinful nature."

No-Chance felt warmed by his father's smile, but it did not ease his agony.

"I have done the one thing forbidden me. I desire to take a wife. Black Storm will never allow it. I will have to leave. If I go, I break my promise to Chickamauga." No-Chance slumped against the tree. "My heart knows Chade's love, and I can never again sit next to her as a brother."

"Merciful heavens! Did not the good Lord beget

Eve for the first man's mate? God, in His goodness, does not mean for man to wander alone. Have ye not been unselfish in your giving? Have ye not put others before yourself? Did yon lass drain ye of your senses?"

Blue eyes twinkling, Alexander shook his head. "What if Jacob, that crafty bard of the Lord's, had not stood firm and persevered for the fair Rachel? Do ye not think by faithful endeavor 'tis possible to soothe the old lion's heart? Nay, Laddie, running away 'tis not the answer."

No-Chance searched his memory for the story of Jacob. "Surely Father, you do not think Black Storm would want me to work for him? He has a slave to do his bidding."

"Are ye blinded by love, John? The sweat of ye brow 'tis not the only thing ye have to offer."

Mist swallowed the image of his father even as he spoke. No-Chance pulled the blanket tight and closed his eyes. Maybe there was a way around his promise.

****

The aroma of coffee intruded on his dreams. No-Chance stirred. Somewhere in the trees, a crow fussed.

"Enough. I hear," No-Chance muttered and sat up to stretch kinks from his spine. The morning air was crisp with wood smoke and the promise of coffee. He looked toward the cabin.

Chade sat in the doorway and smiled. She gathered her blanket close and picked up a tin cup with her free hand. Sunlight, filtering through the sparse foliage, glossed her long black hair. She knelt and held out the steaming cup.

"Mother Earth makes a warmer bed than…" she hesitated, "than the buffalo robe?"

"Chade, I am weak as a newborn pup when you are beside me. My head goes soft and light like Grandfather's eagle feathers. I needed the night air to tell me what to do." No-Chance worked a finger into the looped handle of the cup and took a sip of hot coffee. Heat spread across his chest.

"Unlike your people, I came to this land by choice. I ran from the white man's law. Black Storm allowed me to remain hidden among his people if I made a promise to him."

Dark grounds in the bottom of the cup swirled. No-Chance waited for them to settle before he took another sip. Chade sat, head tilted, mouth parted, as if pondering a question.

He cleared his throat. "I promised the chief I would not take a woman of the tribe. He does not want my seed to dilute the nation."

Drawing back, Chade gasped, "No."

****

"It has been four days." No-Chance paced the length of the cabin, pausing to glance out the doorway each time he passed. "What is keeping them?"

"The worries of each clan and town must be heard." Chade put her sewing down. "Such things take time."

No-Chance pointed to the garment in her lap. "I meant those ribbons for you."

"You must be presentable when you talk with Black Storm. His ears would hear only laughter if you wear that." She nodded at his frayed tunic, shortened too many widths during the Comanche time, and held out a new blue cotton hunting shirt. Dangling scarlet ribbons, the length of a man's hand, marched across the back and front yoke.

No-Chance shrugged, stripped the frayed tunic off, and slipped the new garment over his head. It was stiff and smelled of the trading post.

Chade pushed him into a sitting position and knelt to untangle his hair with her fingers.

"Ouch," he protested. "I feel like a..." he searched for words, "...struttin' rooster ripe for plucking. I'm the same man whether I'm naked or dressed all gussied up."

Chade tilted her head. "A naked man does not command respect. Only laughter." She continued weaving dyed rawhide strips into his braids. "A man in fine clothes has something important to say." She touched the scar on his forehead and pulled the ruffled collar wide to expose the jagged pucker of skin on his chest.

"It is good you have such marks," she said. "It is measure of man's bravery. It will not go unnoticed."

For a moment, No-Chance imagined the likeness of Crazy Bear's scarred face in her large brown eyes and pulled her close to press his lips against hers. He released her and studied the look of surprise on her face, hoping to find himself in her gaze.

Chade touched two fingers to her lips. A slight smile answered his question as she slid her arms around his neck and returned the kiss.

In the distance, Dog barked.

"They come." Chade pulled away, smoothing her skirt, and hurried to the door.

The moment No-Chance dreaded had arrived. If Chickamauga disapproved of his desire for Crazy Bear's widow, he could expect no permission from

Black Storm. He joined Chade at the door to watch the two-wheeled cart emerge from the woods, rumble past the burial cabin, and through the creek.

Poca and Stands-in-Water bumped up and down on the wooden seat as the wheels rolled over rough ground. Cesse peered around her grandfather.

No-Chance stepped out into the yard and walked toward them. He reached for Cesse, hugged, and set her on the ground.

"It is good you come, Stands-in-Water. I see you eat well at the reverend's house," he teased. A broad grin crossed her wrinkled face as he helped her down.

"Old eyes see you pretty boy, now." She patted one of his braids. "Ruth, I am Ruth Stands. Reverend Ward say it good"—she lifted her chin—"good Christian name, praise the Lord."

Poca's gaze swept from the burial cabin to the doorway of the new cabin where Chade waited. "Time of sorrow is put away?"

"You were right about her, Grandfather." No-Chance didn't look up, pretending an interest in dislodging a clump of weeds from one wheel. Better the old man didn't know the truth of the matter.

Chickamauga halted his horse and handed Tampa down to Stands-in-Water. The excitement of homecoming faded as the women entered the cabin and the wagon moved away.

In the sudden quiet, No-Chance bit his lip, searching for the right words. "Finished the roof."

"It is good."

"Started the corral."

"Good." Chickamauga glanced at four knobby posts, leaning in various directions.

"Chade ended her mourning."

"It was time." Chickamauga swung his leg over the saddle and slid from the horse.

No-Chance took a deep breath and blurted, "She shares my blanket."

Chickamauga pursed his lips. He looked over at the new cabin.

"This is Chade's choice?"

No-Chance nodded, "Yes. And mine."

"You go to ask permission from Black Storm?" Chickamauga stepped back to look at him. "Maybe you dress to welcome us home?"

No-Chance shrugged. "Chade thought the chief might not hear the words of someone who did not command attention."

"She is wise woman. I wish tongue of the mockingbird for my brother, that his words sound as music to ears of Black Storm."

Two days later, No-Chance sat atop his horse on the crest of a timbered hill. He watched women hoe weeds in a small pumpkin patch. Most of the pushed-away ones chose to settle together and work in communal fields just as they had in the old lands.

Steam rose from pots suspended above campfires in front of rows of one-room cabins. A group of boys pushed and shoved each other in the rough game of kickball, or as the old men called the game, "the little brother of war."

The Palouse picked her way down the incline. Leading the brown and white pinto, No-Chance headed toward the brush arbor in the center of the square. It was here the chief would spend the day conversing with others of the tribe.

Several women stepped from their doorways to watch him pass.

Proud of the Comanche Palouse, he sat tall. A slight breeze played with the line of ribbons on the new shirt. Chade was right. It was good to make an impressive entrance.

No-Chance tied the horses to a corner post, reached into his saddlebag for a leather-wrapped bundle, and ducked under the thatched roof. The drone of conversation ceased. Three old men, sitting on woven mats, looked up.

Despite the shaded light, Black Storm's imposing presence was strong. Hardship had not humbled the chief. The ever-present scowl wrinkled the three blue tattoo lines on his face.

"I ask to speak with the great chief, Black Storm, about a matter of some importance." No-Chance glanced at the smoke curling from the men's pipes. "I bring tobacco so you know the truth of my words."

The chief's face softened. By the acrid smell in the air, there was more dried bark and crushed sumac leaves than tobacco in the mixture the old men smoked. No-Chance spread his blanket, sat down, and held the bundle out in both hands.

The chief accepted the offering and unwrapped the tobacco. Black Storm fingered the crumbled leaves and inhaled the sweet aroma wafting up.

Each man filled his pipe and settled into discussions about the new land and the poor crops. No-Chance listened to their complaints of the fort soldiers and lack of promised supplies and, though he knew Chickamauga would have told them of the Comanche, answered their questions about the fierce ones. He cupped the warm bowl of his pipe in his hand and glanced out at the changing shadows. It would be impolite to bring up the visit's purpose until certain pleasantries had been observed.

At last, Black Storm put his pipe down and folded his arms. "There is a matter of importance?" The old man's dark eyes held him captive.

No-Chance swallowed. "I will never forget the kindness of the great chief when I came into the nation. I bring him a buffalo pony from the land of the Comanche."

Black Storm's eyes shifted to the pinto. The other two men murmured their admiration.

"My sweat waters the land. I share my harvest that my Mvskoke brothers do not go hungry. In my heart, I am Mvskoke now, and I want the rights of its citizens."

Black Storm frowned.

No-Chance hurried on. "I want to be released from my promise not to marry into the tribe. My mother was a Seminole woman of the Alligator clan. My blood line is honorable."

Black Storm's lips tightened.

No-Chance pulled his knife from the scabbard at his waist. Black Storm did not move. The chief's companions straightened.

"Do not let hatred of the white man cloud your eyes and close your mind." With a sleeve pushed up, No-Chance laid the edge of the knife against his wrist. He dragged the blade across his skin, leaving a thin red line in its wake. Blood oozed from the wound and wrapped around his arm.

"Show me the blood of a true Mvskoke." No-Chance thrust the handle of the knife at Black Storm.

The chief's eyes glared at the challenge, his nostrils flared. Then he clenched his teeth and reached for the knife. In a slow deliberate motion, he cut his outstretched arm. Blood sprang to the surface. Black Storm closed his hand as blood ribboned down his arm.

"Is not the life force within me the color of yours?" No-Chance leaned forward. "Tell me you see a difference."

Black Storm harrumphed.

"The measure of a man is here." No-Chance sat back and thumped his fist on his chest. "Release me from my promise that I might stand tall as any man of the nation." He took a deep breath and commanded, "Or use the knife to end my life now."

In the following silence, the old chief's eyes narrowed. He still held the Celtic blade in his hand.

No-Chance swallowed. Had he pushed the chief too far?

Slowly, Black Storm's eyes relaxed, his face melting into a mask of passivity as he studied the dark spot where blood soaked the ground. One of the old men stifled a cough, but no one moved.

No-Chance had, at first, been numb to the wound, but now the breeze brought the pain alive. Perhaps he would be buried in the blue shirt with scarlet ribbons.

"There are many widows," Black Storm jutted his chin toward several women that passed.

"I only want one," No-Chance answered. "Chade, widow of my gone-away brother has ceased her mourning. Her people are in the darkening land." He jumped to his feet. "In their name, I bring an offering to the chief."

No-Chance hurried to the horses and untied a long

object wrapped in a white blanket behind his saddle. He squatted before the men, laid the blanket on the ground, and unrolled it to expose the new Kentucky rifle traded for Iseeo's horse. A shaft of early afternoon sun worked its way through holes in the brush roof and glanced off the rifle's blue steel barrel.

There was an audible intake of air as the men bent to look at the offering.

Black Storm reached with a bloody finger to touch the polished brass plate on the walnut stock. He ran both hands under the rifle and lifted, testing its balance, then fit it to his shoulder to sight at an imaginary target. The chief's dark eyes flashed as he looked across the rifle at No-Chance.

"My son-in-law knows of your desire?"

"He does."

Black Storm caressed the wooden gunstock with the palm of his hand and studied it for a moment before speaking. "Chickamauga told me you are brothers in blood as well as spirit. Your scars speak of bravery." He stiffened his back and puffed his chest out. "Our people diminish in this land. If you take Chade as wife, you will be bound to fight our enemies."

No-Chance choked back a yell and stuttered, "My heart is full of thanks. I—"

Black Storm held up a bloody hand. He drove the knife into the moist dirt, rose and tucked the gun under his arm. "Obey our laws. And do not remind me of your white blood." Without further ceremony, the chief untied the pinto and led it away.

Was that all? No-Chance reached for his knife and rocked back on his heels. He bought a wife and the right to live amidst these people with a gun and a horse? True, the spotted pinto was a novelty, and the gun, an enviable possession.

He shook his head. No, that was not all. He was not the same man who hid among the Mvskoke. That man was a lifetime away. Happiness teased the corner of his lips, and he broke into a wide grin as he turned the blade in his hands.

Wrinkled and stoop-shouldered, the two old men smiled back.

One reached to pat him on the knee. "Go home," he whispered.

In the distance, ever so faint, a crow cawed.

A word about the author...

M. Carolyn Steele enjoyed a career in journalism and commercial art before retiring to pursue a love of writing and genealogy. She has short stories published in many anthologies and has won a number of awards, which include several creme-de-la-creme wins and nomination for a Pushcart Prize.

Her writings reflect a childhood steeped in Civil War history and Indian lore. Carolyn presents a variety of programs designed to inspire others to commit family stories to paper and authored the book *Preserving Family Legends for Future Generations*, a 2010 First Place winner for Heartland New Day Bookfest.

http://mcarolynsteele.com

Thank you for purchasing
this publication of The Wild Rose Press, Inc.

If you enjoyed the story, we would appreciate your
letting others know by leaving a review.

For other wonderful stories,
please visit our on-line bookstore at
www.thewildrosepress.com.

For questions or more information
contact us at
info@thewildrosepress.com.

The Wild Rose Press, Inc.
www.thewildrosepress.com

Stay current with The Wild Rose Press, Inc.

Like us on Facebook

https://www.facebook.com/TheWildRosePress

And Follow us on Twitter
https://twitter.com/WildRosePress